BIG GIRLS
NEED *Love* TOO

A NOVEL

AUBREY GROSS

Copyright

Copyright © 2015 by Aubrey Gross

All rights reserved.

Book layout © 2015 Aubrey Gross
Book cover © 2015 by Aubrey Gross

Big Girls Need Love Too/Aubrey Gross -- 1st ed.

Epub Edition August 2015 ISBN: 978-0-9962821-4-7

Print Edition ISBN: 978-0-9962821-5-4

To the Seton Hill University Writing Popular Fiction community: this book would not be what it is today without y'all. And to my brain twin: without you pushing me to apply to SHU, this book wouldn't even exist. Thank you.

CHAPTER ONE

Molly Sampson mentally catalogued her flaws. She'd become more than aware of them after being her older sister's maid of honor a few months ago.

Five foot four inches. Forty-eight. Forty. Fifty-two.

Her measurements also served as the numbers to the combination lock she used when she went to the gym. She looked at them as a motivational tool.

Despite having a gym membership, she didn't know what number corresponded with her weight, since she only stepped on a scale when she had a doctor's appointment. She'd done her best to erase the memory of that particular measurement from her mind.

So really, why was she sitting here in Clicks—a smoky pool hall a mile away from her apartment—knowing good and well her best friend Benjamin intended to hook her up with some unknown guy? Especially when the population of their hometown of Waco, Texas consisted of spoiled, rich Baylor brats, men who were already married or single dads who barely managed to pay their child support—if they paid it at all.

What were you thinking, asking Benjamin to set you up on a bunch of blind dates? Molly took a sip of her Pineapple and Parrot Bay. *Oh, yeah, it was that whole trying new things, meeting new people, attempting to date resolution you made.*

She rolled her eyes. Whatever had possessed her to make a New Year's resolution like that—hell, to make one at all for the first time in her twenty-six years of life—was beyond her. But she'd only made the resolution a few days before, and she didn't like to renege on a promise, even if it was a silly one made in the early hours of January first to no one but herself.

She sneezed. Ugh, she knew this had been a bad idea. Not only was the cigarette smoke aggravating her allergies, but she had to have been temporarily insane to agree to meet a guy in a bar of all places. Could she get any more cliché? How romantic could neon Lone Star beer signs and Corona advertisements be anyway? Although she did have to admit that the grass-skirt wearing Spanky the Monkey— the pool hall's mascot who hung from the ceiling in the bar area—did add a certain amount of class to the establishment.

"Earth to Molly. Did you hear a word I just said?"

Her head snapped up at the sound of Benjamin's voice. He stood across the table from her, holding one of the bar's famous Big Ass Beers in his hand, with an impatient expression on his bearded face. Man, she must've really zoned out, because Benjamin rarely got impatient.

"Sorry, hon. I was thinking."

"Stop doing that."

"But thinking is good."

"Not when you're mentally cataloguing every single flaw you think you have."

She tucked a strand of dark auburn hair behind her ear. "What makes you think I was doing that?"

He raised a brown eyebrow.

"Okay, you're right. Get out of my head."

The problem with being best friends with someone you've known since junior high was that they also knew all of the things you obsessed over.

"Moll, you know I love you, but sometimes you just think way too damned much."

"I know. I know. It's just…" she paused, trying to find the right words. "I haven't been on a date in three years. I haven't kissed someone in almost two. And it's been so long since I last had sex that I'm pretty sure I've forgotten how to do it. So right now I kind of feel like I'm jumping into the deep end of the pool and all I know how to do is doggie paddle."

He took a swig of his beer before responding. "At least you know how to doggie paddle. And I know it's a big step, Molly. But don't you think it's time to get back out here in the world and try to meet someone? You're great. Any guy would be lucky to have you."

I don't want just "any guy," though. I want you.

And that was the one thing her best friend didn't know about her—that her other New Year's resolution had been to fall out of love.

Before she could get too lost in her thoughts, Benjamin's deep voice interrupted her again. "Barrett should be here any minute now."

Molly tucked a strand of hair behind her ear again before readjusting her sweater over her stomach. What had she been thinking, wearing something so clingy? Her fingers itched to grab the jacket draped across the back of her stool, but the bar was extremely warm and she kept fighting back the urge to push up her sleeves.

She took a deep breath in a desperate attempt to steady herself and looked at Benjamin. "Am I crazy for doing this? What if he doesn't like me? What if he thinks I'm fat and ugly or too smart or talk too much or have too many freckles or…something?"

He leaned across the round, waist-high table and ducked his head so they were at eye level. She'd always loved how his hazel eyes would change color depending upon his mood. Right now they were green, which meant he was either horny or irritated. Some instinct told her to bet money on the latter. "Molly, listen to me. Stop thinking about your size for just a little while. Despite what you think, you're not fat. And if Barrett doesn't like you, it's his loss."

Molly opened her mouth to object—after all, her combination lock kind of disproved his notion that she wasn't fat—but the door to the bar opened before she could get the words out, and her attention was redirected to the attractive guy who had just walked in. The attractive guy who headed straight towards Benjamin.

He was tall with sandy brown hair and a somewhat large build, the type of guy Molly would usually go for. Well, if she were the type to "go for" it to begin with.

In all honesty, she would be lying to herself if she said her interest wasn't slightly piqued. He had a nice boy look about him, but his piercings added a little bit of an edge. She'd never really been into guys with piercings, but the hoop in his eyebrow and the labret in his lower lip were oddly appealing.

Benjamin must have noticed that Molly's attention was riveted on something—or someone—and turned in the direction of her gaze.

"Hey man, what's up?" he said to the newcomer.

Molly watched as they did what she referred to as the guy hug—a one-armed shoulder pump, back pat sort of thing that vaguely reminded her of a gorilla mating ritual where the two alpha males battled it out over the poor, unsuspecting female gorilla.

"Nothing much," the guy said.

Benjamin grabbed his beer with one hand before saying, "Oh, hey, Barrett, I'd like you to meet my best friend Molly." He turned back to her. "Molly, this is Barrett."

She resisted the urge to rub her palms on her jeans before taking Barrett's proffered right hand in her own. "Nice to meet you." Okay, her voice sounded calm enough. Normal. Even.

He smiled. Molly let go of his hand and promptly gave in to the urge to rub her hands on the thighs of her faded blue jeans before sitting up straighter and adjusting her sweater over her stomach. Again.

"Nice to meet you, too." He sat down on the empty stool to her right.

Their waitress appeared and took Barrett's order, bringing him back a Bud Light after a few moments.

Molly's stomach was a ball of nervous tension, and she gave up on listening to the idle chatter Barrett and Benjamin were making. She couldn't stop looking at him and the piercings in his ear. She wasn't sure what it was about them, but she found the different studs and hoops somewhat fascinating. Along with having his eyebrow and labret pierced, he also had both ears pierced. He laughed at something Benjamin said, and she saw a flash of silver on his tongue.

She shifted slightly in her seat. Crossed her legs. Uncrossed them. Fiddled with her own earring. Picked up her straw and started to chew on it. *Can I like a guy who owns better earrings than I do? More importantly, would he let me borrow them?* He laughed again at Benjamin, and that same flash of silver once again caught her attention.

"So, Molly's a really good photographer."

Molly jumped at the sound of Benjamin's voice. She'd been thinking way too hard about that tongue ring.

"Really?" Barrett asked. "What do you take pictures of?"

She picked up her drink and sipped before answering, trying to pull herself back to the present. "Well, I prefer to shoot kids. Wait a second, that didn't sound right."

He laughed. "I know what you mean, though."

"Good, because that made me sound like some weird mass murderer or something." She smiled and licked her lips. "Anyway, I like to photograph kids, but I've mostly been photographing flowers and plants here lately."

"Really? That's interesting."

"Yeah, she has this really cool photo of a flower in her bedroom—what is it, Molly?" Benjamin asked.

"It's an orchid." She could feel a faint blush warming her ears.

"That's right, an orchid. Anyway," he turned towards Barrett, "she did this really neat effect with it, turned the flower and background itself into black and white, but kept the color of the middle part, so it looks like this big, pink pu—" he cut a look to Molly, "—vagina in the middle of this black and white photo."

"Reeeally?" Barrett asked.

Great. Now he probably thinks I'm a perv. And it's vulva, not vagina.

Barrett's question caused the warmth from her ears to creep into her cheeks. *Well, at least now maybe my freckles aren't standing out as much.* "Yeah. I kind of saw it, but another photographer friend of mine helped me come up with the idea. And I wasn't meaning to sexualize it—actually, the first thing that stood out to me is that there's a part of the flower that looks like a yellow butterfly right in the middle of it, so I wanted to bring that out. It just happened that when I did that, the pink part stood out even more, and I realized that it did indeed look like well, a woman's lady bits. And ever since then, I've never been able to look at flowers the same way."

Barrett laughed. "I'll have to see this photo sometime."

"Maybe, yeah." That would require having Barrett in her bedroom, and she wasn't sure she wanted him there just yet, even if he did have a pierced tongue.

Benjamin stood up and stretched. "I'm going to go to the bathroom real quick."

"Okay," Molly said.

Silence fell over the table as Benjamin walked away, broken only by the sound of Aerosmith blaring from the loud speakers. Several long moments went by before either of them said anything.

"So, are you from here?"

Molly looked at Barrett. "Yup. Born and raised. You?"

"A little bit of everywhere, but mostly Lampasas."

"Fun. Y'know, we went there once in high school for an academic competition, and we kept talking about how everyone in the town looked inbred."

"Um, thanks."

The blush crept further down her face and inched towards her neck. "I so did not mean that the way it sounded. It was just, everybody looked alike, and you know how high school kids are..." Oh, God, this was getting worse by the second. Why couldn't a hole open up underneath her barstool and suck her in?

She glanced towards the other side of the bar, looking for Benjamin. Damn. He was talking to someone. *Guess I'm on my own to clean this one up.* "I am so sorry, Barrett. Everything is coming out wrong tonight."

He chuckled before taking a swig of his beer. "It's okay, don't worry about it. Most of the people there are douche bags anyway."

"Well, okay then. No offense taken?"

"None."

"Good."

His knee bumped hers under the table. She waited for him to move it, to realize he'd accidentally invaded her personal space, but he didn't. Maybe he didn't realize his knee had bumped against her leg, maybe he thought it was the table. She swallowed and almost held her breath waiting for him to move, but still she felt nothing but the warmth of his leg pressing against hers. She frowned. Considering her thus far erotic thoughts, the lack of a physical response to his touch surprised her. *Chalk it up to sexual repression, Moll.* Besides, it wasn't as though the tongue ring fantasy had come out of nowhere—she'd wondered about that ever since someone had explained the jewelry's use her freshman year of college. Which, subsequently, had been long before she'd even experienced the joy that was oral sex. Or, hell, sex period.

God, you're such a good girl.

Realizing they'd been silent for a while, she spoke over the click of balls on the pool tables behind them. "So, what do you do?"

"I'm a cook at Texas Roadhouse."

"Really?" Great, he had a part time job as a cook at a steakhouse. What was Benjamin thinking? She moved her knee away from Barrett's.

"Yeah, it's something to pay the bills while I'm finishing up at MCC."

Okay, that was a little better. Granted, going to the local community college part time wasn't quite the same as going to a university, but it was better than not pursuing higher education at all. "What're you majoring in?"

His knee bumped hers again. "Well, I was majoring in radiology, but it's way too competitive, so right now I'm getting some basics out of the way before I decide on something else."

"My sister was a radiology major for a while at MCC. I've heard horror stories about how competitive some of the students can get." She leaned back and once again moved her leg.

"It can get rough. Plus, I'd lost the passion for it, and I realized it wasn't what I wanted to do anymore." He shifted in his seat, leaning forward just a little bit as he did so.

Their eyes met. Blue green. Huh. She'd always been a sucker for blue green eyes. Too bad she wasn't attracted to him. "I know what you mean about losing the passion for something. I started out in college as a journalism major, but realized I just didn't want to do it anymore. Granted, I'm still a news junkie and would love to have a syndicated column, or write for *RollingStone,* but I'm just not as passionate about it as I was in high school."

"Journalism, huh?"

"Yeah. That's actually where I picked up the interest in photography. I got lucky enough to take pictures from the sidelines at football games, and figured out I had a knack for it. Plus, being so close to all those cute boys in tight pants always gave me a little thrill." She grinned.

"I'm guessing that would be a plus if you're a chick. Did you ever get hit with a ball?"

"I almost did a couple of times, along with almost getting tackled at least a dozen times. Luckily, though, I somehow managed to avoid any injuries, which is odd considering how much of a klutz I am."

He laughed. "Oh, I'm a klutz, too. I swear I trip over my own feet sometimes." His knee bumped hers again. Okay, maybe he really was just clumsy.

"Me, too! I'll wake up with bruises wondering how I got them."

"Oh, really?"

"Well, I know they're not from doing anything fun, but I have to be getting them from somewhere." *Like from your knee if you keep hitting me with it.* She shifted the position of her legs yet again.

"Sleep-walking, maybe?"

"No, I don't think so. Although it wouldn't surprise me, since I talk in my sleep constantly."

He raised his pierced eyebrow in question.

"Yeah. I've actually woken myself up talking in my

sleep. And my mema—that's my grandma—used to comment all the time on how I'd just been yackin' away at someone in my dreams. I was always afraid she was going to hear something she really did not need to hear."

Barrett threw his head back and laughed. "Yeah, that might not have been a good thing."

"No. Especially not with some of the dreams I have."

"And what kind of dreams might those be?"

The waitress walked up before Molly could answer. "Y'all doing okay?"

"Could I get another beer?" Barrett asked.

"Sure." The waitress smiled and turned her attention to Molly. "And you?"

"No, I'm fine. Thank you, though." So far Barrett hadn't tried to play the knee version of footsies under the table again. *Thank God.*

"No problem. I'll be right back with your beer," the waitress said to Barrett before she turned and walked away, gathering empties from several tables as she made her way to the bar.

"So, about those dreams…" Barrett said.

"What about dreams?" Benjamin asked as he plopped down on the chair he'd previously vacated.

"I was just asking Molly about dreams she was afraid of her grandmother knowing about." Barrett shifted his body slightly away from Molly and towards Benjamin.

"You have sexual dreams?" Benjamin asked Molly, fake shock in his voice.

"Yes, I have sexual dreams. Who doesn't?" She rolled her eyes.

"The Pope, maybe?" Barrett suggested.

"Good point," Benjamin conceded.

The waitress returned with Barrett's beer and he pulled a five-dollar bill from his wallet. He handed it to the waitress, who made change and gave him back a dollar and fifty cents. He tipped her a quarter and turned back to the table. Looking at Benjamin, he said, "Susan called me again last night."

"Really? What the hell did she want?"

"Me to come over again." He took a swig of his beer.

"Again?" Benjamin paused. "Wait. Did you fuck her?"

If Molly had been drinking something at that moment, she probably would have spit it out.

"Yeah, once. A couple months ago."

"I can't believe you hit that."

I can't believe y'all are actually talking about this in front of me.

Barrett shrugged. "Katrina and I had just broken up, and I was drunk. She took advantage of me."

"Katrina?" Molly asked.

"Yes, Molly, that Katrina," Benjamin said.

"Katrina the Skank?" That was what Benjamin and a couple other guys had dubbed Katrina a couple of months ago after it got out she'd cheated on her ex-boyfriend and then supposedly given him an STD.

"One and the same."

"Oh, you know her?" This from Barrett.

"Yeah. You dated her?" Molly asked. *Benjamin tried to set me up with someone who'd dated Katrina? Gross. What the hell was he thinking?*

"For a while. Until she cheated on me with some loser from Austin."

"Color me surprised." Locals often referred to Waco as "the biggest small town ever," and Katrina had managed to make quite a reputation for herself—and that was before the STD incident.

The sarcasm must have been lost upon Barrett. "I was surprised. I didn't see it coming at all. I mean, things hadn't been great for a while, but I didn't realize they were that bad, either."

"That still isn't an excuse for sleeping with Susan," Benjamin said.

"Wait," Molly said. "Do I know Susan?"

"Yeah. Susan. Blonde. Big girl. Got her ass kicked at Shot Daddy's by some biker bitch about a year ago," Benjamin said.

"Ohhh. That Susan." She started to put two and two together. "She's kind of got a reputation, too, doesn't she?"

"Slightly, yeah," Benjamin said.

She turned to Barrett. "So you slept with both Katrina and Susan?" If she'd been remotely attracted to him, her feelings would have completely dissipated at this point. "You might want to go get checked out, because there's not much telling how many diseases you've gotten from the two of them combined." She made a mental note to wash her jeans as soon as she got home. Sure, gonorrhea couldn't be passed by clothing to clothing contact, but she felt the need for a heavy dose of penicillin at just the thought of Barrett touching her after sleeping with both of them.

Barrett had just taken a drink of his beer and seemed to have trouble swallowing. After several moments, he finally managed to speak. "You might have a point."

Molly's attention was drawn to the entrance of the bar again as Emery, a Cindy Lou Who look-alike, walked in. Well, if Dr. Seuss had drawn Cindy Lou Who in an oversized sweatshirt, well-worn blue jeans and a pair of beat up Nike's.

She walked up to their table and aimed a beaming smile in Benjamin's direction. He wrapped his arm around her, scooping her towards him so he could lean in and place a kiss on her lips. Molly felt a small pang of jealousy at his open display of affection, and took a quick sip of her drink in an effort to squash her reaction.

Benjamin had been dating Emery for going on three months now, and Molly had avoided her for the first two of those. However, she'd soon run out of excuses (a girl could only wash her hair so many times before people started thinking she was either lying or had a severe dandruff problem) and had broken down and met Emery. To Molly's dismay, she'd found herself liking the other woman, and understanding what Benjamin saw in her.

Emery had recently graduated Summa Cum Laude from Baylor and was currently studying for the GRE to get into grad school. She'd also just taken a high-paying job at a hotel in Dallas as a manager. The only black mark against her seemed to be that Emery didn't watch football, and Benjamin was probably the biggest football nut she'd ever met.

The love birds finally tore their lips away from each other, allowing Emery to turn to Molly and smile. "Hi, Molly. It's great to see you out."

She smiled faintly. "Well, I could only stay in my rabbit hole for so long before I ran out of carrots."

Did I really just say that?

"Carrots? Are you a vegetarian?" Barrett asked.

Was he blind? Vegetarians did not wear a size twenty, or if they did Molly sure hadn't ever seen one. "Hardly."

"Oh. Well, it's just you said you'd run out of carrots."

Molly glanced at Benjamin. She apparently needed to set some ground rules here, the first of which being any guy he set her up with had to at least have the IQ of a gorilla. Or a dolphin. Dolphins were smart.

Benjamin whispered something in Emery's ear.

"Barrett, I'm gonna go play some songs, wanna help me pick some?" Emery asked.

He finished his beer and slid off his barstool. "Sure."

The two of them walked off. Benjamin watched Emery the entire way. *Did he ever look at me that way?*

He finally tore his gaze from Emery and turned towards Molly.

No, he's definitely never looked at me that way.

"Okay, so maybe Barrett isn't the best choice for you, but this was the best I could do on short notice."

She shook her head and pushed away her morose thoughts. "I think saying he's not the best choice for me might be an understatement. I mean, he seems nice enough, just a little slow on the uptake. Plus, there's the fact that he's made some questionable decisions considering he's slept with both Susan and Katrina. It's a bit of a turn-off, hon."

"Why are you doing this anyway? All of a sudden deciding to go out on a bunch of dates is completely unlike you."

Molly shrugged and looked towards the jukebox across the bar. Barrett and Emery were engrossed in their musical choices, so Molly turned her attention back to Benjamin. "I just decided it was time for me to meet someone. Maybe have some fun."

"Except you don't seem to be having much fun."

She squirmed in her seat and reached up to play with the dragonfly hanging from the thin silver chain around her neck. "I'm just not used to this. It's going to take some time. Plus, I'm not sure this even counts as a date. Does it?"

She felt clueless when it came to this whole dating thing. Then again, the only thing she did know was that dating and attraction as an adult weren't anywhere near as simple as when you were a child. When you were a kid and you liked someone, all you had to do to show your affection was pull their hair, kick them in the knee and send them a note asking, "Do you have cooties? Check yes or no." Simple. Straightforward. Not a lot of room for guessing games.

If the *Friends* reruns she loved were any indication, though, dating as an adult was nothing but a series of guessing games.

Benjamin's voice drew her out of her thoughts. "No, I don't think this really counts as a date. This is more you sticking your toes in the water before jumping in headfirst."

A slight pang of jealousy and regret ricocheted inside of her. Benjamin always seemed to know just what to say and do for her. *Does Emery know how lucky she is?*

"Thanks, hon."

Emery and Barrett returned to the table. Emery smiled at Benjamin, who smiled back at her, and they greeted each other with a long, slow kiss as though they'd been separated for months rather than just a few minutes. The jealousy threatened to take over, so Molly averted her gaze.

She desperately needed her Getting Over Benjamin plan to work. Otherwise, she was screwed. And not in a good way.

CHAPTER TWO

Don't do this. Don't do this. Don't do this. Molly repeated the three words to herself, trying to stave off the anxiety attack that threatened to take over.

She pushed the UP arrow on the elevator of the refurbished downtown warehouse and noticed that her hand was shaking. *Deep breaths, Molly. Deep breaths.*

The door opened after what seemed like hours. *Thank God it's empty.* She stepped in and hit the button for the third floor, fighting to keep the nausea at bay.

That was the thing about her anxiety attacks. First she got cold. Really cold. And then she would start feeling sick to her stomach, even though she'd never once thrown up. She'd figured out years ago how to keep a full blown attack from happening and could usually talk herself out of them—mind over matter, really. Once the anxiety attack did become full blown, though, the only thing that helped was lying down flat on her back, not moving, and sleeping.

Unfortunately, sleeping wouldn't pay her rent.

The elevator doors opened and she stepped off onto the third floor and turned towards the glass doors of the financial advisor she worked for. She walked through the left hand door, trying to appear calm and normal. Linda, the company's receptionist, greeted her.

"Good morning, Molly. How're you today?"

She nodded in Linda's direction and managed to get

out a "fine" before heading towards the small work area she shared with Blanche and Sharonda. The three of them handled clients' 401(k) distributions. It wasn't the most glamorous job in the world, and certainly wasn't the most difficult, but it paid the bills.

Blanche turned to Molly as soon as she walked in the door. "Mornin'. You okay?"

Molly set her purse down on her desk and plopped into her chair. "Anxiety attack."

"Another one?"

Molly nodded. She'd finally broken down a couple of weeks ago and let her coworkers know about the attacks.

"Need some Xanax?"

Molly shook her head.

"Need some dick?"

Molly chuckled. Her middle-aged coworker's cure for everything was either Xanax or a penis—or, Molly suspected, sometimes both at the same time. "If only it were that easy."

"Any idea what caused this one?"

She took another deep breath and closed her eyes, felt the nausea start to subside. "None. I was fine until I got out of my car, and then it just hit me."

"Something happen over the weekend?"

Another deep breath. "Nothing other than a pseudo date, really."

"How'd that go?"

She opened her eyes. "It wasn't anything to write home about. The guy was kind of cute in a multiple piercings sort of way, but unfortunately the only sharp thing about him was the spike through his labret."

Blanche wiggled her eyebrows. "Did he have a tongue ring?"

"Who had a tongue ring?" Sharonda asked as she came through the door, looking frazzled as usual.

"My pseudo date this weekend."

Sharonda set her purse down on her desk and turned on her computer. "How'd that go?"

"Nothing to write home about."

Sharonda sat down and looked at Molly. "You look a little pale. Are you okay?"

"I'm getting better. I had another anxiety attack coming in this morning."

"That's not good. You need to get that checked out." Molly's other coworker was a recently divorced mother of two, and tended to be the "mother hen" of their department.

Molly breathed deeply again. "I'm starting to think so myself."

"Like I said, girl, I've got some Xanax. And that boy you went out with this weekend might not be the sharpest tool in the shed, but as long as he can plow your garden does it matter how sharp his tool is?"

Molly's jaw dropped, and she and Sharonda looked at each other before bursting into laughter. One thing was for sure, working with Blanche was never boring. Plus, the woman was great at getting Molly's mind off of her anxiety attacks and onto other things.

"Okay, ladies, time to close down the sewing circle and get to work."

Molly heard their boss Warren's voice and glanced towards the door. Just like that, the nausea returned, and in full force this time.

Warren turned on his heel and walked back out of the room, and the three women looked at each other. Blanche and Sharonda rolled their eyes and turned towards their computers. Molly swallowed the mixture of anxiety and resentment lodged in her throat, and turned to her own work station. As she let her email load, she wondered how she was supposed to work for someone who literally made her feel sick to her stomach.

That Friday afternoon, Molly was walking back into the office and furiously going over her wardrobe in her head. Benjamin had called Wednesday night to tell her he'd found a date for her this weekend. She'd talked to Kody the night before on the phone, and their date was tonight. Unfortunately, she didn't have anything clean in her closet that she would classify as date worthy—her two options were basically "business" and "blue jeans and a t-shirt."

Maybe you should've thought this through a little more, Moll.

She reached her desk, sat down, and removed a calculator from her desk drawer. Adding up what she'd just deposited into the bank, along with what she already had in there, then subtracting the bills she had coming out over the next couple of weeks, Molly figured she could afford to spend, oh, five dollars on a new outfit.

"Damn," she said to the empty room.

Well, maybe she could just wear a pair of her work trousers and a slightly sexy top.

Who am I kidding? I don't own any sexy tops.

Her wardrobe consisted of cardigans, camis, button-down shirts, blue jeans and t-shirts. Sure, she had some great shoes, and she was a sucker for a sexy bra and panty set, but unless Kody was gay he wouldn't care one bit about her shoes. *And he certainly isn't going to get a peek at my underwear.*

Sighing, she opened up her email box and noticed that she had a new message from Warren. She clicked it, and read, "Come to my office when you have a chance." *What could he want?*

She pushed away from her desk and readjusted her shirt around her hips, trying to come up with a plausible reason for being summoned by her boss. To praise her work performance? Somehow she doubted that, considering she'd never received anything but a chilly reception from him the entire time she'd been with the company. At the same time, though, she couldn't think of anything she'd done wrong, either.

Molly stepped up to Warren's office door and knocked lightly. He looked up from his computer screen, wire rims perched precariously on his long nose, and said, "Come on in. And shut the door behind you."

"Uh oh. What've I done wrong?" She tried to make her tone light and even added a smile, but it seemed to have lost its effect on her prickly boss. Her stomach also didn't seem to be paying attention, either. *You cannot have an anxiety attack in front of him.*

"Have a seat."

Molly sat down in the mahogany-colored leather chair across from his desk and waited. *Deep breaths Molly, deep breaths.*

"Molly, I'm going to be honest with you, I have some concerns about your numbers."

"My numbers?"

"Yes. Your distribution numbers have been slipping here lately, and I can't quite pinpoint why. You're obviously a smart girl, so I don't know if there's something you're not grasping or if you just aren't paying enough attention."

"I completely understand everything." *Considering this job's so easy a monkey could do it.*

He sat forward, folded his hands on the navy blue desk blotter in front of him, and gave Molly a look of detached indifference. "I was told when I took over as supervisor of this department to watch you specifically, Molly. Your numbers haven't been high enough, and we've been trying to figure out why."

"I've been in distributions for eight months. Why hasn't something been said to me before about this?"

"I really don't think you can use that as an excuse."

Who the hell does he think he is? "I just think that if someone had seen it before, something should have been said to me. I should have gotten a review at the end of the year." Her voice was surprisingly calm, considering the simmering mixture of indignation and sheer anger she was feeling, not to mention the fact that her pulse was racing so quickly she was starting to feel a bit lightheaded.

Warren sighed. "Molly, you're just making excuses when we both know that the real problem is that you spend too much time on the Internet. There have been several times when I've walked in and you've been on Yahoo dot com or Skype or checking Facebook."

I don't even have Skype on my work computer. Instead of saying that out loud, though, she took a deep breath and said, "Yahoo happens to be my home page, so when I'm done looking up information on a client I go back to it."

He leaned back in his chair, crossed his arms over his chest and looked down his nose at her. "Fair enough. But unless you bring your numbers up, you won't have a job for much longer."

Molly sighed, not quite knowing how to react to any of this. Her body, however, had decided to go into full blown panic attack mode. She swallowed past the dryness in her mouth. "So where do you think my numbers should be?"

"Between fifteen and twenty a day."

But I have been doing that, her mind screamed at her. Instead of saying that out loud, though, she took a shaky breath and resigned herself to her fate as a corporate whore. "I'll see if I can figure out a different process so I can start producing more."

"Good."

Her hands gripped the arms of the chair so hard her knuckles started to ache. "Is that everything?"

"That's all." His gaze flickered to his computer monitor, a clear dismissal. "Have a good day."

She stood up and walked out of the prick's office on shaky legs. Great. Fine. Fan-fucking-tastic. She wobbled back into her office and slumped down into her chair. This was bullshit. Utter and complete bullshit. Warren's comments had been completely out of line, not to mention incorrect and unfair.

Deep breaths, Molly, deep breaths. She closed her eyes and tried to will the nausea away. After a few moments of deep breathing, her stomach calmed slightly. Still feeling cold, though, she grabbed the jacket from the back of her chair and put it on, hoping it would make her feel better.

She grabbed a stack of paperwork out of their inbox and got back to processing distributions. When had she turned into a corporate pen pusher? What had happened to her goals and career ambitions? Sighing, she printed out some extra forms, and thought that there had to be more to life than slaving away for the man and killing fifty trees on a daily basis.

Well, at least she had a date to look forward to tonight. Things couldn't get much worse. Right?

CHAPTER THREE

Upon getting home from work, molly looked frantically through her closet for a shirt that was not only date worthy but appropriate for the chilly january weather. Unfortunately, everything she owned either had short sleeves or made her look like an uptight librarian. Great.

She and Kody were meeting at Johnny Carino's, and luckily the usual patron dress ranged from college student grunge to prom night dinner. After tossing every item of clothing she owned onto her bed, she finally settled on a pair of gray trousers and a scoop necked pink sweater that was not only weather appropriate but showed a subtle amount of cleavage if she pulled it down just enough.

She turned from side to side in front of the mirror that covered the length of her closet door, checking her appearance from every angle. At least her hair looked good, but there wasn't much she could do about the wide hips she'd inherited from her great-grandma Pearl or the tummy pooch she'd had since she'd been, oh, nine. Molly turned away from the mirror, knowing that it did her no good to over-analyze her body, and padded on bare feet into the living room. She contemplated the pile of shoes sitting next to the front door and finally chose a pair of pink, black, white and purple tweed heels that were hell on her lower back but made her legs look less like tree stumps. The shoes went with the outfit and were close-toed. Plus, she'd paid fifty-five bucks for the damned things, so she might as well wear them at least a few times.

She did a few passes through her one bedroom apartment, trying to acclimate her feet and lower back to the three-inch heels, and gave up after the second walk through.

"Screw this." The empty living room absorbed the sound of her voice as she toed the shoes off and returned to the pile at the front door. She tapped a finger on her bottom lip as she once again contemplated her choices.

After long moments filled with Anna Nalick's voice singing from the iPod docking station in her bedroom, Molly finally decided upon a pair of simple black kitten heels that were not only cute, but most of all comfortable. So what if they were open-toed? She'd mostly be inside, anyway, and it wasn't like it was twenty below outside. Hell, it wasn't even below freezing, just hovering somewhere around forty-five.

She checked her appearance once again in the bedroom mirror before deciding she'd done as good a job as she could before turning off the music and overhead light. Molly grabbed her purse off the couch, pulled out her car keys and made sure her cell phone was tucked safely inside before heading out the door.

Although she lived only five minutes away from the restaurant, it took her closer to twenty to get there due to a wreck on Valley Mills Drive. Apparently some idiot had decided to run a red light. Dumbass.

She finally got to the restaurant—ten minutes late— and scanned the area, looking for a guy who matched Benjamin's description of tall with brown hair. She counted approximately twenty-six different tall men with brown hair, so she decided to look for someone who might remotely resemble an accountant.

After a few minutes of scanning the restaurant from the

front reception area, she walked up to the hostess station and asked if there was a Kody who'd already gotten a table. The hostess smiled and said, "Sure. He got here about ten minutes ago. Just follow me."

Molly walked behind the perky blonde, who stopped once they reached a table in a far corner of the restaurant, away from the traffic of servers and patrons. The hostess stepped aside and Molly pulled out a chair and sat down. The blonde told them their server would be right with them, and when she left Molly allowed herself to get her first good look at Kody.

Benjamin had at least been right when he'd said Kody was tall with brown hair, but he'd forgotten to mention the unibrow, thick glasses and scrawny body. Molly managed to hold in her sigh, and smiled instead as she said, "Hi. It's Kody, right?"

He smiled in return, his cheeks flushing pink. "Yeah." His Adam's apple bobbed up and down. "Benjamin didn't say you were hot."

Molly watched, fascinated, as his cheeks went from pink to candy apple red. Wow. Benjamin had also forgotten to mention that Kody was very obviously blind. Maybe he needed thicker lenses, although his eyewear looked to be pushing five pounds already. Or maybe it was the dim lighting in this back corner; Molly had to avoid the urge to squint herself.

"So, um," she picked up the menu in front of her, searching for something to say to break the awkward silence, "Benjamin told me you're an accountant?"

Clever Molly, clever. Where are all those scintillating verbal skills you've always prided yourself on? Wait, can verbal skills even be scintillating?

He sat forward, propped his elbows on the table and pushed his glasses up his nose, reminding Molly of an over-eager puppy dog. "I work for Extraco. A/R and A/P.

That means Accounts Receivable and Accounts Payable. They're a great company to work for. Good benefits. Health, dental, 401(k)." The thick-rimmed glasses slid back down his nose, and a lock of oily-looking hair fell over his forehead as he leaned further forward. "So what do you do?"

She looked down at her menu, contemplated how much to tell him, and looked back up. "I, um, work for a small firm downtown. I'm basically a glorified paper-pusher with a title that makes it sound more appealing than what it is."

"But what do you do?" He folded his hands on the scarred wood table in front of him.

"I generate and fill out paperwork."

"That's it? That doesn't sound like much fun."

"It isn't, which is why I'm trying to find another job." Molly closed her menu. She was ordering the fettuccine chicken alfredo, calories and fat grams be damned.

"Oh really? Doing what?"

"I'm not sure, really. I just decided this afternoon that I needed to start looking elsewhere."

Their waiter appeared—a good-looking, college-aged guy named Bryan—and smiled before asking them what they wanted to drink.

"Water, please," Molly said.

"Iced tea with lemon, unsweetened."

Bryan told them he'd be right back with their beverages and disappeared.

Kody looked over his menu before asking Molly, "Do you know what you're getting?"

"The chicken fettuccine alfredo."

"I'm not sure what I'm going to get. The shrimp linguine looks good, but so does this Tuscan chicken."

"I've never had either, so I can't help you out with that one."

Bryan returned with their drinks a few minutes later and whipped out his notepad. "Y'all ready to order?"

Molly gave the waiter her order and handed him her menu. Bryan turned towards Kody, his pen poised above his notepad, waiting expectantly.

"I'll have the shrimp linguine." He paused. "No, wait. The Tuscan chicken."

Bryan started to write down Kody's order.

"No, no. The shrimp linguine...no, the chicken. No, wait. The shrimp. Shrimp linguine." Kody nodded his head and handed Bryan his menu.

So he's delusional and indecisive, great.

The waiter shook his head and wrote down Kody's order. Kody didn't notice, because he was too busy beaming at Molly and making her increasingly uncomfortable. She slid the dragonfly back and forth on her necklace, trying not to fidget in her chair.

Bryan returned a few minutes later with bread and olive oil, which he set on their table before moving on to the next one.

Kody sat there, still smiling and not saying a word. Molly crossed and uncrossed her legs. Took a nervous sip of her water. Her stomach growled and she fiddled with her necklace.

Why had she decided to torture herself?

Benjamin watched as Molly strode across the bar towards him, wearing gray pants and a pink sweater that made her look like she'd just come from a meeting of the Junior League. She sneezed as a stream of cigarette smoke wafted into her face. He signaled the bartender for Molly's drink, since she'd called him on the way over after her date and asked him to have a Pineapple and Parrot Bay ready and waiting.

Julie slid the drink in front of him right as Molly reached the empty barstool beside him. Molly placed her purse on the bar and plopped onto the aforementioned stool, put her elbows on the bar and rested her chin in her steepled hands. He waited for the heavy sigh, and Molly didn't disappoint.

"Okay, so how bad was it?"

Molly glared at him and narrowed her eyes. "I can't believe you set me up with that guy. He's nowhere near my type!"

"He's smart, nice, has a good job. I figured since you were doing this whole trying new things business you might appreciate being set up on a date that wasn't your usual type."

She took a sip of her drink. "I hate it when you make sense. Stop doing that."

He chuckled. "So what was so bad about Kody?"

He watched as she sighed and then started to toy with the straw in her drink. Give her a few minutes and she'd have the brown swizzle stick in her mouth, chewing it into a mangled piece of plastic.

"First off, does he even know what a bottle of shampoo looks like? I've never seen anyone with hair that oily in my life."

"Now that's just superficial." And slightly amusing, but he wasn't going to tell her that.

"No, it's not. It's true—the guy has oily hair. And all he could do was talk about his job and numbers and accounting and invoices, and oh my God, I wanted to hit him upside the head with a baseball bat to make him shut up."

"I'm sorry."

"And he couldn't make up his mind. It was embarrassing, really, the way he kept wavering back and forth between one thing and the other. I almost ordered for him, but figured that would've been a little rude."

"You think?"

"Shut it." She kicked him in the shin. "He was also completely blind, or maybe he had a severe vision problem because he had the audacity to tell me I'm hot."

"A guy tells you he thinks you're hot so you automatically assume he has a vision problem?" They really needed to do something about her self-esteem.

"Hey, I think his glasses needed to be polished. Or maybe they're just so thick they distort everything."

"You're not allowed to use eyeglasses humor, Miss I-Used-To-Have-A-Lazy-Eye."

"Actually, that gives me more of a right to use eyeglasses humor." She chewed further down the straw, and he thought about how someone could take her actions suggestively if they were so inclined.

"Whatever." He shifted in his seat.

"I know I'll laugh about this a few days from now—how can I not?—but right now, I just don't have it in me."

Julie reappeared, and he ordered another beer for himself and another Pineapple and Parrot Bay for Molly since she'd managed to drink most of her first one while talking. "So what else happened to make today so shitty? One mediocre date isn't going to make you guzzle a drink in less than ten minutes."

"I got a verbal warning at work."

"A verbal warning? What the hell for?"

"Apparently my numbers are too low." She rolled her eyes.

"Your numbers are too low? What kind of bullshit is that?"

"The kind that my new supervisor likes to dish out. According to him, my numbers have been low for quite some time, and he was told to specifically watch me when he took over the department."

"That's crap. If your numbers are so low, why didn't they say something to you months ago? You've been in that department for what, six months now?"

"Eight. It's eight months."

"Eight months and they've never said anything to you?"

"You've got it." Her voice sounded unusually tight.

"So what are you gonna do?"

She shrugged. "Get my numbers up and start looking for another job."

Julie returned with their drinks and set them down on the bar and turned to take an order from a guy to their right.

He pushed the Pineapple and Parrot Bay towards Molly before picking up his own Bud Light. "Do you think you're gonna get fired?"

She took a sip of her drink before answering. "I honestly don't know. All I do know is that I'm pissed off and frustrated."

"I would be, too. You've gone from loving your job to hating it, anyway, so maybe it's time for you to start looking for something else."

"Yeah." She took another drink. "I just don't know what."

"Molly, you could do anything you wanted to."

She snorted. "Not so much, hon."

He took a swig of his beer. "You'll figure something out, I'm sure."

"Yeah, probably." She paused, took another sip of her drink, before saying, "I still can't believe you set me up with that guy. I swear, Benjamin, the next one better be my type and able to make a decision."

"That really did irritate you, didn't it?"

"You know it did."

He pulled a cigarette from the pack in front of him and lit it. "Don't worry, I really think you'll like this next guy I have in mind."

"Hopefully I will."

"Oh, you're gonna like this guy. You're gonna sing my praises after this one." He took a drag off his cigarette, enjoying the taste of tobacco on his tongue before exhaling.

"Whatever."

"Whatever," he mimicked, just because he knew it would piss her off. She punched him in the arm. "You hit like a girl."

"That's because I am a girl."

Unfortunately, he was sometimes all too aware of just how much of a girl she was.

CHAPTER FOUR

The next night Molly found herself sitting at a table in Clicks with Benjamin and Emery, the sounds of balls clacking together and Led Zeppelin pulsating around them as she visually scanned the area. The place is busy tonight. She never really knew just who or what she was looking for, but she'd developed a people-watching habit over the past few weeks. Every now and then she'd see a cute boy, or someone from high school that she had no intention of talking to, but she figured this habit was healthier than her Benjamin habit.

"So how'd your date go last night?"

Molly turned her attention towards Emery. "I'm sorry. What?"

"I asked how your date went last night." Emery raised her voice slightly.

"Oh. Well. It pretty much sucked."

"Really? What happened?"

"He couldn't make up his mind," Benjamin answered.

"What?" Emery asked.

"I can answer for myself, jackass," Molly said.

Benjamin held his hands up in the air as if declaring peace. "Fine, then. I'll just sit here and look pretty."

Molly smiled indulgently at him before turning back to Emery. "He was really indecisive and had the greasiest hair I've ever seen in my life."

"So it wasn't a good date?"

"Not by any stretch of the imagination." Molly gestured towards Benjamin. "He better have something better up his sleeve next week, that's for sure."

"Don't worry, I do," Benjamin said. "Last night was just a warm up. A preseason scrimmage if you will."

"Well, next week better be the start of the season, otherwise no one will be making it to the play-offs."

"What the hell are y'all talking about?" Emery interrupted.

"Football." They answered in unison. Benjamin and Molly looked at each other and laughed.

"Oh." Emery took a sip of her beer. "Yeah, I know nothing about football. I'm a hockey girl."

"Hockey's for pansies," Benjamin said.

"Hey, while I would argue that football is the greatest sport ever invented, I will say that hockey is not for pansies. It can't be too easy skating around on thin metal shoes getting the crap knocked out of you every few minutes," Molly said.

"Well, yeah, but it isn't football."

"Nothing is, hon." Molly still couldn't believe Benjamin was dating a woman who didn't watch football. They must have been making snowmen in San Antonio for that to have happened.

"Speaking of football, are you going to come up here and watch the playoff games tomorrow?" Benjamin asked Molly.

"I might. I don't think I have anything else to do."

"Cool."

Molly looked towards the door of the bar as it opened, letting in a gust of cold January air as another patron entered the building. He was tall and slim with short brown hair and rectangular, black-framed glasses. The cool type, not the hipster type. He walked over to Benjamin, and they exchanged greetings. Unlike most of the guys who knew Benjamin, though, this one didn't participate in the alpha male gorilla dance. He also seemed different from most of the guys who knew Benjamin. He carried himself with a quiet confidence that piqued her interest.

She watched, half-interested, as the two men talked to each other. It still amazed her that Benjamin seemed to know everyone in Waco. The two of them couldn't go anywhere without running into at least one person that knew him. She secretly liked to refer to them as "Benjamin's Fan Club."

Benjamin's groupies also provided her with endless hours of amusement; they all thought they knew him, that they were the greatest of friends. What they didn't know was that the Benjamin they knew was the person Benjamin wanted them to know. Over the course of twelve years of friendship, she had seen so many people come and go in Benjamin's life that she sometimes wondered how she'd managed to become such a permanent fixture.

The guy walked off and Benjamin turned his attention back to Emery and Molly. "So, yeah, what was I saying?"

"We were talking about football," Molly volunteered.

"Oh, yeah, that's right." He took a swig of his beer. "So you're going to come up here tomorrow and watch the games?"

"Yeah, I don't see why not. I need to do laundry at some point in the next few days, but I can spare a few hours for some cute boys in tight pants."

Benjamin rolled his eyes. "You always have to do laundry. And call me crazy, but I don't think that Nate Newton in tight pants is anyone's definition of hot."

"I wasn't talking about him, silly. Besides, he's retired anyway. I was talking about Aaron Rogers." She feigned licking her lips. "Mmmmm. Talk about yummy. That's a whole lot of hot in some very tight football pants."

"He looks like me!"

"Hardly. See, he's hot."

"Hey now! I'm hot."

Molly laughed at Benjamin's attempt to act insulted. "Sorry to break it to you, hon, but you're just cute. Not hot. And definitely not Rogers hot." Oddly, she wasn't lying. While she could argue that Benjamin had a certain attractiveness about him she'd never seen him as drool-worthy.

"I have no idea who y'all are talking about, but I think Benjamin's hot."

Molly turned to Emery, having momentarily forgotten the other woman was there, and said, "Yeah, but you're sleeping with him. I would hope that you think he is."

"Of course I do." Emery smiled at Benjamin before leaning over and pecking him on the lips.

Molly looked away. She was trying. She really was. But even if she could lie to Benjamin and everyone else about her feelings, she couldn't lie to herself, and seeing Emery and Benjamin so happy together made her feel a lot like crying inside.

"Hey, I think I'm fixin' to go home." Molly collected her purse from its place under her barstool.

"Why?" Emery asked.

"Because I'm tired." *Because I can't stand to watch the two of you together right now.*

"I'll walk you out to your car." Benjamin got up from his bar stool.

The two of them walked out of the bar, and Molly removed her keys from her bag.

"You okay?"

She glanced at Benjamin out of the corner of her eye. "Where'd that come from?"

He shrugged one shoulder. "You just seem a little…off tonight. Moody."

"I'm fine, hon. Just tired."

They reached her car, a cute red Ford Fiesta she'd found used online.

"By the way, who was that guy you were talking to earlier?" she asked.

"Which one?"

"Tall, slim, black-framed glasses, brown hair. He stopped by the table and said hi, but then walked up to the bar."

Benjamin looked as though he was trying to remember who all he'd talked to over the course of the night. After a few seconds, he said, "Oh. Joe. That's who you're talking about."

"I guess."

"What about him?"

She looked away. "He was kind of cute, is all."

"But he's not your type."

She chewed on the inside of her lip. "Like you said, I made a resolution to try new things, and maybe the best thing for me would be to veer away from my usual type."

"I don't think Joe really dates, though."

"Never mind. Forget I even brought it up." She turned and unlocked her car door.

Benjamin touched her on her upper arm. "Molly, hold on."

She looked at him over her shoulder and raised her eyebrows.

"I don't know much about him, he's just an acquaintance. He doesn't come out often, in fact this is the first time I've seen him in months. He seems like a decent guy, but I get the feeling there's a lot going on with him right now. He may not be a good option for you."

"Fair enough. It's not like I was thinking marriage and babies with the guy, I just thought he was cute." She got into her car. "Anyway. I'm going to head home. I'll talk to you later."

"Yeah, I better get back inside before Emery starts wondering if I decided to walk to Antarctica or something."

Benjamin closed Molly's car door and she fired up the engine. As she let the car warm up she watched him walk back into the bar.

It was hard watching him with Emery, hard sharing him with someone else. She'd been the only woman in his life for so long, and to say the adjustment was difficult would be an understatement.

But she was happy for him. She really was.

And maybe if she kept telling herself and everyone else that, frogs would start growing hair and cows would learn how to talk, there would be peace in the Middle East and she'd win the lottery.

It could happen. Maybe. On a cold day in hell on the twelfth of never.

A tear rolled down her cheek and she hastily brushed it away. *No use crying, it'll just give you puffy eyes in the morning.*

Another tear rolled down her cheek. She moved the car into reverse and backed out of the parking space. How many dates would it take before she finally got over Benjamin once and for all?

CHAPTER FIVE

"I have your next date set up."

Molly sighed into the phone. "So who's the lucky guy this time?"

"Is that sarcasm I hear in your voice?"

"No, not at all." She didn't even feel like making an attempt at enthusiasm.

"Bull, but whatever." Benjamin paused. "Anyway, your next date's name is Lance. I really think you'll like him."

She shook her head. "After Kody, I think anything could be an improvement. He was horrible."

"I know, I know, but I think this one's a winner. He's smart, he's funny, and he's your type."

"We'll see. So when and where?"

"I gave him your number, so he should call you in the next day or so to set something up."

"Okay. In the meantime, are you coming over tonight to watch TV?"

"You know it. What's for dinner?"

"I'm not sure yet, but I'll have something figured out by the time I get off work."

"Okay. I'll see you later."

"Later."

Molly ended the call and set her cell back down on the desk next to the mouse pad. It was Wednesday, she was at work, and things hadn't been going so well for her.

Molly sighed and went back to eating her lunch. She was miserable. Utterly and completely miserable. Her phone had rung all morning with stupid people calling to ask her stupid questions. Warren had jumped down her throat again that morning–apparently she'd been spending too much time on the phone trying to help clients. She was feeling snappish and mean and petty and if one more person asked her about what freaking forms were needed in order to take their money out of their 401(k), she was going to scream.

She didn't like feeling so mean and nasty, hated feeling so down and depressed and unsatisfied with every little thing in her life. A huge sigh escaped from her lips as she propped her chin on her fisted hand and toyed with the pasta in front of her with her plastic fork. Maybe she could just blame her mood today on PMS and shrug it all off. Unfortunately, there was only so wide of an open window for blaming the ills of the world on good ol' Aunt Flo, and people might start to question her reproductive health if she kept using PMS as an excuse.

As a distraction, she logged onto LinkedIn and did a brief job search. Nothing new, just like every day so far this week. She sighed and went to Indeed, repeated the process, and again came up with nothing.

Dammit. All she needed was a chance, just one chance to prove herself, one person to see her resume and decide to hire her. Unfortunately, the job sites continuously felt the need to inform her of her over- and under-qualifications. Not enough work experience. Too much experience. Oh, you have a degree? Sorry, you're over-educated. Don't have a Master's degree? We apologize, but you'll need to put yourself further into debt in order to be hired here.

Just one more thing that sucked about Waco.

Sighing, she logged off Indeed and checked a few

other sites. A small miracle occurred and she actually found one position that not only seemed remotely interesting but which she also was somewhat qualified for. Deciding she had nothing to lose Molly submitted her cover letter and resume before logging off and checking her personal email as her lunch hour drew to a close.

Yes, she realized looking for jobs while at her current one would probably only garner more dislike from Warren, but at this point she really didn't care.

Screw Warren and his long nose and condescending attitude. Molly threw the uneaten portion of her lunch into the trash and forced herself—and her bad mood— to get back to work.

Hopefully her date this weekend would help her to cheer up, but she wasn't holding her breath.

"Hi, you must be Molly."

Molly looked up at the tall, good-looking blonde male in front of her. Okay, so at least Benjamin had set her up with someone who didn't have greasy hair and who was actually, well, attractive. She smiled and held out her hand in return. "And you must be Lance."

His grip was firm, which earned him another point on her mind's chalkboard. She couldn't stand it when a man gave a woman a weak handshake.

"I've already given the hostess my name, so it should only be a few more minutes."

"Great."

They'd decided the night before to meet up at Buzzard Billy's, which had relieved Molly. It was casual enough so she didn't have to worry too much about dressing up, but she still had room to wear something more than blue jeans and a t-shirt. She'd opted for dark wash trouser cut jeans and a teal empire waist top paired with a cute pair of kitten heels she'd picked up on clearance after Christmas.

Lance sat down on an open bench, and Molly followed suit, not quite sure what to say. Around her friends, she had no problem making conversation. When she was around a good-looking guy she didn't know, however, she always ended up somehow tongue-tied or saying the wrong thing.

"So how was your day?" Lance asked.

She debated how much to tell him. On one hand, she needed to vent. On the other, she didn't want to scare the crap out of this poor guy. "It was okay. Long, but Fridays always are." So it wasn't too much of an evasion of the truth.

The past two days had only gotten worse. Warren was making her life a living hell with his constant snide remarks and watching over her shoulder, and Molly didn't know how much more stress she could take before she snapped.

"Tell me about it. Fridays are the absolute worst. So what do you?"

She shifted in her seat, readjusted her shirt around her midsection. "I work for a small firm downtown. Mostly, I just fill out paperwork for people who don't know how to do it themselves." Wow, that had sounded just a little bitter. "What do you do?"

"I'm a painter."

"Really? My dad's a painter."

"Small world." *He has a nice smile.*

"Yeah. Who do you work for?"

Lance shrugged. "Some guy named David Jones. It's good money, but the guy's a jerk."

"I think I've heard Dad mention him a couple of times, and none of it was very good."

"Yeah, he has a really hard time keeping employees."

"So I've heard." She readjusted the strap of her purse

on her shoulder.

"Lance, table for two." A feminine voice announced over the PA system.

They stood and approached the hostess station and were led to a table in a back corner of the restaurant. Moments later their waiter appeared, and Molly ordered a glass of water while Lance ordered tea. Molly mentally noted that he hadn't opted for alcohol, which was another check mark in his favor.

As they perused their menus, Molly inadvertently studied her date. Tall, with sandy blonde hair, blue eyes and a great smile, he was slightly skinnier than she usually liked, although not so skinny that she felt like a fat cow next to him. Definitely a plus in her book. He had man hands–big and strong and slightly callused–and a couple of flecks of white paint on his knuckles. The faint hint of stubble graced his jaw line, and Molly briefly thought she'd detected a dimple on the right side of his mouth. His khakis and short sleeve, blue button down shirt indicated he at least cared a little bit about his appearance. Maybe Benjamin hadn't done such a bad job after all with this one.

The waiter returned and asked if they were ready to order. Lance gestured towards Molly, so she ordered blacked catfish. Her date ordered the crawfish platter. The waiter left, and Molly had just opened her mouth to say something when the sound of "Big Pimpin'" emanated from Lance's side of the table.

He reached into his pants pocket, grinned, and apologized before taking the call. On a flip phone. Who even used a flip phone anymore?

Molly sipped her water and looked around the restaurant, trying to look interested in the decor rather than his conversation.

"Yeah, no, I'll have it there tomorrow, I swear. I have to talk to my boy first, but I promise you I'll come through."

He paused while the person on the other end of the line apparently said something, and Molly pretended to peruse the drink menu.

"Man, naw. It ain't like that, I swear. My boy just hasn't had anything. Things have been real dry here lately."

Molly barely managed to not raise her eyebrows at that statement.

"I swear, man. I'll bring it to you tomorrow, and it'll be good stuff. My boy's not going to screw me over on this, and he wouldn't give me something bad."

Am I going to have to erase some of those points he's earned?

"I'll have it to you by noon tomorrow, I promise. You gonna have the funds?"

I really hope this conversation isn't what I think it's about.

"Okay, then. Tomorrow, bro." Lance ended the call and put his phone back in his pants pocket. "Sorry about that. Friend of mine wanting to know if I'd located some comic books he's been looking for."

Comic books my ass. Molly had heard conversations like that before, and while they involved paper, it wasn't the type anyone read. "You have a friend who collects comic books?"

Lance shrugged. "Yeah. He's a little bit of a nerd, but I've known him since elementary school, so I try to help him out when I can."

"So you're a comic book dealer?" She asked innocently, and then almost laughed out loud when Lance choked on his tea.

"Yeah, you could say that."

"What kind of comic books does your friend like?"

"Um, well, all kinds, really."

Uh huh. And she had a bridge she could sell his friend

for a real good rate.

Fortunately for Lance, the waiter chose that moment to appear with their food. Molly smiled, said all the right things, picked up her fork and knife and cut her chicken the way her aunt had showed her a couple of years earlier. She'd never forget the day her aunt had told her she cut her meat like she was trailer trash. Molly's rebuttal had been that she'd grown up in a trailer, so if the shoe fit, she would be sure to wear it.

They chewed in silence for a few moments before the sound of "Big Pimpin'" once again filled the air around them. Okay, those points were about to be erased completely.

Lance removed the phone from his pocket and once again took the call after apologizing to her. Yup, there went another point. "Hey man, what's up? Yeah, man, yeah. I talked to my boy, and he's giving me some good stuff tomorrow. I'll hook you up."

He's not even trying to hide the fact that he's making deals in the middle of a wholesome family environment. There are kids around for crying out loud.

"Yeah, man, he's got some 'dro. It's good man, real good."

Molly didn't even attempt to act like she wasn't paying attention anymore. This was getting a little ridiculous.

After a few more minutes, Lance once again ended the call, smiled sheepishly, and returned the phone to his pants pocket. "Sorry. He collects fish and has been looking for a certain type of beta that a friend of mine happens to have for sale."

"You must think I'm an idiot."

He paused, a fried crawfish tail midway between his plate and his mouth. "Why do you say that?"

"You don't have a friend who collects comic books and I've never heard of a fish being referred to as 'dro'."

He set the crawfish tail back down and frowned. "So what do you think is really going on?"

Molly picked her napkin up off her lap and set it down on the table. "You know what I think is going on. Don't assume that I'm some goody two-shoes idiot who doesn't know what you're up to."

"Ooookay." He picked a crawfish tail up and took a bite.

Molly rolled her eyes and stood up. "I'm sorry if you think I'm a bitch for doing this, but I think this date might have been a mistake."

He looked up at her. "Well, I'm sorry you feel that way, but no hard feelings."

The sound of "Big Pimpin'" followed her as she walked away from the table and her half-eaten meal.

♡

"What'd he do?" Benjamin asked. He could tell by the look on Molly's face that something had gone wrong on her latest date, but he couldn't for the life of him figure out what it could be.

She set her purse down on the table a little more forcefully than necessary and glared at him. It took every ounce of will power he had not to laugh–she was just too funny when she was pissed off.

"You set me up with a drug dealer."

A couple of heads turned at her very loud proclamation. "Shhh. Sit down and calm down." He waited for her to take the seat across from him. "Now what's this about Lance being a drug dealer?"

"He was making deals in the middle of the freaking restaurant! There were kids around!"

"And are you one hundred percent sure he was making drug deals?"

She narrowed her eyes and he barely bit back a chuckle.

"Yes, I'm sure he was making drug deals."

"And how do you know that for sure?"

She crossed her arms across her chest. "Benjamin, I'm not stupid. When a guy has 'Big Pimpin' as his ring tone and refers to needing to 'talk to his boy' who hasn't had anything because 'things have been real dry here lately,' he's not having an innocent conversation about comic books, especially when he asks the person on the other end of the line if they'll be paying him tomorrow. And then when the next person calls a few minutes later and the word 'dro' is bandied about, he's not talking about goldfish like he would have me to believe. Not to mention the fact that all of these conversations occurred on a flip phone. A flip phone! Who even has a flip phone these days? I know who. Old people and drug dealers. That's who."

"What the hell does 'dro' mean?"

"It's a type of weed that's apparently really good, called 'hydro.' I wouldn't know, but that's what I've heard."

"You know far too much about marijuana for someone who's never been high a day in her life."

She shrugged. "Yeah, well, that's what happens when you have a family full of potheads. I've heard far too many conversations just like that for me to believe that he was making comic book and goldfish deals."

Benjamin took a sip of his beer. "I hate to break this to you, but he's not a drug dealer."

"How can you be so sure about that?"

He barely stifled his chuckle. "Because I've known the guy for a while now. He bids on stuff on eBay and sells it back to people at a slightly higher rate to make a profit. I'm guessing his 'boy' he was talking about was actually your stepbrother, since they do the bidding and trading together."

Her jaw went slack for a few moments. "Are you kidding me?"

"No, I'm not kidding you."

She groaned and dropped her head onto the table. "I am such a freaking idiot."

"No, you're not. It was a natural assumption to make if he was speaking in generalities, especially considering you have a family full of potheads. Well, except for your stepbrother."

"I suck at this Benjamin. I don't know if I can go out on any more of these dates."

He reached across the table and tugged on a chunk of her hair. He waited until she'd lifted her head and was looking at him before speaking. "I'm still not sure what caused this whole dating idea you had, but if you ask me it's about damned time you started trying to meet new people and have a life. I know your ex fucked you up by cheating on you, and I know I probably didn't help matters either with all my wishy-washiness four years ago, but you deserve happiness just like everyone else, and if you think dating and meeting guys is going to get you that happiness then you cannot give up."

She sighed, one of her heavy sighs that meant she had something seriously weighing on her mind. "But I am an idiot. What's a fat girl doing dating? No one's going to want to be with someone who looks like me."

"You're not fat. I don't know how many times I'm going to have to tell you that before you start to believe it, but you are not fat."

"Yeah I am. I have the measurements to prove it."

"Those are just numbers, Molly. Fucking numbers. Who cares if you wear a size two or a size twenty-two? I don't, and most men don't, either. You're curvy, and in a good way. And I might not be attracted to you anymore but I'm not blind and I know pretty when I see it."

She was silent for a few moments, but instead of addressing his comment asked, "So, where's Emery?"

He sighed. Apparently Molly was either mulling over what he'd said or had chosen to ignore it altogether. "She had to work a little late, so she's on her way down right now." He checked his watch. "Actually, she should be here pretty soon."

"Ah."

"What does that mean?"

"Nothing. Just, 'ah'."

"You're such a horrible liar."

She shrugged. "I know."

"So how was your day before the date?"

"Hellish. I swear to God, I want to break Warren's long, stuck up nose."

"What'd he do now?"

"He's just making my life a living hell at work. He's always looking over my shoulder and he's started to make snide comments. The other day he actually had the audacity to tell me I was spending too much time on the phone helping clients. Seriously! What is this guy's problem?"

"He's a Baylor Brat."

"That pretty much sums it up–a Baylor Brat who's mommy and daddy always paid for everything and who never had to work for anything a day in his life. Hell, this position was pretty much handed to him on a silver platter, even though there are other people in the office who are much more qualified to be our supervisor."

"That's pretty much the way it goes." He reached for the pack of cigarettes on the table in front of him. "The people who have the money make the money, and those of us who don't have the money do all of their work and don't get a damned thing for it."

Molly snorted. "Man, we're getting cynical."

He lit a cigarette and took a drag. "It happens."

The door of the bar opened as he exhaled, and Emery walked in, looking tired. She approached their table and greeted him with a long, wet kiss and a smile. Okay, so maybe she wasn't so tired. She then turned to Molly and did that one-armed shoulder hug thing that women seemed to do.

"How was the drive?"

Emery sat down next to him and lit up a cigarette. "Long. Traffic was a bitch, as usual."

Their waitress approached and Emery ordered a Miller Lite before launching into a story about a customer she'd had earlier in the day at the hotel she worked for. He noticed Molly fiddling with her phone out of the corner of his eye, and turned to his best friend as soon as Emery stopped to take a drink of her newly delivered beer.

"Going somewhere?" he asked Molly.

She looked up at him, but he couldn't quite read her expression. "I don't know. Barrett just texted me, wanting to know if we were up here. I don't even know how he got my number."

Oops. He may have forgotten to tell her he'd given Barrett her number a couple weeks ago.

"I wonder why he didn't text me?" Emery asked.

"I have no idea."

"What did you tell him?" he asked.

"That yeah, we were up here and to join us if he felt like it."

"So are you going to stick around, then?" he asked Molly.

"I guess I can for a while. It's not like I have anything else going on tonight."

"Oh, yeah, how'd your date go?" Emery asked.

"I mistakenly thought he was a drug dealer."

Emery raised an eyebrow and Molly retold the story.

"So you just walked out before you finished eating?"

Emery asked.

"Unfortunately. I was really hungry, too."

Emery turned to Benjamin. "Where do you keep find-ing these guys?"

Benjamin looked around. "Here. Right here."

"Well that explains that," Molly said, sarcasm lacing her voice.

He pointed a finger at her. "Hey, now, Missy. You know you liked him before he turned into the supposed Marijuana Pimp."

Molly snorted. "Okay, you've got me there. He is a good-looking guy, and actually seemed nice and halfway intelligent."

The door opened again, and a cold blast of air hit their table as Barrett walked in.

"Hey man, what's up?" He asked everyone at the table as he made his rounds, hugging Molly then Emery before nodding his head towards Benjamin.

"Nothing much, bro, just drinking some beers and dis-cussing Molly's bad date," Benjamin said.

"Bad date, huh?" Barrett asked Molly.

"Yeah, you could say that."

"What happened?"

For the third time that night Molly retold the story. Anyone else would've been tired of telling it, but not Molly. She loved telling stories, and often forgot which ones she'd told, which meant he got to hear several of them many times over. Usually with embellishments.

"Ouch," Barrett said after Molly finished.

"Yeah."

Barrett took the one empty seat that remained, putting himself between Benjamin and Molly and across the table from Emery. They made small talk, and a few minutes turned into an hour, an hour turned into two, and before Benjamin knew it, the bar lights came on and the manager told everyone to close their tabs and go home.

Their group of four made their way outside, and a few other friends slowly made their way out of the bar and into the cool night air.

"Anything going on tonight?" someone asked.

Benjamin turned around and saw that it was Freddy, an acquaintance who worked for Budweiser delivering beer. "Don't know yet, man."

A couple of other people joined them outside, asked him the same question, and somehow he ended up telling about ten different people to come on over to his place. He didn't know how it happened, but it always seemed to when he'd been drinking.

Within ten minutes, his apartment was crowded with people, alcohol, and Emery's nervously pacing dog.

He looked up, surprised, as Molly walked in. "I figured you weren't coming." Molly never came to his after parties.

She shrugged. "I'm not really tired just yet, and didn't feel like going home."

"Hey, Molly, what's up?" Barrett asked from one of the three couches Benjamin had in his living room.

"Hey, there. Nothing much, just thought I'd join the party for a little bit."

"Cool, cool."

"Anyone got any cards?" someone suggested.

"Nope," Benjamin said as he grabbed a beer from the fridge.

"Damn"

"We could play I Never," someone else suggested.

Benjamin closed the refrigerator door and shook his head. The room swayed slightly, but even in his inebriated state he knew that game was never a good idea. Never.

"That's never a good idea," Molly said.

"Sure it is," Emery said. "It's fun."

Oh, this could get bad. Unfortunately, no one else seemed to agree. God save her from drunk people.

Emery patted the empty space on the couch beside her, and Molly watched as Benjamin made his way over outstretched legs and feet and flopped down on the empty cushion.

"I'll start," Emery volunteered.

Molly groaned inwardly.

"Wait, how do you play this again? I haven't done this since Junior High," Freddy said.

That's because it's a game meant to be played in junior high—not by a bunch of twenty-somethings.

"Well, you say something like, 'I never kissed someone in public.' If you've done it, you take a drink. If you haven't, you don't take a drink. If you're the only person who's ever done something, you have to tell the story behind it," Emery explained.

"Oh, okay," Freddy said.

Emery grabbed her beer from the coffee table in front of her, thought for a few minutes, and said, "I've never had sex."

Everyone in the room took a drink. Not surprising.

"It's your turn now, Benjamin," Emery said.

Benjamin seemed to think for a few moments. "Um, I've never had sex in a public place."

About half the room drank to that. They continued in a circle around the room, and everyone seemed to be getting wasted except for Molly, who was drinking water. *Why am I doing this again? Just get up and go home already.*

They went around the room a couple more times, with every round getting more and more risqué. The game went back around to Benjamin. "I've never lost a condom during sex."

Deep breaths, Molly, deep breaths.

She, Emery, Benjamin and Barrett were the only ones who drank to that one.

"Molly, you've lost a condom during sex?" Emery asked.

Molly felt slightly panicked. Shit. This game was never a good idea.

"Um, yeah." She gulped her water.

"Well, tell us the story," Emery cajoled.

"But I wasn't the only person."

Deep breaths. Deep breaths. Deep breaths.

"Oh, come on, Molly, tell us the story," Freddy teased.

She hesitated, tucked a strand of hair behind her ear. "Well, it was the night I lost my virginity. We were in the middle of, uh, having sex and we realized we'd lost the condom. We looked, couldn't find it, and said 'screw it' and went back to what we'd been doing. A few hours later, after everything was said and done, I, ah, found it."

"Where'd you find it?" Barrett asked.

"Let's just say that when I got up to pee I noticed that something didn't quite feel right downstairs."

"It was stuck in your hoo-ha?" Emery asked.

"I guess you could put it that way." Molly's cheeks felt like they were about two hundred degrees.

Everyone started laughing, and after a few moments, Emery turned to Benjamin and asked him, "So how did you lose a condom?"

Well crap.

"What, what happened was I was fucking this chick, and it just slipped off or something in the middle of it. That was it."

"That's it?" Barrett asked. "Come on, I know you can make that funnier."

Benjamin shrugged. "It was funny at the time, but it isn't so funny now."

Molly gulped down more of her water.

"Oh, come on, baby, tell us the whole story. I don't mind," Emery said.

"Well, you've kind of already heard it."

Why had he just said that?

The water Molly had been gulping went down the wrong way. Emery looked first at Benjamin then Molly, who was in the middle of a spastic coughing fit.

"Wait a second."

Molly could almost see the wheels turning in Emery's head. Crap.

Emery looked at Benjamin. "You took Molly's virginity?"

Shit.

Molly coughed again before shooting up off the couch and almost sprinting into the kitchen.

"Um, yeah."

"You didn't tell me that. I mean, I knew you two had slept together before, but I didn't know you were her first."

Molly grabbed a jug of water from Benjamin's fridge and refilled her glass. Why had she come over here? *Bad idea, Molly, bad idea. You should have gone home when you had the chance.*

"I didn't think it was important," she heard Benjamin say from the living room.

She slammed her glass down on the counter.

"Wait, what I mean was I didn't think it was important to us, you and me. I told you we'd slept together, and that was all there was to it."

Wasn't important? Taking her virginity wasn't important?

"Baby, you don't have to explain. I think it's cool that you were Molly's first."

"What?" Benjamin asked.

Was Emery serious? She couldn't be.

"Seriously. It's cool, doesn't bother me."

Are you kidding me?

"Yes, I'm serious," Emery paused before loudly saying, "Molly, you can come back in here. I'm not upset."

She took a deep breath before walking back towards the living room.

Molly peeked her head around the corner. "Really?"

"Really. Come back in here, sit down, have some fun."

Molly tossed Benjamin a look that she hoped said, "Keep your mouth shut."

Emery took a swig of her beer before looking at Molly. "So was it good?"

Molly could feel heat warm her cheeks and Benjamin groaned. Yup. Never a good idea to play I Never with the best friend you'd lost your virginity to and the woman he was currently dating. No, not a good idea at all.

CHAPTER SIX

"I thought you'd told her about us!"

"I did tell her about us."

"Except you somehow managed to leave out the part about you being my first?"

Molly watched Benjamin rake a hand through his hair and propped her fists on her hips. She tapped a foot and cocked her head to the side as she waited for his response.

Last night had been horrible. Absolutely horrible. Not to mention uncomfortably embarrassing and possibly the worst idea ever.

"I didn't think she needed to know."

"How could you think that, Benjamin?"

"Look, I told her we'd slept together, and she was fine with it. I didn't think it was necessary to go into detail about our past sex life." He plopped down on her couch and grabbed the remote.

Molly bent over and yanked it out of his hand before turning off the TV. As much as she loved him, he could sometimes be the biggest bonehead ever.

"Hey!" he looked up at her.

She glared back down at him. "You're not going to avoid this one, hon, and football can wait."

"But it's the playoffs!"

"I know it's the playoffs and I want to watch, too, but right now, we're having us a little discussion."

"Fine, then." He crossed his arms over his chest.

"Don't get pissy with me. You're the one who didn't tell your girlfriend everything you should have, which put me in the hot seat last night. Do you have any idea how uncomfortable that was?"

"A pretty good idea, yeah."

Molly rolled her eyes. Somehow she doubted that. "You should have told her."

"Why? Is this some weird girl thing or something?"

"Yes, it's some weird girl thing. In case you haven't noticed, we women are kind of—to use your word—weird about that whole losing the virginity thing, and most of us build it up to be some uber important, life-altering event, so we automatically think it was that way for all other women."

"Was it that way for you?"

She sighed. He'd been there. He should already know the answer. "It was important, I'm not saying it wasn't. But the thing is Emery's not going to understand the circumstances or the dynamic at the time. It was what it was. You and I know that, but she probably doesn't."

"And I still don't understand what the big deal is. What happened back then is between us and no one else. I told her we'd slept together—at your suggestion–and she was fine with it. I didn't see any reason to tell her anything else."

Molly sat down on the couch beside him. "That's because you're a guy, hon. Women, well, like I said, we're weird about this stuff. Hell, my own mother told me she wished my first time had been special for me."

"Hey now!"

"I'm not saying it wasn't special, but losing your virginity on Good Friday while watching porn isn't exactly the most romantic thing in the world. Sure, it was special because you're my best friend, but it wasn't special in the hearts and flowers and candlelight way most women think their first time should be."

"Well, I sure as hell never heard you complain about it."

I can't believe he actually has the audacity to be offended. I'm the one whose cherry got popped while watching ridiculously awful porn. And God, that music. The piano set to a porn beat had been distracting rather than romantic. At one point she'd actually had to ask him to turn the volume down because it had been such a mood killer.

Realizing Benjamin was staring at her she shook herself from her thoughts.

"Because the situation fit us, you big dummy. And that's what I'm trying to explain–Emery's going to have this idea in her head that it was some big romantic to-do or something, and it wasn't. But I can guarantee you it's going to make her insecure."

He got up and walked into the kitchen. "But she has nothing to be insecure about. You and I haven't had sex in years."

"True, but you were my first."

Molly turned around and watched over the back of the couch as he grabbed a glass from a cabinet and poured himself some water.

"What's the point of this, Moll?" He asked as he closed the refrigerator door.

"The point is that I'm guessing that the fact that we have a past probably makes her at least a little uncomfortable and that this isn't going to help matters any."

"But why would she say she was fine with it if she wasn't?"

Molly rolled her eyes as Benjamin sat back down on the couch beside her. "You are such a guy. She's going to tell you she's fine with it because she doesn't want to seem like the crazy, jealous girlfriend who can't handle the fact that her boyfriend has a best friend he's slept with, even if it was only one time."

"Really?"

Why am I helping him out again? Seems a little counter-intuitive, Moll.

"Really. It's the way we work, hon, and it's part of the reason I stayed away for so long when y'all first started dating."

"I thought that was because you were jealous of her."

Molly punched him in the arm in an effort to hide that she had in fact been jealous of Emery. Insanely jealous, even. "I didn't want to cause problems by being around all the time." *I didn't want to see you kissing someone else all the time.*

"Ow!" He rubbed his arm where Molly's fist had landed. "That hurt!"

"No it didn't. I hit like a girl."

He grinned. "Yeah, you do. So should I try to explain things to her?"

"I don't know. At this point, it might seem more like you're trying to save face and make excuses rather than reassure her. I hate to say it, but she's probably already suspicious as it is."

What are you doing? Helping or hurting here, Moll? Make up your mind.

"What do you mean?"

She licked her lips. "Hon, she's up in Dallas all week long. That's an hour and a half away. You don't think she's up there wondering if we're going at it like a couple of rabbits while she's gone?" *Guess I'm hurting.*

"She wouldn't think that."

"Why not? Everybody else does." Which was partially true.

"Who does?"

"Well, not so much anymore, but before you and Emery started dating everyone thought we were a couple, or at least sleeping together."

"Yeah, well, that was then. And people are stupid."

Of course they are. Why would you want a fat slob like me when you have the perpetually thin and gorgeous Emery?

"Benjamin. Are you listening to a word I'm saying?"

"Yes, I'm listening to you."

"Okay then. Just be prepared, because I have a feeling she might have a few questions for you." A part of her hoped Emery did have a few questions for him.

"Great. Fantastic."

"I know." Molly handed him the remote, and he turned the TV back on and tuned into the football game that was currently being played out.

"I really did think you stayed away because you were jealous."

She punched him in the arm again. This time she didn't hit like a girl.

That night, Molly lay in her bed, staring up at the ceiling as lights and shadows played against the surface. She couldn't believe Benjamin hadn't told Emery the whole story.

Well, okay, in all fairness, she did partially see it from his point of view. Usually, she took the same stance–what had happened between them was between them and no one else. But she'd always been up front with men about her relationship with Benjamin. She'd always told them that they had a past, that he'd been her first, but that the sex was in the past. And most of them had been fine with that. Well, two of them had been, but considering they'd only been two-night stands, she guessed it didn't really matter what they thought anyway.

Her ex boyfriend, though, hadn't been too comfortable with the past, and that was one reason she'd encouraged Benjamin to be up-front with Emery. Molly's ex—affectionately known as The Asshole to her and Benjamin–had been jealous of Benjamin, and had gone so far as to try to manipulate Molly into pushing Benjamin out of her life.

His plan had worked for a while, and Molly had almost lost her best friend in the process. Luckily, though, Benjamin was stubborn and refused to be kicked out of her life completely. So they just hadn't talked to each other for a few months, and after she and The Asshole had broken up, Benjamin had been the first person there for her. In a weird sort of way, the whole mess had only made their friendship stronger than it had been.

It wasn't until a few months after the break up that Molly had found herself doing some soul-searching, and she'd finally faced the sticky, horrible truth–she'd pushed Benjamin out of her life because she knew she couldn't be with The Asshole while Benjamin was still there.

As blasé as she tried to be about their sexual history, she couldn't lie to herself. No, they'd never actually been officially in a relationship, but they had slept together and she had lost her virginity to him. She had fallen completely in love with him in the process. It hadn't been until after the break up with The Asshole that Benjamin had admitted to her that he'd been in love with her, too, in the time period she liked to refer to as After Sex.

Sometimes she wished she hadn't decided to sleep with Benjamin that Good Friday four years ago, especially knowing he wouldn't commit to her. Looking back on it, she knew that a part of the reason why she'd done it was because she'd been willing to pathetically take whatever crumbs she could get. If she was honest with herself, though, she also had to admit that part of her reasoning had been that maybe sex would make him see the light and admit he was in love with her. Chalk it up to reading too many romance novels as a teenager—or simply being naïve—but at the time she'd believed sex could make him want a relationship with her.

She sighed and turned over onto her side, wrapping her arms around her body pillow and holding on tight.

Sleepily, she thought to herself that someday, someone would come along who would help her get over Benjamin, who could give her all the things her best friend wasn't willing to. There had to be someone out there who could and would be all those things she needed him to be. There had to be.

CHAPTER SEVEN

"I'm thinking about proposing."

Molly's entire body went still, and all she could do was stare at Benjamin for what felt like forever before she finally managed to oh-so-eloquently say, "What?"

"I think I'm going to propose to Emery this weekend."

She looked down at her hands and noticed that the knuckles were white. "What brought that on?"

Benjamin sat down on the couch beside her, shrugged before saying, "It just feels like the right time to do it."

"Uh. Okay."

"I, ah, bought a ring earlier."

Molly felt ice water run through her body. *Great. Not an anxiety attack. Not now. "Really?"*

"Yeah. I need a woman's opinion on it, though."

She watched in a type of fascinated horror as he reached into his pants pocket and pulled out a small white box. She'd often thought over the years of what it would be like to see him hand her a ring box, but even in her craziest fantasies the ring hadn't been for someone else. He pried open the lid and Molly stared down at the piece of jewelry, blurrily saw silver and a hint of a colored stone, and had to blink her eyes to try to regain focus.

"It's, um, interesting."

"That's all you have to say?"

"Interesting in a good way, hon." She looked up at

him, saw the nerves etched across his face, and knew it was important that she be happy for him.

Deep breaths, Molly, deep breaths.

"Do you think she'll like it?"

"Yeah, I think so." She swallowed past the lump in her throat. "At least you didn't choose something obnoxiously big."

"So you like it?"

Probably more than I should.

"Yeah, I like it."

"Guess how much I paid for it?"

She really didn't want to.

"I don't know. Nine hundred bucks?"

"One twenty-five."

She raised her eyebrows. "One twenty-five? Did you get it on clearance or something?"

"Nope." He grinned like the cat who'd just eaten the proverbial canary. "Pawn shop."

Molly stared at him, rapidly blinked her eyes, and then burst into laughter. Oh, this was good. Too good.

"What? What's wrong with buying it at a pawn shop?"

"Hon, you don't buy an engagement ring at a pawn shop."

"Why the hell not?"

"Because, it's bad luck for someone else to have put the ring on before her." Was it bad of her to feel a slight twinge of hope at the thought?

"That's just silly superstition."

"But it's superstition for a reason. Plus, it's kind of, well, how do I put this nicely?"

"You're going to say it's cheap, aren't you?"

"You know me far too well."

"Hey, I have a limited amount of money to spend here, so I did what I had to do."

"You couldn't have saved up the money?" *Like most*

normal people.

"It would have taken me forever to save up enough money to get something really expensive."

"Which would have been plenty of time for you to assess whether or not you really want to spend the rest of your life with her." The argument made perfect sense to her.

He sighed. "But we don't have time. She's applying to grad school, and if she gets in she'll be moving to Oregon in about six months. I would rather do this now and solidify everything, that way if it comes down to it, I can just move up there with her."

Nausea settled in on top of the cold. "You can't move!"

"You did it for The Asshole," he pointed out.

"Yeah, well, I was stupid."

"Well I'm not."

"That's still up for debate."

Benjamin grabbed a piece of chocolate from the candy dish on her coffee table and unwrapped it before saying, "So you think I'm being stupid and moving too fast?"

She thought about it for a few moments before responding. How was she supposed to answer this one? "On one hand, yeah, I do. Y'all have only been dating for a few months, so this is awfully quick. But on the other hand, you're the one in the relationship, and if it doesn't feel too fast to you, then you need to go with your gut and do what you feel is best."

"That doesn't tell me anything."

She grinned, even though her heart was breaking. "I know. So when are you planning on popping the question?"

"This weekend, while we're in Galveston."

"Ah."

"What's that mean?"

"Nothing, just 'ah.'"

They sat together in companionable silence for long moments before Benjamin spoke again. "So, you really think I should do it? Because I really want your approval."

Molly plastered as genuine a smile as she could muster on her face and said, "Yes, I approve. You have to do what makes you happy, and as long as you're happy, I'll be happy for you."

He leaned over and kissed her on the forehead before standing up. "Well, I've got to go meet my dad up at The Shame."

"The Shame" was short for The Crying Shame, a primarily country bar Benjamin's dad liked to frequent. "Tell him I said hi."

"Will do," he said as he opened her front door and stepped outside.

Molly sat there and stared at her front door, lost in thoughts best left alone.

♡

After staring at her door for a good thirty minutes, Molly turned on her laptop and pulled up her blog. She'd started blogging while in college as a way to keep up with friends who had scattered across the country. They would write about the daily goings on in their lives and leave comments for one another, ranging from sympathetic to happy to offering to help cut off the balls of more than a few men.

More than a way to keep up with her friends, though, her blog had turned into a journal of sorts. When she'd been a child she had gone through a diary phase. Every day after school she would get home and write about the day's events, who liked who, her latest crush, classes and even a couple about her favorite boy bands. There was something oddly freeing about being able to write out her thoughts as an adult and choose who got to read them and who didn't. Sometimes she didn't let anyone read her blogs and set them to "private." But she always felt better after writing one.

She took a sip of water, sighed, and placed her fingers on the keys.

Benjamin just left. He told me he's going to propose to Emery, even had the ring with him and wanted my opinion on it.

I wasn't sure what to say or what to do. I felt like I'd been punched in the gut. A part of me still feels like we belong together, even if the rest of me is determined to get over him. But how do you get over someone when they're such a big part of your life?

How do you get over someone when he's always there? When you see him at least three days out of the week and talk to him every single day? How do you get over someone when for years he's all you've been able to think about, all you've really wanted?

Sometimes I think I must've been the world's biggest idiot to sleep with him that night. I knew, deep down, that it would end in nothing but heartache for me. I knew he didn't want a commitment or anything serious. I knew he didn't feel the same way about me that I felt about him. But I did it anyway. And it isn't that I regret my decision that night, more that I sometimes wonder how different things would be now if we hadn't had sex.

Even though I was in love with him, I was the one who decided I would rather have him in my life as nothing more than my friend than nothing at all. At times I want to blame him for the mess I'm in, but I'm the one who never came clean about my feelings. Well, if I'm being honest here, he never did, either. We both kept our mouths shut. Chalk it up to immaturity, fear, or whatever, but we both screwed up and I do wonder what could have been had we just been honest with each other.

So here I am now, four years later, still wondering what could have been. What's wrong with me? I'm I a masoch-

ist? A pathetic chicken shit? A little bit of both?

I don't know. Right now I feel like I don't know anything, other than the fact that I'm tired of feeling this way. I am so sick and fucking tired of feeling this way, of always feeling like I'm on the verge of tears, like I'm just waiting, waiting, waiting for something—anything——to give. I'm sick of waiting for him to see the light. I'm sick of waiting for myself to see the light.

He doesn't love me the way I love him. I need to accept that. I need to move on.

But why does moving on have to be so damned hard?

Molly brushed away the few errant tears that had managed to trickle down her cheeks. What was up with her? She never cried, and yet here lately she'd become a regular waterworks.

Sighing, she read over her entry, set the privacy setting to "friends only" and clicked on "post."

She was not looking forward to this weekend, to say the least.

CHAPTER EIGHT

Molly didn't know how she was supposed to sit through another date while Benjamin was down in Galveston proposing to Emery, so she'd begged off on dates for the weekend, telling Benjamin she was going to concentrate on looking for another job.

Of course, she wasn't actually looking for another job. Instead, she was standing in the romance section at Barnes & Noble at eight o'clock on a Friday night, desperately searching for a way to escape from reality for at least a few hours.

"Are these actually any good?"

Molly had been deeply engrossed in the second page of the latest Susan Elizabeth Phillips novel, and jumped at the sound of the masculine voice beside her. Hand over her chest, as though her heart would leap out of it, she turned to her right to address the person who'd just about scared the living daylights out of her.

"I didn't startle you, did I?"

He was absurdly good-looking in a lanky, geeky sort of way. His dark brown hair was thick and wavy, in that way that only men's hair could be. Clear green eyes behind a pair of rectangular black-framed glasses. Casually dressed in faded blue jeans, a long-sleeved white Henley with a black graphic tee layered over it that said "Inconceivable!" on the front. Dark stubble covered his jaw.

Molly licked her lips and realized she was staring. *What is a hot, geeky looking guy doing in the romance section? Is he lost?*

Mentally shaking herself, she finally responded to his question. "Just a little bit."

They stood there in awkward silence until he finally smiled, causing a dimple to appear. "Sorry about that."

"No, it's okay. I was probably a little too into this book considering I'm standing in the middle of the store."

He raised an eyebrow. "I wouldn't say that. Bookstores are for reading, if you ask me."

She lifted the right side of her mouth in a half smile. "You have a point."

"So *are* romance novels actually any good?"

"You interested in buying some?"

He shrugged. "My mom reads them all the time, which is why I'm here, actually. I've never read one, so I'm a little curious."

Picking up books for his mom on a Friday night? Molly wasn't sure if she should buy it or not, but decided to give him the benefit of the doubt, at least temporarily.

"It depends, really. Every genre has their bad apples, but it's all subjective."

He nodded towards the book in her hand. "I'm guessing that one is pretty good?"

She felt her cheeks grow warm and knew she was probably blushing. "Well, what I managed to read before you scared me was."

Did I really just say that? Man, I really do suck at this flirting thing.

"I am sorry about that."

The warmth in her cheeks spread to her ears. "It's okay." She looked down at the book she still held in her hand and back up at him. "You look familiar for some reason."

"I was thinking the same thing, but I know we've never met."

She raised an eyebrow. "How do you know that?"

"I definitely would've remembered your name had we ever met before."

His voice had dropped to a slightly lower register, and Molly felt the warmth from her cheeks begin to spread through her entire body. Was she seriously attracted to a complete stranger?

He held out his hand. "My name is Joe."

"Molly." She placed her hand in his and shook briefly. Her stomach flip-flopped at his touch. She began to worry, hoping she wasn't about to have an anxiety attack when she realized this wasn't an I'm-about-to-freak-out flip flop but rather a hormones-coming-to-attention flip flop. Her eyes widened. "Wait a second! You know my best friend Benjamin. You stopped by our table at Clicks the other night and said hi to him."

"That would be it." He withdrew his hand. "So Benjamin's your best friend, huh?"

She barely managed to not glance away from him. Just looking at him was making her mouth dry. "Yeah."

Come on, Molly, you can do better than "Yeah."

He gestured once again towards the book she still held in her hand. "So what's this one about?"

She looked down at the cover and tried to remember the plot. "It's the last book in her series about an NFL team in Chicago."

"Da Bears?"

Molly laughed. "Nice impersonation. And that's what you would think, but no, it's a fictional team."

"So there's an entire romance series dedicated to a fictional football team?"

She grinned at the disbelief in his tone. "Oh, yeah. They're very popular, too."

"So is it the tight pants or the actual sport that draws women in?"

"Well, I can't speak for other women, but for me it's the actual sport. You combine football with a flawed alpha hero and a quirky, intelligent heroine with issues and you have me hooked. Plus, her books are hilarious."

"So what other authors would you recommend? Like I said, my mom gave me a list, but it would be nice to surprise her a little bit."

"Well, it depends upon what she likes. What titles did she give you?"

Joe reached into his pocket and withdrew a folded up sheet of notepaper, which he unfolded and then handed to Molly.

"Your mom has pretty good taste in books."

"Well, I'm sure she'll be glad to hear that."

Molly looked up at him and felt her cheeks warm again. "I didn't mean to sound rude—if I did—it's just that some people have atrocious taste in reading material."

"No offense taken. So what would you recommend?"

Molly pointed out several books she thought his mom would like according to the list he'd provided. He chose two, along with a few his mom had requested.

"Thanks. You have no idea how much this means."

She looked at him from the corner of her eye. He sounded genuine, as though he actually meant what he was saying.

"No problem. I kind of enjoyed helping you out."

He smiled and turned, took a few steps in the opposite direction and turned back towards her. "This might sound weird, but do you want to grab some hot chocolate in the café or something?"

Am I really being picked up in the bookstore?

Molly looked down at the novel she still held in her hands and back up at Joe. Oh, hell. What could it hurt?

It was just hot chocolate. With a very attractive man. In a bookstore, which was pretty much her favorite place. "Sure."

After paying for their books and hot chocolate—separately, of course, since Molly would only allow him to pick her up so much—they claimed a table in the far corner of the café.

"So tell me, Molly, what are you doing in a bookstore at eight o'clock on a Friday night?"

"I could ask you the same thing."

His dimple flashed at her when he smiled. "You got me there. But you didn't answer my question."

"I felt like staying in and reading a good book, but I've read everything on my shelves, and didn't feel like re-reading any of them tonight. I still haven't managed to jump on the ebook train, so I decided to make a trip to the bookstore." She took a sip of her hot chocolate, tasted whipped cream and rich chocolate and thought she might be in heaven. "So what about you? What are you doing in a bookstore at eight o'clock on a Friday night buying romance novels for your mom?"

He shrugged. "I'm a nice guy?"

She shook her head. "You're not getting off the hook that easily."

"It seemed like a good time to go to the bookstore. When you think about it, most people are either out or getting ready to go out by this time of night."

"You were hoping to not get caught looking at covers filled with bare-chested men, weren't you?"

"You got me there."

"And then I had to go and ruin that for you." She was having a hard time not smiling at him.

"I wouldn't say you ruined anything for me."

Molly took a hasty sip of her cocoa to cover up the fact that she was blushing like a twelve-year-old girl. *Stupid fair skin and freckles, can't even hide a blush decently.*

"So how long have you and Benjamin been friends?"

His sudden change of subject made her hesitate before answering. "Um, about twelve years. Where'd that come from?"

He shrugged. "Something about the way you looked at him the other night."

The way she'd looked at him? "What do you mean?"

"It just seemed like there might be something going on there."

Molly stirred her hot chocolate with a swizzle stick as she thought about all the different ways she could respond to that comment. "We're probably never going to see each other again, right?"

He knitted his brows together. "Anything's possible."

She sighed. *Screw it, just tell him the whole story. What could it hurt?* "There's nothing going on between Benjamin and me. In fact, he's proposing to his girlfriend Emery this weekend. But there used to be something. I don't know. It was complicated. Well, complicated for me, not for him. For him it was just sex. At least that's the way he approached it. For me, yeah, not so much. He was my first. I was in love with him. He loved me, just not in the same way."

"Friends with benefits?" He raised an eyebrow.

"I think you have to sleep together more than once to be considered friends with benefits." She took a sip of her hot chocolate.

He pushed the sleeves of his Henley up, revealing tanned forearms liberally dusted with black hair. *How did he have a tan in January?* He placed his newly-revealed forearms on the table and leaned forward. "So let me get this straight. You've known each other since at least high school if not junior high, you lost your virginity to him, was in love with him, and yet you're still friends with him?"

She took a nervous sip of her hot chocolate. "I know it sounds a little odd. Most people couldn't have stayed friends after something like that, but it wasn't ever really an issue. Well, at first things were a little weird and awkward, but I got over it. He was my best friend—is my best friend—and I knew he wouldn't commit to me. We've had four years to move past it, and we've done a pretty good job."

"You mean he's done a pretty good job."

She shrugged. He really was too perceptive. "Sometimes it seems like I've done a good job of it myself, tonight not so much."

"So you're still in love with him?"

The swizzle stick snapped in her hands. "He's my best friend. I see him all the time. How else am I supposed to feel? Besides, I made a New Year's resolution to kind of get over him and move on."

"The same one you made last year?"

Molly narrowed her eyes. Maybe he wasn't so nice after all. "If you must know, no, it's not the same one I made last year. In fact, this is the first resolution I've ever made."

"So how's that working out for you?" He grinned at her.

She rolled her eyes. "If you're going to give me a hard time I can get up and leave."

She moved as though to stand. He placed his hands over hers and said, "I'm sorry. I didn't mean to insult you."

She snorted but settled back into her chair. Her stomach was performing those crazy cartwheels again at his touch. Okay, maybe she should leave, because she wasn't sure how she felt about being so attracted to a total stranger who was pushing far too many of her buttons.

"So, really, how's your resolution working out for you?" he asked, his tone gentler.

She hesitated. "Not so well. I had this great idea that

the best way to get over him would be to go out on blind dates, which is completely unlike me or anything I've ever done. The only problem is that I don't exactly know a lot of single men, so Benjamin's been hooking me up with guys. So far nothing's really panned out."

"Maybe you're not going out with the right guys."

She laughed. "Oh, I'm definitely not going out with the right guys. The first one had a unibrow and very oily hair, and all he talked about the entire time was his accounting job at a bank. I don't know about you, but I'm not a big fan of math, much less accounting, so needless to say I was a little bored. Plus, he couldn't make up his mind and was really indecisive. The second guy, well, that was more my fault than his. I mistakenly thought he was a drug dealer and walked out before I even finished eating."

"Yeah, you're definitely dating the wrong guys."

"I know! And to add to all this is the fact that I'm stressed out about my job, have been having anxiety attacks almost every morning and am looking for a new means of employment which just adds more stress. And I have no idea why I'm telling you all of this, especially after you insulted me."

He threw back his head and laughed, his Adam's apple bobbing up and down in his throat. "I call this an L.I.T Moment."

"L.I.T Moment?"

"Have you ever seen *Lost in Translation?*"

"Yeah."

"Well, you know how Bill and Scarlett's characters have this experience away from home that they would've never had if they hadn't traveled and met each other?"

"Oh. So basically, when you meet someone who's a complete stranger but the fact that they're someone you'll probably never see again makes you feel comfortable enough to be your neurotic self?"

He winked at her. "Exactly."

"Well, hopefully my neuroses didn't scare you too much."

"Neuroses? What neuroses?"

Her smile was slow. "It's been really nice meeting you, Joe."

"It's been really nice meeting you too, Molly."

CHAPTER NINE

Molly put down the book she'd been reading and glanced at the clock on her cable box. Five p.m. Benjamin should be getting back fairly soon.

She hadn't heard from him all weekend, and the suspense was killing her. Had he popped the question? Had he come to his senses and decided not to? And if he had popped the question, what was Emery's answer?

Unable to stand the suspense any longer, she picked up her cell phone and typed out a quick text message.

> Molly: Did you ask her?

She exited out of her text messages and set the phone back down on the coffee table. Warily, she got up from the couch, grabbed her empty glass and walked into the kitchen to refill it. She gulped down the cold water, and re-opened the refrigerator and once again filled the glass.

She jumped slightly when Benjamin's ring tone echoed through her apartment. With something akin to dread, she walked back into the living room and picked up her phone.

> Benjamin: Yes.

Short answer. Didn't tell her much.

> Molly: What'd you say?

A few minutes later, he responded.

> Benjamin: No. She and Barrett ended up hooking up.

Molly cocked her head to the left and drew her eyebrows together. Was he being serious or just messing with her? He had to be messing with her; Emery wouldn't do something like that. She wasn't the type. Still, though, she had to ask just to make sure.

Molly: Are you serious?

Almost immediately, she received a response.

Benjamin: No, I'm not serious. She said
yes.

Molly sat down on the couch and stared at the phone in her hands, not sure if she wanted to congratulate him or start bawling her eyes out. A tear plopped onto her hand and she guessed she'd opted for the latter. Since Benjamin wasn't there to see her cry, and because she was his best friend and wanted him to be happy, she texted him back.

Molly: Well, congratulations.

She locked the phone's screen, slowly set it back down on the table, and leaned back into the deep cushions of her couch. She grabbed a throw pillow—a soft, red chenille she'd bought on sale from Target—and hugged it to her tight.

The phone rang, and Molly hit the button to silence it. Tears began to stream down her cheeks. She took a deep, shuddering breath before allowing a sob to escape.

There was a tightness in her chest, like a big ball of despair that threatened to overwhelm her.

Engaged. He was engaged. To someone other than her. To some thin, perky, gorgeous woman who probably didn't have a single cellulite dimple on her butt. Who could shop anywhere she wanted to, wear the cute bras and panties from Victoria's Secret and not worry about whether or not she was too chubby to wear a thong.

What's wrong with me? What does she have that I don't have? Why am I alone? I'm so tired of being alone.

Sobs wracked her body and Molly held the pillow tighter, closer to her body. She curled into a ball on the couch, her knees drawn up almost to her chest, and tried to remember to breathe. Instead she just cried harder.

All these years. All these years of being so sure he would come to his senses, waiting for him to realize they were meant to be together. And instead he proposed to someone else. After all his talk about liking thicker girls, all his insistence that he liked curves, he'd proposed to a skinny woman.

Molly squeezed her eyes shut, felt more tears stream down her face, over the bridge of her nose and into her hair. A drop of water tickled the inside of her ear. She breathed deeply, tried desperately to get air into her lungs.

"Calm down, Molly. You have to calm down." She hiccupped to herself and the empty—very empty—room.

She opened her eyes.

Took a deep breath.

The tightness eased a little bit. She sat up and felt light-headed. Closed her eyes again. More deep breaths as tears continued to roll down her cheeks, slower now but still too fast for her to control.

She cupped her forehead with her hands and asked the empty room, "Am I ever going to get over Benjamin?"

She sniffled. At least she wasn't crying quite as hard now. She grabbed a tissue from the box on the coffee table and blew her nose.

Damn him for making me cry. Now my eyes are going to be red and puffy and my face will be splotchy and I'll be blowing my nose for the next thirty minutes. Stupid boy. Stupid me.

Molly threw the used tissue into the trashcan. She wished she could throw her feelings away just as easily.

♡

Benjamin waved good bye to Emery as she pulled out

of his parking lot. He was engaged. Holy shit.

Anxious to talk to Molly about it, he quickly walked back into his apartment and pulled his cell phone out of his jeans pocket. He tapped on her name, and waited for her to pick up.

"Hello?" She finally said.

"What're you doing?"

"Um." There was a pause on the other end of the line. "I'm reading a book."

"Are you okay?"

"Yeah. Why wouldn't I be?" He heard what he could have sworn was a sniffle.

"Are you sure?"

And there, that was a sigh. "Yes, I'm okay."

"No you're not. You sound like you've been crying."

"My allergies are bothering me. I think I'm getting sick." That was definitely a sniffle.

He wanted to call bullshit on her since he was ninety-five percent sure she was lying to him, but he couldn't quite figure out just why she would be lying to him, so he decided to not press the issue.

Instead, he said, "That sucks. So how was your weekend?"

He heard Molly clear her throat. "Um, it was okay. Read some books. Watched a movie."

"Wow, don't sound so excited."

"Benjamin, you know how I am when I get sick—it's hard to get me excited about anything."

Something definitely wasn't okay with her. "So you just relaxed?"

"Yeah."

He walked into the kitchen and grabbed a beer out of the fridge. "Meet any guys this weekend?"

There was a brief hesitation and another sniffle. "Um, no."

"Well why the hell not?" He teased.

Another sigh—this one much heavier than the last one. "Because I suck where men are concerned."

"No you don't."

"Yes I do."

"If you say so." He tipped the beer bottle up and took a swig.

She sighed again, and he could imagine her facial expression—she would have her irritated Molly face on, the one where she cocked her head, drew her eyebrows together and looked up at the ceiling in exasperation.

"So, um, she said yes?" He heard her ask.

"Yup."

"Don't sound so excited." She mimicked his earlier statement.

"I am excited, just tired. I've barely gotten any sleep this weekend."

"Well then go to bed."

"It's six in the evening."

"So?"

He finished off his beer and threw the empty bottle in the trashcan. "So, it's too early for me to go to bed."

"If you say so." There was a slight pause. "Hey, hon, I've gotta go, someone's beeping in."

"No, you're not allowed to," he teased.

"Whatever. I'll talk to you later, bye."

He waited until she'd hung up to hit "end call" on his phone. Something was wrong with Molly, and he was willing to bet that it wasn't a high pollen count. He knew her, and it sounded like she'd been crying, but he couldn't for the life of him figure out why.

♡

Molly blacked out the screen and slowly set the phone

down on the coffee table. She took a deep, shaky breath, and waited to see if the tears were going to come back.

She shouldn't have answered the phone just then. Benjamin knew her too well, and he probably knew she was lying through her teeth when she said nothing was wrong. Of course something was wrong. Everything was wrong.

She sighed and picked up the remote control, flipping through channels before stopping on a *Say Yes to the Dress* marathon.

Despite her feelings for Benjamin, she really did want him to be happy. Sure, there were times (okay ninety-nine percent of the time) when she felt she was really the only woman who he would be happy with. And there were times when she wanted to shake some sense into him, ask him what his problem was where they were concerned.

Molly's thoughts swirled as she stared at the image of a woman in a wedding dress on the television screen. Things had gotten so complicated between them, and she wasn't quite sure when that had happened. Some would say it had all started back in high school, when he'd asked her to be his prom date. Others would say it was right after the first time they'd kissed each other—on a bet, no less. Sometimes she wondered if it had been when they'd lived together with two other roommates for a brief period of time during their early college years. Lord knew the sexual tension had been unbearable even back then. Most people, though, would say it had gotten complicated that Good Friday a few years back, when they'd finally given in and slept with each other.

Her heart and stomach did this funny lurching thing at the memory of that night. Despite the fact that there hadn't been candlelight or roses, the experience had still meant something to her. While her first time hadn't necessarily been emotional or soul-bearing or even spectacular in the way some people thought it should be the evening had been special. Not every woman could say she'd lost her virginity to her best friend.

Benjamin had known just what to say and do to keep her from over thinking everything. The few times they'd fooled around prior to that night, she'd tensed up, been nervous and had slammed on the brakes. To this day, she still wasn't entirely sure just what had caused her to make the decision to sleep with him that night, other than the fact that it had simply felt right. She'd been relaxed and enjoying herself and had decided the time was right, so why not?

She didn't regret that decision, either, even if doing so had complicated things immensely.

Actually, if she really thought about it, she could say that the day things got so complicated was the day he'd looked at her and really, truly, seen her. They'd been standing outside in a friend's front yard. He was smoking a cigarette and she was standing on the top porch step, leaning against the rail. They'd been talking about something—she couldn't remember what now, but the topic was probably music or movie related—and he'd just kind of stopped, cigarette in mid-air, and looked at her. A half smile had played over his lips, and for just a few seconds, he'd looked at her the way she'd always wanted him to.

And then the expression was gone. Just like that, the cigarette had finished its course to his mouth, the smile had disappeared and the look in his eyes was nothing more than a distant memory.

It hadn't been until a good two years later—after she and The Asshole had broken up—that Benjamin had admitted to her that that day, at that moment, he'd looked at her and realized he'd fallen in love with her.

And that was when things had gotten complicated.

"Are you okay?"

Molly looked over at Blanche with what was probably a slightly confused look on her face. "Yeah. Why?"

"Because you look like hell."

"Thanks."

"You look like you've been crying," Sharonda piped in.

Molly turned around fully in her chair and faced her two coworkers. She looked at Blanche and then Sharonda, and felt her upper lip start to quiver. Oh, God. Not now. She couldn't start crying now.

She sucked in a deep breath, braced herself, and blurted out, "Benjamin proposed to Emery and she said yes."

"Are you shitting me?" Blanche asked.

"That asshole!" Sharonda said.

"No, I'm not shitting you and he's not an asshole, just blind."

Sharonda got up and closed the door to their office space. She sat back down, leaned over, and patted Molly on the leg. "He'll come to his senses. He'll realize he really loves you."

Molly shook her head. "I don't know if he will. And besides, I'm the one who decided to get over him. I should be fine with this, rather than crying my eyes out."

"Well, he's obviously stupid for not being with you," Blanche said.

"Thanks. Doesn't help much, but thanks."

Sharonda hugged Molly. "It'll be okay. Even if he doesn't come to his senses there are other fish in the sea."

"I know, I know. So far I just haven't caught one worth keeping." Joe's face flashed across her mind. Now where the hell had that come from?

"Well y'know, honey, you can always catch one and then throw him back once your done with him." Blanche wiggled her eyebrows suggestively.

Molly and Sharonda looked at each other and choked back laughs. Blanche got up and opened the door, and Molly turned back to her computer.

She glanced at the time. She'd only been at work for twenty minutes and already she was itching for her lunch break to hurry up and get here so she could email the cover letters and resumes for positions she'd bookmarked over the weekend.

She heard Warren's voice out in the hallway and shuddered. If she couldn't get out of her personal hell she could damn sure get out of her professional one.

CHAPTER TEN

Molly set the treadmill to a nice, steady pace, increased the incline just slightly and opened up the book she'd brought with her.

When she'd first started coming to the gym she'd thought people were crazy for bringing books and magazines and reading while on the various stationary equipment. But then she'd tried it and found that reading while walking was much easier than one would think.

She'd read about five pages when a masculine voice pulled her out of the very hot sex scene she'd been in the middle of.

"Do you have any idea how sexy multi-tasking is?"

She turned her head and almost pulled a Bridget Jones.

Joe reached out a hand to steady her—unlike Molly he had no problem balancing on a swiftly moving treadmill—and said, "Sorry, I didn't mean to startle you." He peered at her book. "Whatcha reading?"

She marked her page and swiftly closed the novel. "The same book you interrupted the last time."

"Imagine that."

He continued to stare at her as he walked. Just her luck. She never saw anyone she knew at the gym, and yet here Joe was, viewing her in all of her makeup-less glory. Not to mention the ghost-white legs that peeked out from athletic shorts. And, oh man, her boobs were flattened.

Well, as much as they could be, at least, all things considered. Stupid sports bra. She'd figured out that some women could manage to look attractive while they worked out. She, however, just looked hot. Literally.

She continued walking and turned her head so that she was once again looking forward. From the corner of her eye, she could see that Joe was still watching her. "So are you stalking me now or something?"

He laughed. "Not at all. This is just a happy coincidence."

"Sure it is."

"So was this another resolution you made this year?"

"Hardly. I've been coming here for almost a year now, figured working out would be a good way to reduce my stress levels."

"How's that working out for you?"

"Right now not so well." She looked pointedly at him.

He laughed again. "So are you saying I'm stressing you out?"

"The fact that you're stalking me is."

"I swear I had no idea you were a member here."

"Uh huh."

"Really, I didn't. I usually come in the mornings before work, or sometimes during my lunch break."

"Then why are you here at six o'clock in the evening?" She wasn't sure why she was being so bitchy, other than the fact that he seemed willing to let her get away with it. That, and she was uncomfortably aware of him. And she was hot and sweaty with flat boobs. Not exactly her best look.

"Because this morning was insane and then some stuff came up at lunch that I had to take care of."

"'Some stuff,' huh? Sounds mysterious."

"Hardly. Just bills and...stuff."

"Again with the stuff. Next thing I know you're going to pull out a water bottle that can also be used as a hand grenade and a spyglass."

"Did you really just say 'spyglass'?"

She smiled. "I have no idea where that came from."

"So you think I'm hiding something, huh?"

"I wouldn't say that. You just haven't shared a lot about yourself, and yet twice now we've just randomly bumped into each other. So you might be hiding something." Her grin spread across her face. "Or you could be stalking me."

He rolled his eyes. "I am not stalking you. But if you want me to leave to prove it to you I will."

He reached towards the control panel as though to turn off the treadmill. What was she doing? Here was this cute, intelligent guy flirting with her and she was trying to push him away. Was she crazy? "You don't have to leave. I'm just giving you a hard time."

"Why would you want to do that?"

She had a feeling he knew why, but answered anyway. "Because that's what I do. It's kind of my thing."

"You're thing?"

"Yes, my thing."

"Care to explain?"

"I'm not even sure I can."

"So how was that sex scene you were reading a few minutes ago?"

Her jaw dropped.

"My mom does the same thing—closes books really fast—if I walk into the room while she's in the middle of reading one."

She handed the book to him. "You want to know? Here."

He raised an eyebrow but took the book from her, opened it up to where she'd had it marked and flipped back a page to where the scene began.

Molly tried not to watch as he read, but a part of her

was really curious to see his reaction. In high school, her guy friends would always grab whatever book she was in the middle of and somehow always manage to open it up to a love scene. Which they would then read out loud. To everyone. Her cheeks would turn red, she'd either feel like crying or hitting someone, and would worry that people thought she was the fat girl living vicariously through romance novels. As she'd gotten older, she'd learned to stop caring so much about what others thought about her reading choices.

But still, there was something oddly…intimate…about watching an attractive man read a sex scene. Intimate and apparently arousing.

She looked away from him, uncomfortable with the butterflies that had started to dance in her stomach. Maybe she needed some water. She grabbed for the bottle next to the treadmill's control panel, took a long drink and set it back down.

Nope, that hadn't helped. Crap.

She glanced at him again. He was still reading and walking, his face not showing much of what he was thinking. Or feeling. *Is he feeling anything like what I'm feeling right now?* She looked down. *Did I really just do that? Did I really just check to see if he had a hard-on?*

She looked forward again. She was horrible at this. Horrible. It was no wonder she'd been single for so long.

Joe cleared his throat before handing her the book. "Well, that was certainly interesting."

"Interesting how?"

"Well, is it romance standard for the guy to have a huge penis?"

A bark of laughter escaped from her. "Generally, yes."

"So basically these novels are just disproving what you women always tell us."

"And what would that be?"

"That size doesn't matter."

She laughed. "Any woman who says size doesn't matter is lying through her teeth."

"You'll actually admit that?"

"Yeah. I'm not saying the bigger the better, because honestly there is such a thing as too big. But at the same time, well, generally during sex you want to be able to feel it."

He laughed. "You do bring up a good point."

"I know I do." She smiled at him. "So what else did you find interesting about that scene?"

"The fact that there was a lack of man roots and glistening centers."

The only thing that kept her from doubling over in laughter was the fear of falling off the treadmill. "Romance has changed a little bit since the days of the bodice ripper."

"Apparently." He nodded towards her treadmill. "Your time's almost up."

"Yeah, I know. But you're not too far behind me."

"No, I'm not. Not at all."

She glanced over at his curious tone. "Are you sure you're not stalking me?"

"Nope. Although I am beginning to wonder what I have to do to get your phone number."

Phone number? He wanted her phone number? "I'm surprised you even want to talk to me after everything I told you the other night."

"Why wouldn't I want to talk to you? You're funny, intelligent, and honest. Plus, I have to admit you're pretty easy on the eyes."

Easy on the eyes. The Asshole had told her she was easy on the eyes. She swallowed and tried to keep her tone light. "See, now, if you are stalking me and I give you my phone number, who's to say you won't be able to figure out where I live?"

"If I'd really wanted to know that I could've just followed you home the other night."

"You have a good point."

"Besides, if I was really stalking you wouldn't I already have your phone number?"

She thought about that for a second. "This is true."

"So, see? I'm not stalking you. I'm just a nice, ordinary guy who bumped into an interesting woman in a bookstore who I would like to get to know a little better."

"Fair enough."

The treadmill hit the cool down period and slowed. Usually, she was watching the time and was prepared for the sudden drop in speed, but since she'd been distracted hadn't been prepared. Once again, she almost fell off.

"In case you've failed to notice, I also have all the grace of a drunken moose. I don't know if that's going to change your mind at all or not, but I figured I might as well let you know."

He laughed. "Y'know, that could be a deal breaker. I'm not sure I could ever be interested in a woman who has trouble staying on a treadmill."

His machine hit the cool down period right as he was finishing up his sentence. He stumbled slightly, and Molly giggled. "Pot, I would like you to meet my good friend Kettle."

"Nice to meet you." He regained his footing and grinned at her.

Molly's stomach performed another somersault she was pretty sure the Russian judge would have given at least a nine point one. "So do you still want that phone number?"

He whipped his cell phone out of his gym shorts pocket and tapped the phone icon. "You better believe it."

She rattled off her cell phone number and watched as he keyed in her information. Moments later her own phone rang. She removed it from the ledge on the treadmill and checked the caller ID. "Is this you?" she asked Joe.

"That would be me."

"Thanks."

Her treadmill stopped and she stood there, trying to get used to the feeling of the ground not moving beneath her again. She took a drink of her water as Joe's machine came to a halt.

They stood there, awkwardly watching one another. "Well, uh, I have to go grab my stuff from the locker room."

He nodded. "Me too."

Neither of them moved.

"So, uh…"

"I'll give you a call some time this week."

She swallowed. "Okay. That sounds good."

After long moments she finally stepped off of the treadmill. Joe followed suit. They walked to the locker room area together in silence. He turned towards the men's area, she towards the women's. She looked back, and he was standing in the doorway, watching her. She smiled. He smiled back. Her stomach did another somersault.

Deep breaths, Molly, deep breaths.

For the first time ever, though, she smiled as she opened her combination lock.

He called the next evening. Molly saw Joe's name flash across the caller ID screen and felt surprised shock rush through her body. She tapped the green phone icon to answer.

"So you're not one of those guys who does the whole wait two days to call thing?" she asked without preamble.

He chuckled. "Well hello to you, too. And no, I'm not. I've never seen any point in that. If I get a woman's phone number it's because I want to talk to her, not play a bunch of high school games."

How refreshing. "So do you get a lot of women's numbers?"

"Not really. Yours is the first I've asked for in a while."

Now that was interesting. "How long is 'a while'?"

"Too long." He sighed. "Probably at least six months, if not closer to a year."

Now that was even more interesting. "A cute guy like you has a hard time getting phone numbers? I find that hard to believe."

"You think I'm cute?"

She sighed. Leave it to a man to focus on that one little thing. "In a geeky sort of way, sure."

"Geeky? I'm not sure if I should be flattered or insulted."

His tone was teasing, so Molly teased back. "Well, from some women that would be an insult. For those of us who are more evolved, though, we like our men with a dash of geekiness."

"You still didn't answer the question at hand."

"Well, I'm talking to you, aren't I?"

"Yeah, but that could be simply because you don't want to hurt my feelings."

"Uh huh. And you never answered my question."

"Remind me what it was again? I started wondering what you were wearing and got distracted."

She almost choked on the sip of water she'd just taken. "You what?"

"I'm just teasing you, Molly."

"Oh, okay."

"I've been wondering that since before I called you."

She rolled her eyes and looked down at her blue flannel pajama pants and white t-shirt. "Nothing but a smile."

Where had that come from?

It was apparently Joe's turn to choke. She waited a few moments before asking, "You okay over there?"

He coughed. "Well, I was."

"So what are you wearing?" *What the hell are you doing, Molly?*

"Nothing but a smile. Wanna join me?"

Her stomach did a slow roll. "Um…"

"I was teasing again. Although you joining me doesn't sound like a bad idea now that I think about it."

"I'm really wearing blue flannel pajama pants and a white t-shirt," she blurted out.

He laughed. "I'm actually wearing green boxers and a black t-shirt."

Boxers. Good to know. "You never answered me."

He sighed. "You know, you'd make a great interrogator."

She laughed. "I'm determined and curious, what can I say?"

There was a pause on the other end of the line before he finally answered. "I just haven't had time to date or even think about dating. Work, family stuff, you know how it is."

"So now you do have time?"

"Not really, but something keeps telling me to make time for you."

Her stomach dipped and rolled again. He wanted to date her? Oh, baby. "Um, well then."

"I'm not making you uncomfortable, am I?"

She cleared her throat. "Uncomfortable" wasn't exactly the word she would use. "No, not really. I'm just, well, a little surprised."

"Why? I've told you before, you're an attractive, intelligent woman with a great sense of humor. What's so odd about me wanting to get to know you a little better?"

"I just…I'm not used to this. It's all so," she paused,

trying to find the right word, "strange."

"What are you doing right now?"

"Looking for jobs online."

"Found anything good yet?"

She sighed. "No. There isn't a whole lot out there right now. I've found a couple and emailed my cover letter and resume, but that's it."

"You never did really tell me why you're looking for another job, just that this one has you stressed out."

"Stressed out is probably an understatement."

"Want to talk about it?"

Did she ever. She launched into the story, telling him all about the boring paperwork that a monkey could do, Warren's snobby behavior, the anxiety attacks, everything.

"You definitely need another job."

"Yeah, no kidding. Finding something is proving to be a little bit more difficult than I'd thought it would be, though."

"Have you had any interviews yet?"

"Not yet. I'm hoping something will eventually pan out for me."

"I'll keep my fingers crossed."

"Thanks. So what are you doing right now?"

"Loading dishes into the dishwasher."

"Mmmm. Sexy." She slapped a hand over her mouth. Had she really just said that?

"Well, if you think that's sexy, you should see me wield a mop."

"Well, there is all that hard…length."

What in the world had gotten into her? She never talked like this.

She heard him clear his throat. "The end of which gets wet. Really, really wet."

Her stomach decided to perform a double vault somersault just then. "And there's the back and forth motion."

"Sometimes I have to do it hard, really get in there."

She closed her eyes, and the image that popped into her head had nothing to do with mopping floors. "So, um, how 'bout them Cowboys?"

"Are you sure you don't want to come out and play?"

She swallowed. She wanted to. Oh, did she want to. But she wasn't sure she was quite up to Joe's level just yet. "I, ah, not tonight."

She banged her head against the desk. *Not tonight? Come on, Moll, you can do better than that!*

"The Cowboys, huh? So who do you think is better, Aikman or Romo?"

She released the breath she hadn't even realized she'd been holding. Now this was familiar, comfortable territory. "Well, both quarterbacks have a certain skill set."

"Very true."

As they talked about who was better Molly felt some of the tension she'd been carrying drain from her body. Sure, her insides were still doing funny things every time Joe spoke, but at least she felt more in control, on safer ground. Even though they were tossing stats back and forth, Molly knew she'd only managed to buy herself a small piece of comfort, a little bit of time. He'd backed off for now, but she had a feeling that wouldn't last for long.

And he'd called *her* persistent.

CHAPTER ELEVEN

"So how'd the interview go?" Blanche asked.

Molly closed the door behind her and rolled her eyes. "It was the most God-awful experience of my life."

"What happened?"

Molly turned her head towards Sharonda after placing her purse on the desk. "I got hit on."

"And that's awful why?" Sharonda asked.

"Because she was the ugliest woman I've ever seen, that's why." Molly sighed and sat down in her chair, dropped her forehead into her hands and wasn't sure if she should laugh or cry.

The past hour had been a wasted one—sixty minutes of her life that she could never get back. She'd received a call the day before asking her to come in for an interview, and she'd gladly jumped at the opportunity. Granted, she'd had to schedule it during her lunch break so that Warren didn't get suspicious, which also meant her stomach was now rumbling like a train over wooden tracks, but it had been an interview and her possible ticket out of hell.

Unfortunately, the interview had been more like a ticket into hell.

Despite the fact that she'd lived in Waco for basically her entire life, there were still some companies she was clueless about. And even more unfortunately, Roscoe Printing was one of those companies.

She should have known something was amiss when she'd pulled into the parking lot of the small, dingy building in a not-so-great part of town. Hell, she should have been clued-in when she'd noticed the large, broken chicken sign resting against the side of the building beside it, but it had been years since prostitutes had frequented *that* particular poultry restaurant (which had years ago been closed down due to an unfortunate cockroach manifestation in the frying grease, or so the rumor said), and it was easy to forget about something that had happened when she'd been in high school.

At any rate, though, she should have been clued in. She should have known. Her sixth sense or *something* should have told her to run away and run away now, because this place was bad. But desperation and months of dealing with Warren's uppity behavior had apparently completely whittled away that sixth sense, and Molly had stupidly gone ahead with the interview.

The inside of the building hadn't been so bad, and the foyer had reminded her somewhat of a cheap motel she had stayed in with her mom and brother as a kid. Bare floors, a thinly-padded arm chair with an overly large and faded floral pattern, a crooked landscape hanging on the wall.

Yup, she so should have run when she'd had the chance. Unfortunately, though, the receptionist had spotted her and said, "You must be Margie."

"Um, Molly." Margie? That was a new one.

"Oh, I'm so sorry hon." The receptionist's voice was typically Texan, polite and laced with gallons of syrupy sweet tea. The owner of the voice, however, was a balding man in his mid-50s who also happened to be wearing what had to be the worst shirt ever created or worn–neon green and hot pink stripes covered by random black triangles and squiggles. Apparently he had failed to get the memo about the '80s being over some time ago.

She'd smiled graciously, though, and said, "That's okay." He'd handed her a clipboard and an application, which she'd quickly filled out. Moments later, she'd been ushered into a nondescript office.

The woman behind the desk had hefted herself out of her chair, extended a hand and said, "You must be Molly."

At least she'd gotten Molly's name right. "Yes, ma'am."

The woman had gestured for Molly to take a seat, which she had done.

"Well, I'm Roscoe, and I have to say that I was very impressed with your resume and cover letter."

Molly had barely managed to hide her surprise. Roscoe was a woman? What the hell? And moreover, what was up with the mustache? Seriously, Roscoe looked like she was trying to give Tom Selleck a run for his money in the facial hair department.

The interview had continued, and as the minutes passed, Molly had grown increasingly uncomfortable. Maybe it had been the fact that she was sitting in a very hard wooden chair with arms that dug into her hips, maybe it was that very bushy mustache that no man—much less woman—should ever have, or maybe it was the fact that Roscoe seemed to be staring at Molly's chest, but something had made Molly uncomfortable.

It only got worse, though, when Roscoe had looked Molly up and down as though eyeing a particularly juicy piece of chicken, and had asked, "So, do you have a boyfriend?"

"Excuse me?"

"Do you have a boyfriend? Or a girlfriend?"

"I don't see how this is relevant to the job."

Roscoe had licked her lips, and her eyes had most definitely moved up and down. "Oh, honey, it's very relevant."

Oh, my God.

"Because I can't hire someone as hot as you, because then I'd be dealing with possible sexual harassment lawsuits left and right. And we can't have none of that, now can we?"

What? Molly had gripped the arms of the chair and squeezed tight, not sure if she should run away or call the Better Business Bureau. "Um, s-ma'am, I think this job might not be a good fit for me."

She'd shot up, grabbed her purse and bolted before Roscoe had even had a chance to heave herself out of her own chair and waddle her mustache to the door.

And now here Molly was, back at her actual job, and still not sure if she should laugh, cry, call the Better Business Bureau or go home and take a shower. Damn, did she feel dirty.

She retold the story to Sharonda and Blanche, who were appropriately horrified and yet amused, and who both reassured her she would get more interviews.

"But how many? And when? Employers aren't exactly crawling out of the woodwork, begging me to come work for them."

"Roscoe probably would have begged."

"Okay, Blanche, that was a little uncalled for." Molly rolled her eyes.

"But you gotta admit it was a little funny," Sharonda said.

"Well...." Molly looked from woman to woman. "Okay, yeah, it was at least a little funny."

But when would something pan out for her? She couldn't go on like this much longer, constantly stressed and anxious, waiting for the axe to drop. She was barely sleeping anymore, and thus was a virtual zombie every morning when she got to work. She swore she'd gained about five pounds from over-consumption of chocolate, and the half-full bottle of Parrot Bay in the back of her fridge was beginning to look more and more appealing as a breakfast substitute with every day that passed.

A shudder ran through her body as she thought back to Roscoe's office and the hungry gleam in the woman's eyes. Okay, so maybe she wasn't starving after all, which meant she should at least be a cheap date later that evening.

♡

"Are you sure that's all you want to eat?"

Molly looked at her date across the table, and then down at the plate in front of her. They'd decided to go to Applebee's, and due to the incident with Roscoe the Ugly Lesbian Printer earlier she still didn't have much of an appetite so she'd ordered a small salad for dinner. She had, however, been seriously debating asking their waitress for one of the tempting alcoholic beverages displayed in the drink menu.

The only thing that held her back was the knowledge that even one drink would most likely give her date Larry the wrong impression. Plus, after the day she'd had, frustration mixed

with alcohol mixed with the inevitable horniness that liquor usually caused mixed with the fact that Larry was actually pretty attractive probably wouldn't add up to very good results.

So she'd decided to refrain.

But damn, did that blue drink with her favorite coconut rum in it look really, really tempting.

"Molly, did you hear me?"

"Oh, yeah. Sorry. It was a really bad day, and my mind is just about gone." She gave him what she hoped was a sweet, apologetic smile rather than the smarmy grin she was afraid would play across her face. "But yeah, this is all I want to eat. After what happened earlier, I'm not sure I'll be able to eat again for at least a few days."

He set his fork down and leaned back against the booth, his brown eyes sympathetic. "What happened?"

If Molly's gaze hadn't been fixated on his mouth, she probably wouldn't have even known he'd asked her a question. *What is up with you Molly? Get a grip and stop staring at the man's mouth. You're horrible. Although, his lips do look pretty kissable. I wonder if he's a good kisser. Well, Moll, only one way to find out, and Lord knows that probably won't be happening.*

Crap. He was still waiting for her to answer and here she was staring like a starving woman at a buffet. "Well, I had a job interview that went very, very bad. Actually, it was almost like an episode out of the *Twilight Zone.*"

"Really? What happened?"

She speared a cucumber slice and forced herself to not stare at his lips again. "Well, to give you the short version, I got hit on by what had to be the ugliest woman I've ever seen in my life."

Larry paused, fork in midair, and asked, "So what'd you do?"

"I told her that her behavior was inappropriate and ran out of there as fast as I could." She took a bite of cucumber and chewed thoughtfully before swallowing. "And to make matters even worse–or even more unbelievable, if you will–her name was Roscoe."

"Roscoe? As in *The Dukes of Hazzard* Roscoe?"

"Yes, like that. Except she wasn't an older man, but rather a middle-aged, really fat, extremely ugly lesbian with a mustache."

Larry's laugh washed over her, causing an effect similar to what she suspected that blue drink would have caused had she been brave (or stupid) enough to order one. "Wow. That sounds like the interview from hell."

"Oh, it was."

"So are you just looking for a new job because you hate your current one, or are you gainfully unemployed?"

Molly laughed. "I hate my current one. My boss is, quite frankly–" she stopped and looked around to make sure none of her coworkers were in the restaurant–"a dick."

"Oh really?"

"Yes. He's horrible, and I'm starting to wonder if he's just trying to get me to quit."

"Why would he do that?"

Molly shrugged and dragged a carrot slice through ranch dressing. "I have no idea, other than the fact that I don't think he likes me very much."

"That doesn't make any sense to me."

She tilted her head to the side and watched him cut off another piece of chicken fried steak. He actually knew how to hold his fork and knife correctly, whereas she was con-stantly getting onto Benjamin for his improper silverware etiquette. "Why is that?"

He looked up at her and grinned, causing the corners of his eyes to crinkle slightly with laugh lines. "Because you're a likable person. If I had to put money on it, I'd say he's intimidated by you."

She chuckled. "My mom says the same thing, but I'm not quite sure I understand how I could intimidate anyone. I mean, look at me–I'm five-four with freckles. How could freckles intimidate anyone?"

"You're obviously intelligent, and you don't seem like the type to easily back down or let someone run over you. Some men get intimidated by smart, strong-willed women."

"Oh. Well, thanks." She took a sip of her water and wondered if he got intimidated by smart, strong-willed women. "Hell, you're probably right to a certain extent, but I've never had a problem with a male boss like this."

"How many male bosses have you had?"

"Quite a few. Plus, most of my friends are men and I

don't always get along with other women–they're far too catty at times–so I usually click with male bosses really well. Warren, though..." She shrugged. "...he just doesn't seem to be very receptive to me or my effervescent charm."

"I like that–effervescent charm." He smiled at her, and Molly felt her cheeks grow warm. Maybe she was just tired, but everything about this man seemed to have a mind-numbing effect and his smile was more potent than any amount of blue drinks could ever be.

"I do what I can. I'm always here to entertain." She smiled back at him, tucked her hair behind her ears. "And I'm tired of talking about myself and bitching about work, so tell me about you. What do you do?"

He took a sip of water before replying. "I actually work out at the airplane manufacturing plant."

"I have a couple of friends that work for them. So do you put the planes together or anything?"

"In a way, yeah. I help put the interiors together on the big private jets."

"That sounds interesting. So do you like lay carpet or install the seats or something?"

He threw back his head and laughed, his Adam's apple bobbing up and down. "I actually do the woodwork on the private jets."

"They have wood in private jets?"

"Yes, they do."

"I never knew that. Then again, I've never been in a private jet, so that probably explains why."

"You have the best sense of humor."

It really was a good thing she hadn't ordered that blue drink, because it was right about then that she felt every-thing inside her go warm. At this point, she might just let the guy get away with trying to kiss her.

"Well, thank you." She swirled the straw in her glass of water, thankful that she could at least act casual enough to make him think she wasn't sitting there wondering what kind of a kisser he was. "I've found that having a sense of humor about life makes it a lot easier to get through."

"You definitely have a point."

They looked at each other, and Molly could feel the sexual tension slowly start to hum through her, the sensation not exactly surprising considering she'd been thinking about kissing him, but still unexpected in some weird sort of way. The fact that she'd felt physically attracted to two completely different men within the same week made it all the more weird and confusing yet exciting.

"So what else do you do, besides put wood in airplanes?" She desperately needed to get her mind off of sex, but talking about wood certainly wasn't going to help fix that particular situation.

"Well, I play on the company softball team every spring. My friends and I will get together on weekends sometimes and go out to Cameron Park for some Frisbee golf. Watch some TV, read. Y'know, the usual stuff."

"I've never played Frisbee golf. It always looks like so much fun, but my hand-eye coordination is pretty much nonexistent."

"It doesn't really take that much, just some practice and getting used to the game. Maybe you could join us one weekend when it gets warm enough to go play."

Oh, it was definitely warm enough to go play. At this rate, she was definitely going to have to go home and have a second date with her good friend BOB, who'd been getting quite a bit of action since she'd met Joe the weekend before.

"Sure, I would love to."

"So what do you do besides deal with your asshole boss and get hit on by women named Roscoe?"

She giggled—actually giggled—before answering. "Watch some TV, read. Sometimes I'll pull out my camera and go take photos around town, especially when the blue-bonnets and Indian paintbrushes are blooming."

"Are you one of those people who stops on the side of the highway and takes pictures of your dog and little kids?" His tone was teasing.

"No. Although I have thought about taking my niece and nephews out and getting some shots of them in the bluebonnets. The people who stop on the side of the road are annoying as hell, though, and they're almost always from out of state."

"No kidding. They don't stop to think that they could get bit by a rattler, either."

"Exactly. They're just asking to get bitten by some-thing. But you have to admit, bluebonnets do make for great pictures."

"Oh, yeah. I'm not arguing that at all. People just need to use some common sense when it comes to that stuff."

Their waiter came by and picked up their dishes. "Would y'all like dessert? Some coffee?"

Larry looked at Molly from across the table and nod-ded towards the dessert menu. She shook her head, thinking that the last thing she needed right now was the aphrodisiac known as cheesecake, and he smiled up at the waiter. "No, thank you. I think we're good."

"Okay, then. I'll be right back with y'all's ticket."

The waiter stayed true to his word and was back within minutes. Larry picked up the receipt and pulled his wallet from his back pocket. Molly reached for her purse, and Larry held up a hand. "I've got it."

"Thanks."

"No problem. We're on a date, and while I know you're a feisty, independent woman of the twenty-first cen-tury, I also think the guy should pay for the date."

"It's a good thing I'm not a militant feminist, otherwise you might be in trouble for that," she teased.

He smiled back at her as he left a twenty on the table. "You ready?"

"Yeah."

As they left the restaurant and walked to the parking lot, Molly felt the tension gathering in her muscles. Granted, it was a good kind of tense, but she was tense nonetheless. All those sexual thoughts were definitely getting to her.

They reached her car, and he smiled. "I had a good time tonight."

"Me, too." Surprisingly, she wasn't lying or stretching the truth in order to be nice like she'd done on most of her previous dates.

He crowded in a little closer and reached for her hand. "Maybe we could do this again?"

She tilted her head. "Maybe."

Their gazes connected, and somewhere in the back of her mind Molly realized his intent seconds before his lips softly brushed over hers. It was just a quick movement, over before it really began, but it was enough to make her realize just how long it had been since she'd last kissed someone, and how much she missed it.

He backed away, and the spell was broken. "I'll call you."

"Okay."

He pecked her on the cheek and let go of her hand before turning and walking towards his car. With shaky hands, she reached into her purse and grabbed her car keys.

As she headed home, she replayed her date over and over again in her head, committing to memory every little detail. Hell, it wasn't every day that she had someone who looked like that actually kiss her, and she figured at the very least it would give her something really nice to think about while having that follow-up date.

CHAPTER TWELVE

Molly turned on her laptop immediately upon getting home. Knowing the computer would take a couple of minutes to fully boot up, she walked to the bedroom. She sighed as she took off her date wear and tossed it onto the bed.

Her brain was going crazy after kissing Larry, and she didn't know how to make it stop.

She grabbed a t-shirt and pulled it over her head before walking back into the living room. She sat down in the comfy red chair she'd bought from IKEA and pulled the laptop onto her outstretched thighs before opening her blog editor.

I must have been crazy to ever think this blind date thing was a good idea.

Okay, maybe not crazy, but still, I am so freaking confused right now. And guilty.

Why do I feel guilty? I kissed someone tonight. Well, he kissed me, but I kissed him back. It was the polite thing to do. But what surprised me even more was that I enjoyed it. Sure, sparks didn't fly and the earth didn't move, but it was nice. Plus, when it's been as long as it's been for me a make out session with just about anyone sounds like a good idea.

But for some weird reason I feel guilty. On one hand, I feel like by kissing Larry I've somehow betrayed my feel-

ings for Benjamin—which is stupid considering I'm trying to get over him in the first place. On the other, I feel guilty because right after kissing Larry I wondered what it would be like to kiss Joe.

He called me the other night, which I wasn't expecting. I keep asking myself what a guy like that is doing talking to a girl like me, even though we've only bumped into each other twice and talked on the phone once. But I keep thinking about him. He makes me feel things I don't think I've ever felt before, it's like my body…comes alive just at the sound of his voice. That scares me, the reaction I have to him. Scares me and fascinates me all at the same time.

Benjamin doesn't know about Joe. For some reason, I haven't told him yet. All of this is so completely illogical I don't even know where to begin to sort it all out. On one hand, I have my best friend, who I've loved for what seems like forever. Then over here I have this new guy, who gives me butterflies and really seems to listen to me. And now Larry's gone and kissed me and thrown that into the mix.

I don't know how to handle this. Not that there's anything to handle anyway, considering I'm probably making a mountain out of a molehill. But still, I'm not used to this unfamiliar territory. I'm navigating in uncharted waters here and my GPS system is totally on the fritz and there are no cute Coast Guard boys in sight. Okay, well, there are cute boys, they're just not in the Coast Guard.

But that's completely beside the point. Or maybe it is the point. I don't know. All I do know is that I cried like I haven't cried in a long time the other night when Benjamin told me he was engaged. I felt like I'd been punched in the gut and couldn't ever quite catch my breath. It hurt, to see something I'd held onto for so long disappear so quickly. Even if I am trying to get over him, it still hurt.

Then the next day Joe was there at the gym, making me laugh and asking for my phone number and telling me I'm easy on the eyes even though I was covered with sweat and didn't have on any makeup and my hair was frizzing around my face. The only eyes I would've been easy on at that moment were a blind man's eyes, and Joe definitely isn't blind. And when he called me Tuesday night, I forgot all about Benjamin and Emery and their engagement. I just enjoyed talking to him and flirting, even if I did get flustered, which only helped to reiterate how inept I am at this whole dating thing.

Seriously. I suck at this stuff. Why else would I be writing a blog that probably all of one person will read? Sometimes, I feel pathetic, clueless, like Little Red Riding Hood lost in the woods. Except the only big bad wolf out there is myself.

Molly slowly woke up, becoming more aware of the sound coming from somewhere behind her head. What was that noise? Cell phone. It was her cell phone. "Everybody's Fool" by Evanescence. Which meant Benjamin was either calling or texting.

Blurry-eyed, she turned her head and glanced at the alarm clock across the room. She managed to make out the green glow of eleven forty-five and groped for the phone on the headboard behind her. She powered up the screen and saw that it was a text rather than a call. Wavering between curious and irritated, she opened the message. What she read had her sitting up.

> Benjamin: I need you.
> Molly: What? Why?

Seconds later, she received a response.

> Benjamin: Bitch just broke my heart. I
> need you, Moll.

Wait. What? Was he talking about Emery? What the

hell was going on?

     Molly: What's going on?

Amy Lee's voice greeted her a few minutes later.

     **Benjamin: We got into a big fight. Bitch
broke my heart.**

     Molly: A fight about what?

She set the phone down on the bed before getting up to go to the bathroom.

The phone started ringing again as she dried off her hands. She quickly walked back into her bedroom and picked up her phone. Benjamin was calling her this time. "Hello?"

"Bitch broke my fucking heart."

Was he crying? "What happened, hon? What's going on?"

"We got into a big fight." Sniffle. "She threw the engagement ring at me and now I can't find it."

Molly shook her head, trying to piece everything together in her still half asleep brain. "Where are you?"

"At The Shame. Bitch broke my heart."

"Are you drunk?" He was calling Emery a bitch far too many times to be sober.

"I've been drinking."

"Is she drunk?"

"Yeah."

She sighed and tried to get enough pieces of the puzzle to put it together. "Where is she now?"

"Dancing with Barrett."

"She just threw your ring at you and now she's dancing with Barrett? Have I missed something here?"

"He didn't want either of us leaving because we've been drinking and we're both mad so he's trying to calm her down and told me to get some air."

"Oh. You might want to get some water, too, hon."

"You're not being very sympathetic right now, Molly."

She rolled her eyes. "Benjamin, honey, I have nothing but sympathy for you, but the fact of the matter is you're both drunk and odds are you'll end up kissing and making up tomorrow when you're both sober. What were y'all fighting about anyway?"

"Fuck if I know. One minute everything was fine and the next she was yelling at me, throwing the ring at me and telling me she didn't think I loved her as much as she loves me."

"Did you say something to her to piss her off?"

"I told her she needed to slow down on the drinking a little bit so she didn't get cut off."

"I don't think that would have pissed her off, hon. Did you say anything else that you can remember? Check out another girl?"

"No. All I said was I wish you were here."

"Why would you say that?"

"Because you're my best friend. And that's all I meant by it. You're my best friend."

"I know, hon. You're my best friend, too." But why would Emery get mad at Benjamin for a comment like that? Strange.

"So you really think everything will be okay tomorrow? Because I don't want to lose her, Molly. I love her too much. Hell, I fucking proposed to her."

Molly closed her eyes and took a deep breath. "I know hon. I know. Just go back inside, drink some water and try to sober up. Do you need me to come get you and take you home?"

"No, Barrett said he will."

"Good. Neither of you needs to drive."

"I know." She could hear Benjamin's sigh.

"Just go sober up, hon. And call me if you need me."

"I will." He paused, and Molly could hear him take a drag from a cigarette. "I love you, Molly. You're my best friend and I know you'll always be there for me no matter what."

"I love you, too, hon. Now go drink some water."

"Okay. Bye."

"Bye."

Molly ended the call and took a deep breath. What the hell had just happened?

Shaking her head, she hooked the phone back up to its charger and placed it on the headboard. As she crawled under the covers, she felt another surge of guilt—something she was getting all too familiar with here lately. Instead, this time, it was because a part of her hoped that this was the beginning of the end for Emery and Benjamin.

A small voice in the back of her head whispered that if she really loved Benjamin, then she wouldn't want to see him get hurt. Another voice in her head, though, whispered that she, Molly, was really the only woman who was right for him. Molly tried her hardest to ignore both of them until after she'd had enough sleep to be able to think clearly.

♥

Benjamin watched Emery's taillights fade away, jiggling his car keys in his hand as he did so. After she turned onto Valley Mills off of Wooded Acres, he looked down at the toes of his shoes, mentally noting that they were getting a little worn. Maybe he could get Molly to go shopping with him. He needed some new sandals too.

Not liking the feeling churning in his gut, he turned around and climbed into his truck. A few minutes later he was knocking on Molly's door.

After a few seconds, he could hear the locks turning. He counted them. One. Two. Heard the security bar being flipped. The door opened and Molly stepped back to let him in.

"Hey," she said as he stepped over the threshold.

"Hey." He plopped down on her couch and he heard the door close behind him, the locks all being turned again. Then he felt the cushions on the other end of the couch dip down, turned his head and looked at his best friend.

"You look like hell, hon."

"Thanks." He closed his eyes and rubbed his hands over his face.

"Sorry. It's just, you do. You look like hell. Is everything okay?"

He could hear the sympathy in her voice and it killed him. Well, on one hand, it killed him. On the other hand it made him feel really damned good to know that at least one person cared about him enough to worry. He breathed deeply. "I don't know."

"What do you mean, you don't know?"

"I mean I don't know. She just left to go back up to Dallas. Things seemed to be okay, but we've agreed to slow down a little bit."

"Does that mean the engagement's off?"

"Not entirely. Well, kind of. Fuck if I know." He got up from the couch and paced across the living floor. "I never found the ring. She never found the ring. No one ever found the ring."

"That sucks."

"Yeah, I know. Then again, maybe it's a good thing. Maybe giving her that ring just put too much pressure on our relationship, made things more serious than they need to be right now."

Molly shrugged. "Maybe. But maybe it's also a sign that you moved too fast."

"Maybe. Hell, who really knows? I feel worn out today, though. Worn out and tired and really hung over."

"I'm sorry."

"I'm the one who drank so much."

"This is true."

He paced across the living floor some more, not entirely sure what to say or think. Finally, he stopped pacing, turned back towards Molly and said what had been on his mind for at least the past twelve hours. "I think you might have been right."

"Right about what?"

"Emery not liking the fact that you and I had slept together before."

"Why do you say that?"

He ran his fingers through his hair. "Because of the way she reacted when I said I wished you were there. All I'd meant was that I wished you would've come out and gotten out of the house for a while and had some fun. I think she took it another way entirely."

"So y'all were fighting over me?"

"I think we might have been, but I was so drunk I couldn't really figure out what we were fighting about."

"Y'all almost broke up over me?"

Exasperated, he asked, "Isn't that what I just said?"

"There's no need to get pissy, I'm just trying to figure all of this out."

"You and me both."

She sat there and silently chewed on her lip for a few minutes before asking, "But things are okay between y'all now?"

"I think so."

"Do you need me to stay away for a while?"

He looked at her. She looked uncertain. "No, you don't need to stay away for a while. She knew about us from the beginning."

"But she didn't know about the virginity thing."

He threw his hands up in the air. "I know! I know I fucked up on that! I should have fucking told her from the get go rather than letting her find out during a stupid fucking game of I Never. But I didn't, because I didn't think it mattered. I didn't think it was that big of a deal or that it would bother her."

"If y'all are fighting because of an innocuous comment you made about me, then it's obviously bothering her."

"Don't you think I know that now?"

"Stop yelling."

"I'm not yelling!"

"Yes, you are. Stop yelling. I'm not the one you should be mad at."

He took a deep breath. What was wrong with him? He rarely lost his temper. "I know, Moll, I know. And I'm sorry, I didn't mean to yell."

"I know. You're upset and hurt and confused. Just don't take it out on me, okay?"

He sighed.

"And look at it this way, maybe this is one of those fights that only strengthens your relationship. Better to get this out of the way now rather than waiting until after the two of you get married."

"I know. Hell, I've been thinking the same thing, anyway." He sat back down on the couch. "I can't believe she lost the goddamned ring."

"I can't believe she threw it at you."

"I know. Hit me right in the middle of the forehead with it. I'm surprised I don't have an indention from the diamonds right between my eyes or something."

Molly laughed. "Can she really throw that hard?"

"No, not really. She throws like a girl. But still, those diamonds hurt."

"Maybe someone will find it and give it back to you."

"I doubt that. Hell, I don't know if I even want the damned thing anymore."

He felt Molly's hand pat his thigh and looked over at her.

"Maybe it's better that this happened. You never

know."

"I know. I just have the feeling this isn't all of it," he said, rubbing the spot where the ring had hit him the night before. "I feel like I should be listening to some particularly bad emo music right now."

Molly laughed.

"Isn't this the part of the movie when REM starts playing and I walk around the rainy streets while 'Everybody Hurts' plays quietly in the background?"

"At least you have a sense of humor about it."

"I have to, otherwise I might have to turn in my man-card."

He felt Molly's hand on his back, rubbing gently.

"Hon, you're entitled to a breakdown right now."

He tunneled his fingers through his hair and sighed. "I know, Moll. I just really hope this isn't the beginning to the end."

"I know. I hope you're not right, either." Her hand rubbed a little harder on his back. "But look at it this way, if you are right, at least it's ending before you marry her."

"I'm not sure if that helps or not, but you do have a point."

"Sorry. I'm trying to be positive here, hon."

"I know. And thank you for that."

"Hey, that's what best friends are for."

"I know." He reached over and grabbed her glass of water, took a sip and set it back down on the table before nodding towards her laptop. "Hey, do you think you could cue up some appropriate music? I know you have plenty of depressing crap in there."

"Hey now! Not everything I listen to is depressing." She slapped his arm.

"Yeah, but most of it is."

"Whatever." But she got up and started playing around on the computer, and a few moments later he heard The

Used's "All That I've Got."

He raised an eyebrow. "This is the best you have?"

"Oh, no, it gets better."

"Let me guess, you have plenty of Evanescence cued up." Molly had a weird thing for rock and emo music from the previous decade.

She grinned at him. "You know it."

He sighed dramatically. "I guess I need to go put on my skinny jeans, black and white striped t-shirt and slick my hair back then, don't I?"

"Don't forget glasses. You'll definitely need some hipster glasses."

"So I would look like Rivers Cuomo?"

"Well, if Rivers Cuomo gained at least fifty pounds and grew some back hair."

He smacked her upside the head with a pillow, already feeling better than he had before.

CHAPTER THIRTEEN

Molly nervously smoothed the wrinkles out of her trousers before walking into the hotel.

It was Tuesday morning, and she'd been asked to interview for a job the afternoon before. She'd had to quickly make up a story to tell Warren about why she would be running late, but she figured a doctor's appointment was a great excuse—not to mention the fact that he couldn't fire her for medical reasons.

She walked up to the hotel desk and smiled. "Hi, I'm Molly Sampson and I'm here to see Mister March."

Okay, so this one had a funny name too, and Molly kept wondering if he appeared on a calendar somewhere.

"I'll let him know you're here." The front desk clerk picked up the phone and dialed an extension. A few seconds later she hung up the phone and said, "Just have a seat and he'll be with you shortly."

Molly smiled again. "Thank you."

She chose a seat close to the front desk and sat down, made sure to cross her legs at the ankles the way she'd been told "proper young ladies sit" by her aunt. She barely kept from rolling her eyes at the memory.

Long moments ticked by as she gazed around the reception area. The hotel was decorated beautifully, with lush green plants spilling out of urns, soft lighting and big, plump couches that looked soft enough to sink into.

She wondered if the plants were real or silk. The smell of freshly brewed coffee permeated the air, and a few people were seated in the dining area, taking advantage of what the hotel boasted to be their free continental breakfast.

She shifted her resume folder to her left hand, switched the position of her crossed ankles so the right was in front of the left now, and was just thinking about reaching out and touching one of the plants when an attractive black guy walked up to her.

He smiled and held out his hand. "You must be Molly. I'm Dennis March."

She stood up and shook his hand. "It's nice to meet you."

He led her back to one of the hotel's conference rooms, across the lobby from the receptionist desk and closed the door. There was a table and two chairs, with several others stacked in rows against the far wall. He motioned towards one of the chairs by the table. "Please, have a seat."

Molly sat, placed her purse on the floor beside her and tried not to look too nervous. He looked down at the print-out of her resume on the table in front of him. "I see here you're still currently employed."

"Yes, sir."

"So tell me, why are you looking for another job?"

Because my boss is an ass and I need something that challenges me. "To be honest, I feel like I've reached a plateau as far as the company's concerned. There isn't a lot of room for upward movement, and I'm not sure this is the career I want to have."

"So opportunity for growth is important to you?"

"Very much so."

He wrote something down before asking his next question. "I see here you graduated from North Texas. How'd you like it there?"

She chose her words carefully, not sure if this was a

conversational question or if it actually pertained to the job she was interviewing for. "I loved North Texas. The environment was wonderful, very open and accepting and intellectually stimulating. I met some amazing people while I was there, and took some very interesting courses."

"Tell me about some of those."

Somehow she didn't think he wanted to hear about the anthropology course on the evolution of human sexuality she'd taken her junior year. "Well, I took quite a bit of business and communication courses in subjects such as entrepreneurship, human resources management, business communication, gender and communication, along with some psychology and English courses."

"Sounds like you had a pretty diverse education." He scribbled something else in the margin of her resume. "So why did you choose North Texas? Why not Baylor?"

This was a question she always hated having to answer. The problem with living in Waco was that everyone either loved or hated Baylor, there was no in between. And if you accidentally said the wrong thing to the wrong person, it could totally screw you over. She swallowed. "Honestly, Baylor was a little too expensive for me. I had a great scholarship through North Texas, I loved the campus when I went to visit, and I felt getting out of Waco and experiencing other places would benefit me more than staying here in a bubble."

He smiled at her then. "You seem so much more mature than most people your age."

She barely managed to hide her shock at his statement. "Oh?"

He dropped his voice to a conspiratorial whisper. "No offense, but people under thirty seem to be the biggest bunch of ungrateful, good-for-nothing, spoiled brats I've ever met in my life. Half the time they don't come to work, and when they do they don't do anything. I even had one kid's mom call in sick for him because he was hung over. Can you believe that?"

How did she answer that question? "Well, I can assure you that my work ethic is much better, and I never drink enough to be remotely hung over."

"Good, good." He wrote something else on her resume.

"So, um, Mister March, what position are you hiring for again?" She already knew she wouldn't take the job, even if he offered her a substantial pay increase.

"Oh, I'm sorry."

"That's okay, it's just that the ad in the paper wasn't too clear." *Probably purposefully did that to lure people in.*

"We're currently hiring for the front desk. We need someone who can greet people warmly, answer phones, handle check-ins and check-outs and any little issues that might pop up." He set the pen down and leaned forward. "Of course, there is room for advancement. I started out at the front desk four years ago and now I'm the hotel manager. We believe in promoting from within, and as long as you have a good work ethic and are dedicated, odds are you'll move up fairly quickly."

"Do you mind if I ask what the starting pay is?"

"Not at all. Starting pay is eight fifty an hour, which is actually much higher than the starting pay of most local hotels."

She balked internally, but kept a friendly smile plastered across her face. Once again, she was completely wasting her time.

Mr. March continued. "However, we do give out frequent bonuses depending upon the number of room nights we have booked. For example, if we stay at ninety percent capacity for an entire month, the hotel will receive a pretty large bonus. This usually comes out to an extra couple of hundred dollars a month for our front desk workers."

"What about benefits?"

He frowned. "We do offer health insurance, but it's admittedly a bare bones plan. You do, however, get a steep discount if you stay at any of our sister hotels across the United States, along with ample vacation time."

Like anyone could afford a vacation on eight fifty an hour. "Discounts are good."

"I have to tell you, Molly, I think you would be a great fit for this job. I know it's a little below your skill level, but I have no doubt you would move up quickly. You're sharp, you listen very well, have polite, thoughtful answers and a pretty, friendly face."

What the hell was she supposed to say to that? "Well, thank you."

"At any rate, I'll be getting back in touch with you. I have a few more people to interview and we should be making a final decision at some point within the next couple of weeks. If you don't get a call from me by the middle of next month, it's safe to assume we didn't pick you for the second round of interviews."

Not that she would come back if they did choose her.

He stood up and Molly followed suit. They shook hands and he said, "Thank you for your time, Molly."

"You're welcome. Thank you."

He continued to an office across the hall, and she made her way to the front doors. The receptionist nodded at her and smiled, told her to have a nice day. "Thanks, you too."

It wasn't until she was under the covered portico that Molly realized it had started to pour while she'd been inside. Crap. Her umbrella was in her car, which was parked way across the parking lot. She cast a wary eye towards the sky, which was the color of cold steel and sighed. Great. Just great.

She stuck her resume folder under her shirt, hoping doing so would keep it from getting wet, and pulled her purse as close against the front of her body as possible. *Here goes nothing.* She jogged across the parking lot, finally made it to her car and fumbled with her keys trying to unlock the door.

"Come on, Molly, get a grip woman."

She finally managed to unlock the car and climbed in, soaking wet from head to toe. Not to mention freezing. She turned on the defroster, waited for the interior to warm up before buckling her seat belt and backing out of the parking space. A hank of thick, wet hair fell across her forehead and she brushed it away.

Great, just great.

CHAPTER FOURTEEN

"Molly, could you step into my office please?"

She sighed again—she'd been doing a lot of that today—and turned into Warren's office rather than the area she shared with Blanche and Sharonda. She plastered a fake smile on her face as she walked through the door and politely said, "Yes, sir?"

"Why are you so late coming into work?"

"I told you yesterday I had a doctor's appointment this morning."

He looked pointedly down at his watch and then back up at her, one brow arched perfectly as he stared at her from his beady little eyes. "Yes, but it's ten-thirty. Didn't you say you would be in by nine-thirty?"

"When the appointment was first scheduled I'd been told it should take no more than an hour, but my doctor wanted to run some additional tests that took a little bit longer." She was getting too good at this lying to Warren thing.

He arched his other eyebrow. "What kinds of tests take that long to run?"

"Forgive me if I sound impolite, but I don't see how it's really any of your business just what kinds of tests my doctor decided to take." Which was true, really, because health privacy laws said so.

"Considering this is the second time in two weeks you've missed work due to doctor's appointments, I do think it is my business."

"I have the PTO, though. And I asked for your and HR's approval beforehand. I don't see what the issue is here."

"The issue is that you're being paid to do a job that you're not here to do."

"Because I had a doctor's appointment."

"I want proof."

Crap. "No."

"Why not, Molly?"

"Because the receipt they give me contains private health information that quite frankly is none of your business." Which was also true. Thank God for employment law courses.

"Then I'm afraid I have nothing left to do but give you a final warning."

She felt her stomach drop and her body go cold. Shit. She could not have an anxiety attack in front of Warren. She swallowed and noticed her mouth was dry. Damn. "For what? Having a doctor's appointment? Because underneath the Family Medical Leave Act it's illegal to fire someone for missing work due to their health or their family's health issues." Wow. She'd managed to sound surprisingly calm.

"No, not for having a doctor's appointment. For insubordination." He leaned back in his chair and folded his hands over his chest, a malevolent grin on his face.

"Insubordination? That's bullshit!" She saw one of her coworkers pause out in the hallway and belatedly realized Warren's door was still open. Oh, well. At this point she was pretty much fed up. "I am sick and tired of your constant derision and condescension. I don't know what the hell I ever did to piss you off, but if you ask me you're doing a piss poor job at being a supervisor. You've had it out for me since day one and for no reason at all. I do my job. I do my job damned well. Why you have a problem with that

I will never know, but as of now I'm no longer your problem to worry about."

Warren leaned forward in his chair. "What are you saying, Molly?"

She took a deep breath and said the words before she lost her nerve. "I quit, Warren. I deserve more respect than I'm getting from you. I deserve to be treated like someone who does her job well, not like a child. I deserve to have a boss who is fair and who doesn't have a personal vendetta against me and who doesn't make me feel like I'm less than the dirt he walks on. And frankly, I'm sick and tired of having anxiety attacks every single morning before I walk into this place, thinking about having to put up with your rude, snobby ass and wondering if this will be the day you get tired of playing your little mind game and get rid of me."

"You can't just quit without giving notice, Molly. And if you walk out, don't expect a glowing recommendation when you start interviewing for new jobs."

She raised an eyebrow and calmly said, "Like I would list you as a reference anyway, jackass."

She pivoted on her heel and left his office, took another deep breath and crossed the hallway before stepping into the space she'd occupied for the past eight months of her life. The looks on Blanche and Sharonda's faces pretty much said it all——they'd heard the entire exchange between her and Warren.

"You go, girl," Blanche whispered.

Sharonda got up, closed the door and hugged Molly. "I am so sorry."

Molly shrugged and tried to appear calm, even though she was visibly shaking. "It's okay. You both know I've been looking for another job anyway."

"How'd that pan out this morning?" Blanche asked.

Molly stepped away from Sharonda and looked at her other now former coworker. "Not so well. I was over-qualified and the manager had a serious vendetta against Baylor and Baylor students."

"Lovely." Blanche said.

"Yeah, I know." Molly took a deep breath and looked around, tried to get a hold on her nerves and not think too much about what she'd just done. "I guess I need a box so I can clean up my desk."

Sharonda grabbed one from under the table that housed the fax machine. "Here you go."

It was an Office Depot box, one that held reams of paper but then could be re-used as a filing box of sorts once it was empty. "Thanks." Her tone was wry. "I've always wanted to carry my desk stuff out in a box like they do in the movies."

She stepped up to her desk and started placing items in it. Photos. Pens. Pencils. Coffee mugs. A few pads of Post-It Notes courtesy of her newly former employer.

It only took her a few minutes to gather up her belongings, which saddened her a little bit. But she stepped back and looked at the desk space that had been hers up until fifteen minutes prior. She sighed and looked up at the wall where her diploma hung. Resolutely, she took it down and placed it, too, in the red and white box.

When she turned around, Blanche and Sharonda were looking at her with sympathy and what looked to be a little bit of jealousy. What was that all about?

"You guys okay?" Molly asked.

"Yeah, just sad you're leaving us. And a little jealous that you're getting away from this hell hole," Sharonda replied.

"I just wish I'd had something else lined up, and that I hadn't just burned that particular bridge. I've never quit a job without giving notice before."

Blanche shook her head and twirled her glasses by the ear piece. "There's no shame in it, honey. That prick out there has had it out for you ever since he became our supervisor, and I'm surprised it took you this long to finally boil over. You give 'em hell."

"Thanks, Blanche, but now I'm stuck without being able to use this place as a reference, which sucks since I've been here for a year and a half."

"So? You have other references you can use. Or just give them our names, we'll give you a good referral," Blanche said.

Molly shook her head and grinned, already feeling a little bit better about the situation. "I'm really going to miss y'all."

"We're going to miss you, too, believe me," Sharonda said.

"No shit. Now who's gonna handle those damned divorce distributions?" Blanche asked.

Molly laughed. "You'll just have to get someone to show you how to do them. But I don't envy you, believe me."

"Bitch," Blanche teased.

A knock on the door interrupted their goodbyes, and Pat, the HR director poked her head in. "Sorry to break up the party, ladies, but I have to escort you out of the building, Molly."

"Is Warren afraid I'm gonna blow it up or something? Rearrange his calculator drawer?" It was kind of liberating to be able to speak her mind.

Pat grinned wryly. "We know you won't do anything like that, Molly, but it's company policy."

"Since when?"

"I'm still trying to figure that out myself," Pat said, shaking her head.

Over the HR director's shoulder Molly could see Warren standing in the doorway of his office, arms crossed over his chest with what could only be described as a glower on his face. She'd never seen an actual glower before. But she rolled her eyes and followed Pat out the door, turning around once to wave goodbye to Blanche and Sharonda. "Keep in touch, guys. I'll email you as soon as I get a new job."

"We'll miss you, Molly." Sharonda said.

"Bye, Molly. Go getcha some tonight. That'll make you feel better," Blanche said, causing Molly to shake her head and grin. She really was going to miss these two.

As they walked past Warren's office, Molly stuck her nose up in the air as though she'd smelled something particularly foul and walked right past him without saying a word. They exited the office and made their way to the elevator, and as they stood there Pat asked Molly, "Anything you want me to tell anyone?"

The elevator arrived, the doors opened and Molly stepped into it. She thought for a few seconds and said something she'd heard Benjamin say dozens of times, "Yeah, tell Warren I'm sorry he has a bigger vagina than I do, but he might want to get some of the sand out of it."

The doors closed on the image of Pat's gaping mouth, and Molly closed her eyes. Had she really just said that? Hell. That reference was definitely shot.

Molly had just started her car when she felt her cell phone start to vibrate. She picked it up and glanced at the caller ID. It was an unfamiliar local number.

She flipped the phone open and answered "Hello?"

"Molly Sampson?"

"This is she."

"Hi, this is Sheila with the *Waco Times Dispatch.* We received the cover letter and resume you sent in yesterday and were wondering if you were available for an interview."

She barely strangled a desperate laugh. *Am I ever.* "Yes, ma'am, I am."

"Would today be okay with you? I know this is short notice and if you can't make it until tomorrow that's perfectly fine."

"Today would be great. What time would you like to see me?"

"Actually, Mister Charles has an opening in thirty minutes. Is that too short of notice?"

"Not at all. I can definitely be there."

Sheila gave Molly the newspaper's address. "Be sure to bring an extra copy of your resume, dear."

"I will certainly do that. Thank you, Sheila."

"Thank you. I look forward to seeing you down here."

The call ended and Molly placed her phone in her purse, breathed deeply. How was that for some timing?

She took another deep breath—something she'd been doing a lot of that day—and checked her appearance in the rear view mirror. At least she'd gone home and changed clothes after getting caught in the downpour earlier, and luckily the clouds had scattered and the sun was now shining.

Talk about irony, she thought as she put the car into reverse and backed out of the parking space.

Fifteen minutes later she was parking in front of the newspaper's offices. She'd been there once as a high school student, back when she'd received the invitation to write guest columns as a teenager. Steeling herself, she grabbed her resume folder that she kept in the passenger seat and her purse, exited the car and started towards the building.

Please let this work out. Even if it only pays eight dollars an hour it's better than nothing until I can find something that pays more. She probably shouldn't have been so willing to turn her nose up at her previous job interview.

She opened the door and walked up to the front desk, where she was greeted by a grandmotherly woman wearing a sedate floral print dress. The older woman smiled and said, "You must be Molly. I must say, you sure did get here fast."

"Well, I was already out when you called."

"That's perfectly fine, dear. I'm Sheila, and you'll be interviewing with Mr. Charles today." Sheila handed Molly a clipboard that held an application and a pen. "If you'll just fill this out for me and attach a copy of your resume I would greatly appreciate it."

"Thank you, Sheila." Molly took the clipboard and sat down in a vacant chair across from the receptionist's desk.

Ten minutes later she'd filled out everything, double-checked the paperwork and attached her resume. She'd debated briefly about crossing out the word "present" and writing in today's date on her most recent job experience, but decided it might be better to simply explain the situation when it came up in the interview. Handwriting just looked so tacky on a nicely typed and formatted resume, anyway.

A few minutes later she was escorted to Mr. Charles' office, where she was greeted warmly by a middle-aged man wearing a bad toupee.

"Hello, Molly. I'm Mr. Charles. I have to say I was very impressed with your resume."

Molly almost tripped over her own two feet as she made her way into his office. She quickly regained her composure, though and managed to respond. "Thank you, sir. Hopefully you'll be equally impressed with my interview skills."

Mr. Charles smiled and sat down in a chair in front of his desk and gestured for Molly to sit as well. "See! I like you already!"

Molly smiled. "Thank you."

He looked down at the clipboard in his hands, glanced over her resume and looked back up at her. "So you have no professional copy editing experience?"

"No, sir, not unless you count editing web site content and letters to clients. However, I was editor-in-chief of my high school newspaper for three years, and copy editor my freshman year of college."

He glanced back down at the clipboard, this time at her application. "Well that's good. I see here you were an original Teen *Times Dispatch* contributor?"

Molly smiled. "Yes, sir, I was. I do believe I had three columns published on the editorial page when I was in high school."

"That certainly helps." He looked back up at her. "Why do you want to be a copy editor for the *Times Dispatch?*"

Because right now I have no other options. "Well, Mr. Charles, I've always had an affinity for the English language. I love to write, but I also discovered through newspaper in high school that I love to edit. Considering the Times Dispatch's importance to the community, I think it's important that the stories are easy to read, of good quality and free of as many errors as possible. I'll be honest, there are times when I read the paper and catch two or three mistakes in the lead paragraph alone. That turns off readers, which causes declining newspaper sales—not only from the newspaper stands but through subscriptions, too. I have friends who prefer to read The Dallas Morning News or The Houston Chronicle over the Times Dispatch, and it's primarily because of editing. Although, I do have to say that the Times Dispatch is much better than the Chronicle."

She awaited his response, hoping she hadn't offended him and that she'd at least come across as being somewhat genuine.

"You have a point, Molly. Good copy editing is very important to a newspaper. We can't catch everything, but it has been below sub-par here of late and we're trying to remedy that." He turned and grabbed a piece of paper and a pen from his desk. "I'm going to give you this. It's a short piece of copy, and have you edit it."

Molly tucked a strand of hair behind her ear as he secured the piece of paper onto the clipboard and handed it and the pen over.

She quickly read over the story, catching two verb tense changes, five misspelled words and a dangling modifier. She circled the verbs and the spelling errors and rewrote a few lines to make them flow better. Corrected a few punctuation mistakes and substituted better words for some poor ones.

The look on Mr. Charles' face when he saw what she'd done was priceless, and she could have sworn his toupee almost fell off due to how high his eyebrows were raised. He looked over her work, nodded in places, looked up at her and smiled. "You've got the job."

"I do?" she asked, her surprise obvious.

"Yes, ma'am. I've never seen copy editing like this before, at least not from someone who hasn't been trained professionally to do it. Considering you don't have any professional experience, though, I'm going to give you a probationary period to see how you work out."

"Why, thank you." She tucked a strand of hair behind her other ear and smiled. A probationary period sounded more than fair to her at the moment, not to mention a lot like a life saver.

"Well, first we probably need to discuss salary and benefits before you make a final decision."

"Yes, sir."

Mr. Charles beamed at her, and Molly suddenly felt herself feeling a whole lot better.

That feeling only grew over the next ten minutes, and she thought her face might just crack from the smile that was stretched across it. More money, better benefits and doing something she would actually enjoy? This was awesome.

As she exited Mr. Charles' office with the promise to be there at eight o'clock Monday morning for her first day of work (he was totally okay with the fact that she'd just quit her job), she walked right into a hard, warm body. A set of masculine hands wrapped around her arms to steady her. She looked up, her mouth open and ready to apologize.

"Joe? What are you doing here?"

He looked startled. "I work here. What are you doing here?"

"I, uh, had a job interview." His hands were still wrapped around her arms, and her stomach was doing those freaking somersaults again. She desperately tried not to blush as she recalled their conversation from the week before.

"For the open copy editor position?" He swallowed, and his Adam's apple bobbed up and down.

"That would be the one."

"So how'd your interview go?"

She smiled. She simply couldn't help it. "Very well. I got the job!"

He grinned and hugged her. "That's great!"

Molly hugged him back, and then promptly realized she was hugging Joe and tried to figure out how to disentangle herself without making it seem awkward. Instead, he released her just as quickly as he'd wrapped his arms around her.

She looked up at him and searched her brain for something to say. At least he'd stopped touching her; that should make thinking at least slightly easier. "So, um, how long have you worked here?"

"A few years now. When do you start?"

"Next Monday."

"Wow, that's quick. You're not going to give your boss a two week notice?"

She cleared her throat and looked at a far wall over his shoulder. "Actually, I, ah, quit about an hour and a half ago."

"You quit?" His tone was curious rather than judgmental.

She looked back at him. "Yes, I quit."

"Well, then, I guess that means congratulations are in order."

"You could say that. Considering just an hour ago I thought this was going to be the worst day of my life, I'm very pleasantly surprised with the way things have turned out."

He laughed. "Hey, I'm on my way to grab a bite to eat for lunch. Do you want to come with me? My treat, as congratulations on getting a new job."

She hesitated briefly, then decided to hell with it and said, "Sure."

As they walked out into the bright afternoon sunshine, Molly smiled and thought that today was quickly becoming the best day ever.

CHAPTER FIFTEEN

"So what caused you to quit your job?"

Molly dragged a French fry through the pool of ketch-up on her plate and looked up at Joe. "I just got fed up. Warren's behavior had become even more asinine over the past week or so, and I couldn't take it anymore. And what happened today was just ridiculous. I'd told him I had a doctor's appointment this morning and that I should get to work around nine or so. Well, I was a little late and he wanted proof that I'd been at the doctor and basically told me he was this close to firing me." She held up her index finger and thumb, about a millimeter apart from each other for emphasis.

"Did you give him proof?" He looked at Molly over the hamburger he was holding in front of his mouth.

"Not exactly."

"Why not?"

She grinned before popping the ketchup-covered French fry into her mouth. "Because I hadn't been at the doctor."

"Ohhh."

"Yeah. I'd actually been at a job interview—yet another bad one, by the way—but I couldn't very well tell him that. It had run a little late to begin with, and then I got caught in a sudden downpour on the way to my car and had to go home and change into something dry."

"That sucks. So how'd you get out of proving your whereabouts to him?"

"Told him that under the Family Medical Leave Act it was illegal for him to fire me for having a doctor's appointment."

"Devious and smart. I like it."

Molly felt her cheeks warm. "Well, it really would be illegal. Unfortunately he wouldn't leave it alone and just kept sitting there looking down his nose at me with that condescending attitude he has and I couldn't take it anymore. So I told him to shove it and walked out of his office."

"You just quit? With no backup plan, nothing lined up?"

She swallowed past the lump in her throat. "I think that sums it up."

"What if you hadn't gotten lucky with this job offer? What would you have done?"

"I don't know. I admit quitting like that was not the smartest move I've ever made, and was completely unlike me. But I would have figured out something. Hopefully, I would have figured out something."

"What if you hadn't?"

She shrugged. "I don't know. Sold myself on Elm Street?"

Joe threw back his head and laughed, drawing Molly's attention to his neck and chin. The faint shadow of stubble coated his jaw line, and she could barely make out the indentation of a dimple in his cheek. His smile was genuine, and his laugh simply made Molly feel good just by hearing it.

"Has anyone ever told you that you have a great sense of humor?" Joe asked once he'd contained his laughter.

She smiled. "A few times, but I always appreciate a compliment."

He looked back at her with warmth in his eyes and said, "This could get interesting."

She cocked her head to the side. "Why do you say that?"

He dragged a French fry through ketchup, popped it into his mouth and chewed before answering. "Because I'm attracted to you and I'm pretty sure you're at least mildly attracted to me."

"I'm not. I'm not attracted to you at all." *The lady doth protest too much, Moll?*

His dimple winked at her and he chuckled. "Keep telling yourself that."

"You sure are cocky, you know that?"

"Not cocky, just fairly good at reading people."

"If you were so good at reading people you would see that you need to back off a little bit." Unfortunately, her words didn't hold as much heat as she'd intended.

"See, that's where you're wrong. You want me to back off because you know I'm right. You are attracted to me, and it makes you uncomfortable that I'm attracted to you and not hiding that fact."

She barely managed not to squirm in her seat. Instead, she rolled her eyes. "You think you're so smart, but you couldn't be further from the truth. Sure, you make me uncomfortable, but not for the reasons you stated."

He dragged another fry through ketchup. "Then what is it?"

Crap, she was no good at this. Furthermore, she had a feeling he would see right through any self-protective lie she attempted to tell. So she stayed silent and bit into her cheeseburger instead.

He reached across the table and touched her hand. When he spoke, his tone was low, apologetic and almost sympathetic. "Molly, I don't want to make you feel uncomfortable. If I'm coming on too strong let me know and

I'll back off. I just don't want to give you any chance for uncertainty here. I like you. You're smart and funny and pretty and you have the most amazing smile. I want to get to know you better, but I can't do that if you're keeping me at a distance. I'm not into game-playing. What you see is what you get, and I'm going to be honest with you even if you're not exactly used to that."

She swallowed. What was wrong with her? Here was this smart, funny, very attractive guy who was obviously interested in her—and, yes, who she was very interested in—and yet she kept wanting to push him away. Was she really that self-destructive? "I don't know how to handle you."

"I can think of a few ways." He winked and Molly felt her face warm.

She wanted to look away, but her gaze was riveted. He really did have the most amazing eyes.

"I'm just teasing you, Molly."

God, she really didn't know what to do with him. Sure, her body seemed to have a few good ideas if her physical reaction was any indication. But mentally and emotionally she was clueless.

"How about we go out Friday night and give you a chance to figure out how to handle me?"

"Why does that sound vaguely suggestive?"

He smirked. "Because you want it to."

She rolled her eyes. "I'm busy Friday night."

"Who's the lucky guy this time?"

Was that the slightest hint of jealousy in his voice? Interesting. "Ted. Sadly, that's all I know about him, that his name is Ted."

"How about Saturday night, then?"

"Should we really go out on a date considering we're about to start working together?"

"The paper doesn't have a dating policy. There are actually a few couples working there."

"So now we're going from one date to coupledom?"

"No, I'm just trying to knock down all of your arguments."

"Fair enough."

"So what do you say? You and me on Saturday night?"

A part of her wanted to say no, just because something about Joe made her feel like she was dangerously close to the edge. Edge of what she didn't know, but she knew she was afraid of going over it.

On the other hand, she needed to stop being a scaredy cat.

"Why not?"

"Good. I'll pick you up at seven."

He winked at her again, and Molly's mouth suddenly felt as dry as west Texas in the middle of summer. What was she getting herself into?

The "One with the Prom Video" is on right now.

I love this episode of Friends. It's the one where Phoebe explains her lobster theory to Rachel and Ross, and why they're meant to be together. Soul mates.

I used to believe Benjamin and I were soul mates. I used to believe he was The One, my lobster.

He obviously isn't. I mean, if he really were my lobster he wouldn't be engaged to Emery.

I can't believe he proposed. I can't believe she said yes. Now I know he'll never be mine.

Sounds counterintuitive, right? I'm the one who decided to start dating other men in a desperate attempt to get over him. I guess it's worked to an extent. While none of these dates have been what you could call stellar, they have opened up my eyes a bit. There are other men out there. And some of them might even like me.

Right now, though, I just feel confused. Deep down I know that Benjamin's a safety net for me. He's comfortable. I know I'm going to get hurt by him, but knowing what to expect somehow makes it seem not quite so bad.

How self-destructive can I be, right?

The thing, though, is that there's this guy. I met him at Barnes & Noble a couple of weeks ago. I didn't think things like that actually happened in real life, that chance meetings in bookstores were the stuff of fiction. But there I was in the romance section, and there's this hot guy talking to me and asking me to help him pick out books for his mom.

I know. I was skeptical, too. But he had a list, and he seemed genuine, and after I helped him pick out some books we sat in the café and had hot chocolate and I told him way more than I should have. I figured I would never see him again, though, so where was the harm.

Of course I saw him again. The next Monday at the gym, in fact. I had on no makeup, was hot and sweaty from being on the treadmill and did not look pretty. He got on the treadmill beside me. Later on he got my phone number. He called the next day and actually flirted with me. With me!

I figured that would be the end of it, though, that once he figured out how messed up I am he would run away screaming. He didn't though.

And now we're working together, on top of everything else.

Yes, I just said we're working together.

Long story short, I kind of got fed up at work today and quit. I guess fate or God or Buddha or whoever must've been working overtime today, because I got a phone call before I'd even managed to leave the parking lot asking me to come in for an interview. I went in, interviewed for a copy editor position for the local newspaper, and miracle of all miracles got the job. Sure, it's on a probationary period since I haven't edited since college, but it's a start.

It's better than putting up with Warren day in and day out, having anxiety attacks on a daily basis and feeling like my life is going nowhere. Plus, the pay's better and so are the benefits.

I ran into Joe—that's the guy, by the way—as I was leaving the newspaper. I gave him the details, he asked me to have lunch with him and I did.

I think he wants to date me.

Why, I have no idea. I mean, this guy is hot. Well, hot in a geeky sort of way. Hot in a way that makes my stomach do funny things but not so hot that I'm blinded by his beauty. That kind of hot. And he's smart. Funny. A good listener.

I know, I know. I was wondering, too, if he was gay. But he's not. I almost think it would be easier if he were gay, though. I mean, I wouldn't be so freaking confused if that were the case.

At any rate, he's hot, smart, funny, a good listener and now my coworker who wants to date me. Why would he want to date me? That's what I don't quite understand. Like I said, he's hot. And I'm so...not. Why would the fantastic, skinny hot guy want to date the insecure fat chick who has more issues than the New York Times? It just doesn't make sense.

The girls he's dated in the past have all probably been tall, thin, gorgeous women with perfect teeth and hair, never a pimple or stray eyebrow hair in sight. Their skin was probably flawless and freckle free. They probably never had problems finding clothes that fit them right. They all probably had flat stomachs and perfect C-cup boobs that didn't require molded cups and underwires to look perky. They probably never laughed too loud or over-thought everything or doubted themselves the way I doubt myself. Those are the kinds of women who date guys like Joe. Not women like me, the imperfect ones with too wide hips, tummy pooches and bras with cups so big they could be used as an umbrella. Hell, he's probably never seen a woman with stretch marks or cellulite before. So again, what could he find so interesting about me?

I have some major self esteem issues. I know that. I'm not sure what it's going to take to get beyond those issues, either. And logically I know that even skinny women have body image issues, that there are things about themselves they would love to change, too. I know that I need to stop allowing myself to think such self-destructive thoughts, and to give Joe—and these other dates—a snowball's chance in hell.

I know that. Deep down, I know that. But knowing I need to give them a chance and doing it are two completely different things.

It doesn't help that I think I could really end up liking this guy. That scares the crap out of me. I've wanted Benjamin for so long, clung to the safety net that is his constant wishy-washiness that I'm still not sure how to let go completely. I need to let go. I want to let go. But I don't want to get hurt. I'm afraid to hope. After all, hope is a four letter word. It's an evil word. It makes you think that things might be different this time around, that maybe even fat insecure girls get their happy endings.

All hope has ever done for me is leave me with a broken heart.

CHAPTER SIXTEEN

"So we're going through Darkshire and all of a sudden this huge dragon comes out of nowhere and completely obliterates our party."

This guy is nuts. "Oh, really? That's, um, very interesting Ted."

So far her latest date was a disaster. Molly wasn't sure what Benjamin had been thinking when he'd set her up with Ted, the apparent King of World of Warcraft and rogues across the gaming universe. Whatever the hell a rogue was.

Ted leaned forward and propped his chin up on his steepled fingers. "Yeah, that was the same night the guild leader decided to quit and disbanded us, so we have to rebuild from the ground up. Completely new people." He grinned. "Which is cool because my new rogue is going to be better than ever."

Oh, sweet baby Jesus.

"Actually, I'm almost thinking about changing from a rogue to a mage. Or maybe even a healing class. Ooh. Yeah. A healing class would be a great idea that way the next time we face that dragon I could heal everyone and the party would survive."

Molly seriously considered ordering a raspberry margarita since they were at La Fiesta, and everyone in town knew La Fiesta had the best frozen raspberry margaritas around. However, she had a feeling that alcohol wouldn't be such a good idea when trying to wrap her brain around what her date was saying.

"That could work." Okay, so she had no clue what the hell he was talking about, but she figured that as long as she smiled and nodded everything would be fine.

"Oh, it would definitely work. And we could totally take Warsong Gulch by storm. That damned horde wouldn't know what the hell hit them."

Molly desperately willed their waiter to bring them their food ASAP. Maybe if she wished hard enough she could be back home, curled up on the couch with a good book rather than sitting across from Ted the Magical Roguish Healer.

As her date continued to go on and on about his guild she studied him. It really was too bad he thought World of Warcraft was real and had seemingly nothing else to talk about, because otherwise he might be a semi-attractive guy. He was tall and slender without being too skinny. Sure, his skin was a little pale, but she honestly had no room to talk about anyone having fair skin since hers was white and liberally dotted with freckles. Freaking Irish heritage.

He had reddish blonde hair and clear green eyes. Where was Benjamin finding all these green-eyed men anyway? At least he'd gotten that part right.

"And then when the dragon attacks us again Braden can cast Molten Armor and bounce the fire right back at the dragon. It'll work beautifully."

Molly surreptitiously looked down at the cell phone she'd set on the booth beside her. Ted had been talking about his video game for fifteen straight minutes. Wonderful. Where was the waiter with their food?

"So what guild do you belong to?"

Molly looked up at Ted, momentarily confused. "Excuse me?"

"What guild do you belong to?"

Should she tell him the truth or try to make something up? "Um, I don't." Apparently she was going with telling the truth.

Ted recoiled in what looked to be horror. "You don't belong to a guild? What kind of Warcraft player are you? All the best players belong to a guild."

She really wished she'd ordered that margarita. And seriously, where the hell was the waiter with their food? "Um, well, to be honest I don't really play."

"You don't play?" He blinked back at her.

"I don't play."

"But Benjamin told me you were a cool nerdy chick. All the cool nerdy chicks play Warcraft."

Molly almost spit out the drink of water she'd just taken. Instead, she somehow managed to swallow without choking and looked back at Ted. "Benjamin told you I was a cool nerdy chick?"

"Well, yeah. I only date nerdy girls. I told him that."

Was she supposed to be flattered or insulted here? "Um, Ted, I'm not entirely sure how to tell you this, but I think Benjamin might have misled you a little bit."

"So you're not nerdy?"

Molly chuckled. "I wouldn't say that, just apparently not the type of nerdy you're looking for. I'm a word nerd." There was a new one. And yet it was oddly accurate. "But I'm not really a gaming nerd. I mean, I can kick your ass at Mario Kart if I'm driving with Yoshi, and I'm the queen of Bejeweled and Words with Friends, but that's about the extent of my gaming experience."

"But I only date Warcraft players."

"I'm sorry?"

"I told Benjamin I only date Warcraft players, and he assured me you were the kind of girl I would be interested in."

Benjamin had flat-out lied to this guy?

Ted sipped his water and looked at something over Molly's shoulder. "I'm sorry, Molly, but I just can't date you."

"What?"

He slid out of the booth and stood. "I can't date you."

He withdrew his keys from his pocket. *Is he really going to just leave me here by myself?*

"I'm sorry Benjamin made you think I'm somebody I'm not."

"Oh, it's not your fault, but this date obviously isn't going to go anywhere considering you don't play Warcraft. Better to end it now and cut our losses."

"You're leaving?" She looked up at him.

He nodded his head. "Nice to meet you, Molly."

And with that, he walked off. Molly sat there, dumbfounded. Had that really just happened? Had she really just been rejected for not playing a stupid video game?

She rubbed her chest, expecting it to hurt under the surface. It didn't.

Their waiter finally appeared with their food—about five minutes too late—and set their orders down in front of them. "Could I get y'all anything else?" the waiter asked.

"Actually, could you bring me a raspberry margarita? And take his back, ends up he won't be joining me after all."

The waiter looked at her quizzically but picked up Ted's order and took it back to the kitchen.

Molly stared down at her plate of chicken enchiladas. The smell of sour cream sauce wafted towards her nose, and she picked up her fork. She looked around, but no one was staring at her with pity in their eyes. In fact, no one was even looking at her. She chewed thoughtfully. Rejection hadn't been so bad, at least not this time.

CHAPTER SEVENTEEN

"Should I wear boy shorts or hipsters?" Molly asked herself the next evening as she was getting ready for her date with Joe.

It was times like these when she really wished she had a close female friend. While she could talk to Benjamin about most anything, he just didn't seem to grasp the importance of wearing the right underwear. She'd tried to explain to him once that the bra and panty set she chose in the morning could set the mood for her entire day. He'd looked at her like she'd just told him there were flying rabbits outside her apartment.

She chewed on her bottom lip and tightened the towel that was knotted between her breasts. Glanced at the alarm clock on her dresser. She had twenty-five minutes until Joe arrived to pick her up, and along with getting dressed she still needed to brush her teeth, blow dry and fix her hair and put on makeup. First, though, she had to figure out what underwear to put on.

She looked at the selection she'd laid out on her bed. Pink hot shorts with black polka dots and a cute key hole in the back that was topped off with a little black ribbon. Black hipsters with hot pink stripes. Black lace thong. Pink and tan string bikini. Turquoise lace cheeky panties. Black and blue lace cheeky panties. Red g-string.

Hey, just because she was curvy didn't mean she

couldn't appreciate sexy underwear, even if no one else ever saw them.

The problem, though, was figuring out if she even wanted to tempt herself by wearing something that remotely begged to be seen and appreciated by someone else— namely Joe. Did she even want Joe to appreciate her underwear? Okay, yeah, she definitely wanted Joe to appreciate her underwear.

Maybe she should go with the hipsters. They were cute cotton, comfortable but not very sexy. Definitely not something she would necessarily be overly eager to allow him to appreciate. No sense tempting fate.

Aren't you supposed to be living more in the moment, Moll?

Yeah, but I'm not sure I'm ready to live that much in the moment. Not yet.

Deciding the hipsters were her best bet she undid the knot at her breasts and set the towel down on the end of the bed before picking up the black and pink panties and pulling them on. She found her black balconette bra in her closet, hanging among her twenty-seven other bras, and put it on.

Lingerie had become a sort of obsession for Molly over the past few years. It had been her junior year of college when she'd discovered Cacique, and had fallen in love almost immediately. For some reason, the concept of bras that provided excellent support along with actually looking pretty had fascinated her. Her slightly compulsive self had squealed internally with delight when she'd discovered that she could also buy matching panties in various styles and cuts according to her pant size rather than some arbitrary number Hanes Her Way had made up. The irony of wearing a size eight panty when she was in fact a size twenty in pants had never failed to amuse yet frustrate her.

Wearing pretty under garments, though, had given her

self confidence a much-needed boost, and even on the days when she felt her lowest she secretly reveled in the fact that under it all she was wearing sexy red lace. It was her little secret, and sometimes she thought that little secret had helped to keep her from sinking too far down where her self-image was concerned.

She checked out her reflection in the floor-length mirror, turning from side to side as she did so. Overall, things really weren't all that bad. Hell, they could certainly be worse. And she'd been trying to tell herself that even though she had extra wide hips and a bit of a tummy pooch at least she had nice boobs to balance everything out.

Since there wasn't exactly much she could do to flatten her stomach or shave off a couple of inches around her mid-section in the short amount of time she had until Joe arrived, Molly moved away from the mirror and picked up the dark wash boot cut jeans she'd laid out on the bed.

Once they were buttoned she bent at the waist and unwrapped the towel she'd had on top of her head. She dried her hair vigorously before standing back up straight, grabbing the other towel from the bed and walking into the bathroom.

She quickly brushed her teeth before moving to her makeup, which she applied with somewhat shaky hands.

Deep breaths, Molly. Deep breaths.

She set her eyeliner down on the counter, closed her eyes and followed her own advice.

After a few minutes she felt more in control and opened her eyes, picked the liner back up and got to work putting on her makeup.

Fresh eyeliner and shadow applied, Molly removed the hair dryer from its hook on the wall, bent at the waist and turned it on.

Diffusers were another invention she'd come to appreciate. Her thick, naturally wavy hair had always frizzed

when she'd blow dried it in the past. It hadn't been until
she'd had a stylist suggest a diffuser to her that she'd tried
one, and again, she'd fallen in love almost instantly.

She flicked the hair dryer off and straightened her
body, placed it back on the hook on the wall and looked
at her reflection in the mirror. She finger combed her hair,
smoothing it out a little. It could have looked better, but it
also could have looked worse.

Knowing there was little else she could do in the
small amount of time she had left, she moved back into her
bedroom and picked up the three-quarter length sleeved,
v-neck tee she'd decided to wear. The dark teal of the shirt
looked great with her hair color, and somehow did wonders
for her skin tone.

She glanced at the clock. Ten minutes. She breathed
deeply again. Why was she so nervous about going out with
Joe? It was just Joe, for crying out loud.

Exactly, Molly, it's "just Joe."

She grabbed a pair of black and teal argyle patterned
knee highs from her sock drawer and walked into the living
room, where her shoes were. Molly grabbed her black,
calf-length stacked heel boots from the shoe rack beside
the door and sat down on her couch. The shoes had been
a Christmas gift from her mom, and even though Molly
hadn't worn boots since, well, ever, she'd immediately appreciated the extra two and a half inches they added to her
height. They were also one of those great pairs of shoes that
looked fantastic with trousers or jeans, and were perfect
for the cooler months when she was forced to abandon the
open-toed sandals she preferred.

She zipped up first the left one, then the right, and
pulled her pants legs down over them. Stood up and
smoothed out her clothes. Remembered that he'd said to
bring a jacket.

Molly walked back into her bedroom and removed the

black, three-button corduroy jacket she'd bought on clearance from her closet.

She was checking out her reflection in the mirror,
thinking that Stacey and Clinton of the unfortunately now
defunct *What Not to Wear* really were right when they said
jackets could make you look thinner, when she heard the
knock on her door.

Butterflies danced in her stomach, and she pressed a
hand to her tummy and mentally attempted to settle them.
For whatever reason, the butterflies decided to be uncoop-
erative.

She rushed into the living room, looked through the
peep hole of her front door, quickly glanced around the
apartment to make sure nothing embarrassing was lying
out, and turned the locks.

♡

Joe knocked on Molly's door and realized his palms
were sweating.

*Come on, Joe. Get a grip. You act like you've never
been on a date before.* Except, well, this was Molly. And
for whatever reason she'd quickly become the most fascinating woman he'd met in a long time. A very long time, in
fact.

After what seemed like an hour but was probably only
a minute or so, he heard locks flip on the other side of the
door. And then he saw Molly's smile. Rubbed his palms on
his jeans again. She looked even better than he'd remembered, even though he'd seen her just a few days ago. The
jeans she wore hugged her curves, and the v-neck shirt
showed a subtle hint of cleavage.

He was honest enough to admit that he wanted to see
more.

He cleared his throat. "Hey."

Her smile widened. "Hey. Come on in. I just need to grab my purse and turn out the lights."

He stepped inside and she closed the door behind him. He looked around, took note of the numerous framed photos hanging on the living room walls, the plants that seemed to cover every empty surface and the colorful spines of what had to be at least a hundred books filling up one very large bookshelf along with a smaller shelf beside it. He also noticed that her jeans really did hug *all* of her curves. It amazed him how she was so completely unaware of the appeal of her body, but just glimpsing the curve of her ass made him want to grab hold and never let go.

Molly walked back into the living room, purse in hand, and he motioned towards the shelves. "I knew you were a reader, but wow."

She smiled. "Sadly, that isn't all of them."

"You have more?"

"In storage, at my grandma's house, at my parents' house, in bins out on the balcony. I have a really hard time parting with books. I never know when I'll want to read one again, y'know."

"True." He stepped up to the shelves and took a closer look, turned around with a raised eyebrow. "*Best New Erotica?*" So Miss Molly wasn't quite as innocent as she wanted people to believe. Interesting.

Her cheeks immediately turned bright red. "Shouldn't we get going?"

"Nah. The place we're going doesn't close until eleven." He wasn't sure why he liked teasing her so much, except that she was really cute when she got flustered.

"Where are we going, by the way?"

"It's a surprise." He grinned at her.

"I probably should have told you this, but I'm not a big fan of surprises."

"Why not?"

She shrugged. "A general fear of the unknown, I guess."

He walked the few steps across her living room floor, until he was standing directly in front of her, and said, "Well, Miss Molly, I think that's a fear we might have to work on getting you over."

"I'm pretty sure that sentence wasn't grammatically correct."

Her eyes crinkled at the corners and a smile played across her lips, so he knew she was teasing him. "It probably wasn't. But I took off the editor's hat when I left work yesterday."

She laughed. "Point taken. So have you had a close enough look at my shelves or is there anything else you want to know about my reading habits?"

"Close enough for now." He glanced down at his watch. "You ready?"

They exited Molly's apartment, and he waited while she locked the door then jiggled the handle. She turned around, looked at him sheepishly and dropped her keys into her purse. "It's a compulsive thing. I have to check the door before I leave to make sure it's actually locked."

"And five minutes from now you're probably going to wonder if you really did lock the door, right?"

"Um…how'd you know that?"

He shrugged. "My mom's the same way. Actually, so am I."

They walked down the stairs in companionable silence and made their way towards the parking lot. He led her to his car—a three-year-old black Toyota Corolla—and pressed the unlock button on the key fob he held in his hand. He held open the passenger side door for Molly, and closed it once she was settled in. He rounded the hood of the car, got in on the driver's side and buckled himself up.

"So are you planning on telling me at any point tonight

where we're going?" She asked as he backed out of the parking space.

"You'll find out when we get there."

"You're exasperating, you know that, right?"

He grinned. "It's just one of my many appealing qualities."

She shook her head and laughed. "Keep telling yourself that."

An hour later Molly found herself trying to hit her red ball through the whirling blades of a miniature windmill. She totally hadn't expected Putt-Putt, but she had to admit that it was the most fun she'd had in a while.

She drew back her putter and tapped the ball, held her breath as it rolled towards the windmill. It barely slid past one of the wooden blades.

"It's about time."

She looked over at Joe and narrowed her eyes, which caused him to burst into laughter. "Hey, give me a break. I haven't played Putt-Putt in like six years. Whereas you are apparently a frequent Putt-Putter, Mr. I-Can-Make-A-Hole-In-One-Every-Single-Time." It had unfortunately taken her eighteen tries to get her ball through the treacherous windmill.

He shrugged, but the dimples playing at the corners of his mouth prevented her from being anywhere near mad at him. He was sporting his usual five o'clock shadow, except it was slightly darker at seven p.m. than during the workday. He'd pulled the sleeves up on his long-sleeved Henley, and every time Molly glanced at the dark hair dusting his forearms she felt compelled to reach for her bottle of water.

After a mere thirty minutes of miniature golf Molly had come to the conclusion that spending time with Joe could be a very, very dangerous thing.

He had been touching her ever since they'd arrived at Lion's Park. An elbow graze here. An arm brush there. And one time he'd even gotten behind her, wrapped his hands around her own and showed her how to hold her golf club better. Who knew Putt-Putt could be so sexy?

Wait a second. She was having slightly lascivious thoughts while playing miniature golf. Something seemed so wrong about that. *Like maybe the fact that this place is packed with five- and six-year-olds who couldn't even begin to comprehend the sexual nature of hitting balls into holes with sticks?* It seemed that golf—along with pool—must've been created by someone with a very dirty mind.

Or maybe it was just her.

"You gonna take your next shot or not?" Joe's voice roused her from her thoughts. Molly briefly forgot to breathe as she looked at him and the teasing grin on his face.

What was a guy this damned hot doing interested in her?

And why do you keep asking yourself that?

Both were questions that were probably best left for another time.

"Sorry. You caught me thinking."

"Those must've been some pretty deep thoughts."

She could feel her cheeks grow warm. What was it about him that made her blush like a twelve-year-old talking to her first big crush?

Molly made her way around the windmill, located her ball, lined up the shot and hit it towards the hole. It rolled and bounced off the backstop, away from where it needed to go.

"I apparently suck at Putt-Putt," she said as she hit the ball again.

She wasn't surprised when she didn't make it that time,

either.

"You're hitting the ball too hard," Joe said from beside her. "Just try to gently tap it in."

She glanced at him from the corner of her eye. "Well, you would know." She took her time lining up the shot before following his advice.

The ball rolled right in.

Joe wrote down the number of strokes she'd taken on the scorecard. "That puts you at plus six and me at minus seven."

"I'm pretty sure my score should be much worse than that."

He grinned. "I probably should've mentioned that my math skills are a bit lacking."

She grinned back at him. "For some reason I'm not buying that."

They headed towards the next hole.

Joe placed his ball on the green and settled into his golf stance, which Molly had become fascinated with about four holes back, primarily because of the fact that he wiggled his butt before taking a swing. She wasn't sure if he was aware that he did it, and she would be embarrassed as hell if he happened to catch her checking out his ass every time he putted, but she couldn't seem to look away.

His ball seemed to glide effortlessly up the hill on this particular hole, but somehow didn't manage to find its way into one of the three holes at the top.

She stepped up to the putting surface and set her ball down. "Don't start going easy on me now."

She stood up straight.

"You distracted me."

"How'd I distract you?" She pulled her putter back.

"I could feel you looking at my ass."

Her ball flew off the course and barely missed grazing the ear of a little boy putting the next hole over. The boy's mom picked up the ball that had landed at her feet. Molly walked to where the other woman stood and said, "Sorry. A bug flew into my face just as I hit the ball."

"Oh, it's okay. You can't come to Putt-Putt and not expect some errant balls flying around."

"You have a point." Molly took her ball from the other woman. "At any rate, I'm very sorry, but very glad I didn't accidentally hit your son."

"Don't worry about it."

The woman turned back to her little boy, who'd started tugging on her pants leg, and Molly went back to the hole she and Joe been playing.

She could tell he was barely containing his laughter. "Go ahead. Laugh. It's okay."

He burst into laughter.

She swatted him on the arm with her hand. "I almost hit that kid!"

"Hey, you're the one who was checking out my ass."

"You're the one who keeps wiggling it!"

She set her ball back down on the putting surface, swung, and luckily kept the ball on the green this time around. Her ball had somehow managed to land closer to one of the holes, so Joe took the next shot. He sank his.

"If it makes you feel any better, I've been checking out your ass, too."

Molly stared at him a few seconds, trying to figure out why he would be checking out her ass since, in her opinion, it wasn't all that great. "I'm not sure if I should laugh or just putt."

"Why not both?"

She laughed. "I don't know what to think about you sometimes."

His dimples flashed her. "I could give you a few ideas."

Her stomach dipped and rolled. "I'm sure you could."

She walked towards her ball. Joe reached out and grabbed her hand, pulling her to him. His green eyes crinkled at the corners behind those sexy black frames, and those damned dimples were still teasing her. Seconds later Molly felt his lips brush over hers, soft and somewhat hesitant, gone before it really hit her that Joe had just kissed her.

She blinked up at him, her mind blissfully quiet for at least a few seconds.

He smiled down at her. "Just so you know, you can check out my ass any time you like."

The tension broken, Molly took a slow step back. "Noted."

Great, now she'd been reduced to one-word sentences. And it hadn't even been a *kiss kiss*.

Absently, she turned back towards her ball and swung. The ball rolled right in. Of course.

They played the remaining holes, and Molly somehow managed to get her score back down to par. Joe, of course, was way under that and therefore won, but amazingly enough that didn't bother Molly too much. For someone who'd always been way too competitive, she was surprisingly okay with losing at Putt-Putt.

The rest of their evening was fairly uneventful. Joe took her to Poppa Rollo's, where they ate some excellent pizza before he dropped her off back at her place.

He walked her to her door, and as she turned the key in the lock she tried to figure out if she was supposed to invite him in for a cup of coffee, kiss him goodnight or let him go on his merry little way.

She opened the door and stepped inside, set her purse down on the side table next to the door where she usually placed her mail.

"You're welcome to come in for some coffee or tea or water." Could it be any more obvious that she didn't do this often?

He smiled. "Thanks, but I think me going home would probably be the best idea right now."

"Why?"

He raised an eyebrow.

Molly searched his face questioningly.

He cleared his throat.

What he wasn't saying finally hit her. "Oh. Okay then. Um." *What am I supposed to say now?* "Well, uh, good night then?"

"Yeah. Good night."

They stood there, the silence anything but empty, looking at each other.

God, he really is hot. Why's he standing on my porch again?

Stop thinking like that, Molly!

Joe finally reached out, and his hand grazed her jaw before capturing her chin. He leaned towards her, and this time Molly met him halfway. Their lips met, soft, sweet. She barely remembered to breathe as his mouth slowly moved over hers. Instead of feeling butterflies this time she just felt warm. Warm and tingly all over, like she could wrap her arms around him and melt against him and never come up for air again.

He pulled away, and she licked her lips, could still taste him faintly there.

He kissed her on the tip of her nose before backing away and putting more distance between them. Silence hung thick in the air until finally, she couldn't stand the intensity any longer.

She swallowed. "I really did have a good time tonight, even if I did almost give that little boy a concussion."

He chuckled. "I had fun, too. Want to do it again next weekend?"

"I don't know about Putt-Putt again."

"Doesn't have to be Putt-Putt."

"I think I could manage to pencil you in," she teased. "What night works best for you?"

"How's Friday sound?"

"Friday sounds good. Why do I have the feeling you already have something in mind?"

"Because, Miss Molly, we are definitely on the same wave length."

He kissed her on the lips again—quickly, this time, a peck more than a kiss, really—and said, "I'll see you on Monday."

"Yeah, Monday." She smiled. This new job was definitely looking like a good thing.

CHAPTER EIGHTEEN

"And this," Joe paused, "is your cubicle."

Molly poked her head around the partition and took a look at what was to be her new office space.

It wasn't too bad, at least as far as cubicles went. Plenty of space, what looked to be a good rolling chair, a new-ish Macbook and a large L-shaped desk that offered plenty of work room.

"I think I can make this work." She grinned at Joe, trying not to appear as nervous as she felt. Although, to be fair, she wasn't sure if the nerves were a result of this being her first day at a new job, or because Joe was standing so close she could smell the scent she was beginning to associate with him—the light scent of aftershave combined with pure, unadulterated male.

"It isn't much, but around here we call our cubes home."

"I'm not sure if that's depressing or reassuring."

He chuckled, which caused the dimple in his cheek to play a quick game of hide and seek behind the faint shadow of stubble. Did the man shave just enough every morning to maintain the perfect amount of five o'clock shadow or was his facial hair just naturally Marlboro Man-esque? Furthermore, what aftershave did he use because man did he smell good.

"It's a little of both, honestly. But hey, at least we get

to decorate them however we want. Well, we can't have anything indecent, but feel free to bring photos or artwork or anything you want to make the space your own."

"Awesome. I have tons of photos that are just sitting around in boxes that I can bring. Is it okay to hang my diploma?"

"Oh, definitely. You probably want to be careful with it, though, and make sure the cubicle wall can support it. Actually, come with me to my desk and I'll show you how mine is hung."

Had he deliberately made that sound dirty or was her head simply that far in the gutter whenever she got around him? "Um, sure. That would be nice."

Joe led her to a cubicle a few rows down, closer to the back of the room, and said, "And here's my space."

His diploma was hanging on the partition wall behind his desk. Summa cum Laude from Texas Tech, B.A. in Journalism with a minor in Advertising. Molly raised an eyebrow.

"Summa cum Laude, huh?"

He actually looked slightly embarrassed as he ran a finger under the collar of his shirt. "Yeah."

"Why didn't you mention that before?"

He shrugged. "Didn't seem important."

"How is that not important? You had to have worked your tail off to graduate Summa cum Laude."

He tugged a little bit on his tie, loosened the knot slightly. "Yeah. A little bit."

Molly raised an eyebrow. "You sure are being close-lipped about this."

Joe shrugged again. "It just isn't something I tend to brag about. I sometimes end up feeling like an ass when-ever it comes up, like I'm rubbing it in to everyone that I graduated with honors and they didn't."

"It's not rubbing it in, it's being proud of yourself.

Hell, if I'd graduated Summa cum Laude I would probably be sure to mention it at least once a week, just to remind myself that I am smart and that my college education got me something more than a stack of student loan debt."

"You do have a point. I'm just not the type to brag about stuff."

"I get that."

Molly took a good look at the rest of Joe's work space. Other than the diploma, there was a Macbook similar to hers, except his was turned on. He had papers neatly stacked and filed in trays and folders, a Texas Tech coffee mug holding pens, pencils and a pair of scissors, a Post-It Note cube and that morning's issue of the newspaper folded in half on a corner of his desk. The walls were decorated with neatly lined-up photos, some of places, others of people.

She gestured towards one with him, a middle-aged woman with short, graying hair and a brown-haired little girl who looked to be around five years old. They were all smiling and looked to be incredibly happy, and the little girl was staring up at Joe adoringly. "Who's this?"

He hesitated slightly before a smile lightly played across his face. "My mom and my niece. We'd just gotten back from Annabelle's sixth birthday party at Putt-Putt. She was hyped up on cake and Dr. Pepper and rubbing it in that she'd beat me."

Molly looked at him over her shoulder and smiled. "I'm guessing you let her win?"

"She won fair and square." He winked at her.

"Uh huh." She knew what his miniature golf skills were like.

"She did! Little brat has a fantastic putting ability."

Molly chuckled. "You're really close to her, aren't you?"

Joe turned towards his desk and straightened a folder

in one of the trays. "You could say that."

The three feet between them suddenly seemed like ten, and Molly couldn't figure out why. "Okay." Uncomfortable with his sudden withdrawal, she stuck her hands in her trouser pockets and rocked back on her heels. "Well, I guess I'm going to go back to my cubicle now, get to know it better."

Joe turned back towards her, and his good-natured smile was back in place. Odd. "Do you want to go grab lunch together later?"

"Um, sure." Jesus the man was throwing her off balance. "That would be nice."

His dimple winked at her again. "Good. It's another date."

Molly slowly backed out of his cubicle. "Yeah, see you in a few hours."

She turned and walked towards her own work space, trying to figure out what she'd said or done to put Joe off like she had.

Damn. Damn. Double damn.

Joe sat down in his desk chair, propped his elbows up on the desk and dropped his head into his hands. What the hell had caused him to withdraw like that when Molly had asked him about Annabelle?

He should have known she would ask. Molly was the observant type, always watching and listening and really paying attention. Hell, it was one of the many things he liked about her. And sadly, she was the first person at the paper who'd even bothered to ask about the picture. She was probably the first person who'd actually noticed, truth be told.

Not that he didn't like his coworkers—some of them

were really great. But they were all so busy concentrating on getting ahead, on being the one who broke through and became a page editor, and then a section editor that they barely paid attention to what was really going on in the day to day lives of their fellow copy editors.

Joe paid attention, though, had from the beginning. The people here were interesting. They all had their little dramas, and paying attention to their little soap operas helped to keep his mind off his own.

He looked over at the picture of his mom, Annabelle and him and smiled wistfully. That day had been one of the last fun, carefree days they'd had together. There were times—like now—that he would give most anything to go back to that sunny April day two years ago.

Joe felt his throat start to itch, cleared it and turned back to his desk. He opened up his email and resolutely got to work. Now was not a time to take a trip down memory lane.

He glanced back over at the photo, looked at Annabelle's smile with its missing front tooth and once again wished the past year had been different.

The sound of his Inbox announcing incoming mail drew his attention back to his computer. He smiled when he saw it was from Molly, opened it and read, "Lunch is on me this time. No arguments. ☺"

Joe hit reply and quickly typed out a response. "What did you have in mind?" He clicked on send and continued to check his email.

A few minutes later he received her response. "Ninfa's sound okay?"

"Ninfa's sounds great. Unfortunately we can't have any margaritas."

Joe got through a few more emails before Molly responded.

"True. That's okay with me, though, since Ninfaritas

make my cheeks feel fuzzy."

He chuckled and shook his head before typing out a response. "They make your cheeks feel fuzzy? Please tell me how your cheeks feel 'fuzzy.' ;-)"

Her response time was much faster on that one. "They just do. It's hard to explain. But trust me, they feel fuzzy. Warm and tingly yet kind of numb. It's an odd feeling."

"LOL. Must be the Everclear."

"Or the tequila," she said a few seconds later.

"Good point. You know what they say about tequila, right?"

"No, what do they say?"

He debated sending his next response, but decided to anyway. "Well, there is that song. What's it called? Oh, yeah. 'Tequila Makes Her Clothes Fall Off'."

Please don't let me get fired for sexual harassment.

A few minutes later his inbox alerted him to a new email.

"HAHA. Trying to be clever, huh? ;-) For the record, tequila does not make my clothes fall off."

Joe read Molly's response and tried to figure out if she was mad or teasing him. Damned email conversations. They could be so ambiguous sometimes.

He'd just hit reply when he received another email from her, which he decided to open before responding to the previous one.

"However, tequila does make me feel really warm. Too warm, sometimes."

Oh, now that was interesting. "Really? So what do you do when it makes you feel too warm?"

Her response took a few seconds. "Cool down. *wink*"

He responded with an "LOL" and finished reading his other emails.

Cool down, huh? He thought of all the ways she could

cool down. He shifted in his seat. Something told him working with Molly was going to get a little, well, hard at times.

Molly wasn't sure how she'd managed to work up the courage to tell Joe that lunch was on her, or to actually make a decision about where to go, but there she was sitting at a table across from him at Ninfa's.

The distance from earlier was gone and Joe's usual good humor seemed to be back in place. Molly wanted to know what had caused him to have his earlier reaction, but she also figured that now was not the right time to get nosey.

"So how's your first day going so far?" He piled strips of grilled chicken onto a tortilla before adding peppers, cheese, sour cream and green sauce. He deftly rolled it all into a neat fajita and took a bite.

"It's going well. You know how first days are, though—a little nerve-wracking yet easy," Molly said before taking a bite of her chicken fajita quesadilla.

"Yeah. It's almost like the first day of school, only not as scary."

Molly swallowed before laughing. "Very true. The first day of school was always the worst."

"Really? Why? I never really thought it was the worst, just not a lot of fun." He took another bite of his fajita.

"New teacher, new grade, new classes. Plus, there was all the pressure to have the perfect first day of school outfit."

"That's right. You girls always made such a big deal about what to wear on the first day. It was almost as bad as prom."

"Very true. Girls made such a big deal out of the dumbest things back then." She polished off a quesadilla wedge.

"Yeah. The funny thing, though, is that y'all still do stuff like that."

"How so?"

He gestured towards Molly. "You look really good today—not that you don't usually look good anyway—but your shirt looks like it might be new or at least newish. In fact, I'm willing to lay down money that you debated that outfit all day yesterday."

Molly's cheeks warmed and she wasn't sure which part of his comment to address first. "Um, thanks. And you're right—the shirt is new. I thought about it yesterday and decided around four o'clock last night that I just needed to go buy a new one."

"Damn, I'm good."

Molly grinned. "Either you're psychic or you just know women really well."

"A little bit of both." He winked at her before making himself another fajita.

"Psychic, huh? So what's my fortune? Are there any tall, dark, handsome strangers coming my way?" She teased.

Joe's expression turned thoughtful before he looked at her and said, "My sources say yes."

"Oh really? And how, exactly, am I going to meet this tall, dark, handsome stranger?"

He chewed on a bite of fajita and swallowed. "By chance."

"Doesn't everybody meet by chance?"

"Right you are."

"Your sources aren't very good."

He shrugged. "I do what I can with what I have."

Oh really? "Don't we all?" Molly looked at him as she polished off her last quesadilla wedge. He really was a good-looking guy, not to mention intelligent, funny and easy to talk to. She kept wanting to pinch herself to make sure this was all really happening and she wasn't in the middle of some long, really excellent dream.

"Yeah, we do." He took a sip of his sweet tea.

The waiter appeared with their ticket, and Molly dug her debit card out of her purse and handed it to him.

"Are you sure you want to pay? I'd be more than happy to."

"Yes, I'm sure I want to pay. You've paid for the last two meals we've had together."

"Fair enough, but the next meal's on me."

Her body warmed as his gaze slid over her. He somehow managed to linger over all the right parts without making her feel like nothing more than a sex object. Instead, she felt wanted, desired, appreciated, as though he simply enjoyed looking at her. That was a new sensation, one she wasn't entirely sure she was comfortable with just yet.

She stared back at him, though, enjoying the way his dark hair fell over his forehead and how his constant stubble made him look like some sort of ruggedly hot geek. She'd always appreciated a guy in a dress shirt and tie, and had to admit that Joe definitely looked good in business attire. The deep blue of the shirt was a great contrast against his coloring, and his tie with subtle blue and green polka dots was fun without being obnoxious.

The waiter returned with Molly's debit card and the receipt, breaking the silent tension between them. Mentally shaking herself, she turned her attention to the receipt. She doubled the tax and wrote that on the TIP line, added it all up and wrote down the total before signing the bottom.

"You ready to go?" Joe asked as Molly was putting her debit card back in her wallet.

Molly shoved her wallet back into her purse and slung the bag over her shoulder. "Sure am. Let's get back to work."

As they walked out of the restaurant Molly couldn't resist looking at Joe's profile from the corner of her eye. Her new coworker was definitely a nice piece of eye candy. How many more days until Friday and their next date?

Too many, she thought as his hand brushed against hers before grabbing hold. Butterflies danced in her stomach and she glanced over at him again. He was smiling and watching her.

"What?" She asked.

"Nothing," he said before he stopped walking so that he could lean over and kiss her lightly.

He straightened back up and started walking again. She tugged on his hand, which was still wrapped firmly within her own. He turned to look at her, and Molly pulled him closer. They stood there, in the middle of the parking lot, just staring at each other for long moments before Molly lifted up onto her tiptoes and brushed her lips over his own, one, two, three times before backing away and smiling.

For the first time, Molly thought she might have managed to catch Joe off guard, rather than the other way around. He looked a little shocked. But then he gathered himself and flashed one of his amazing smiles at her, and Molly was glad she was holding on to his hand because otherwise she might have melted into a puddle on the ground.

The sound of a car honking broke the spell that seemed to have been cast over them, and they started walking towards her car again.

Oh, man, she was in trouble. The best part, though, was that for once she didn't mind.

CHAPTER NINETEEN

"Uncle Joe?"

He turned towards the kitchen table, where Annabelle was currently working on her homework. "What, sweetie?"

"I just remembered I have to have Valentine's cards for my class tomorrow."

"Valentine's cards?" Tomorrow was Valentine's Day? Crap.

"Yes, Uncle Joe, Valentine's cards. I have to give them to *everybody* in the class, even William Stevens who's a stinky boy with cooties."

Oh, God, please do not tell me my niece has a crush on a boy already. I'm not ready to start polishing the shot gun. Or buy a shot gun, for that matter.

"How long have you known you needed cards?"

She shrugged and pushed her pencil across her sheet of notebook paper. Her dark hair tumbled over her shoulders, reminding him of his sister—her mom—on a daily basis. "For a while. But I forgot."

He sighed. "Do you just need cards or are you supposed to take cookies or something, too?"

This school year had definitely been a learning process for him. It seemed like there was always a party or some reason for Annabelle to have to take cookies or cupcakes to class. He definitely had a greater appreciation for everything his mom had gone through raising two kids.

"Oh, yeah. That's what I was forgetting. Cookies."

He shook his head. He loved his niece, he really did. Sometimes, though, he wanted to rail against the powers that be who had put him in the position of playing single dad at the age of twenty-eight to a precocious—and yet sometimes forgetful—eight-year-old girl.

"We'll go to the grocery store after dinner and pick up cards and cookies. How's that sound?"

She beamed at him. "I love you, Uncle Joe."

"I love you, too, sweetie. Now finish up your home-work while I finish cooking supper."

A year ago he'd never thought he would be spending his weeknights cooking and helping Annabelle with her homework. Then again, eight years ago he never would have thought anyone other than his sister and her husband would be raising Annabelle. He'd learned the hard way that life sometimes threw you curveballs, and that if they hit you just right they hurt like hell.

Annabelle's voice drew him from his thoughts. "Uncle Joe?"

"Yeah?"

"Is four times four sixteen?"

"It sure is, sweetie, it sure is."

After dinner, the two of them piled into his car and headed towards the grocery store. Hopefully there would still be something for her to choose from card-wise. Other-wise, he wasn't sure what they would do.

As they stood in the middle of a very picked-over Valentine's Day aisle, Annabelle's small hand in his own, Joe's gaze kept wandering over to the more adult offerings. Should he get Molly something? Valentine's Day was one of those things he'd never been good at. As a guy, he could really care less about all the hoopla, but some women got completely bent out of shape over it all. He didn't think Molly was the type to place too much importance on a commercial holiday, but since they were dating, and since he really liked her, maybe he should get her something.

But what?

"Can I get these, Uncle Joe?" Annabelle had grabbed a pink box that she was currently thrusting towards him. Vaguely he saw that they had Dora the Explorer on them.

"That's fine, sweetie. Let's see how many are in there."

Twenty-four. Annabelle's class had thirty-two kids in it. He found another box of similar cards and grabbed them, too.

"Okay, let's go find you some cookies, now."

They walked back to the bakery, where luckily there were containers upon containers of red, white and pink cookies in all shapes and sizes and varieties. He picked up a couple containers of heart-shaped sugar cookies coated in red icing and placed them in the shopping basket slung over his left arm. "Anything else you can think of?"

She shook her head. "Nope. Just cards and cookies."

They headed back to the front of the store, cutting through the produce section. As they neared the produce area check out, the floral displays to his left caught his eye. There were roses everywhere, spilling out of vases, bunched in clear plastic wrap, attached to balloons or stuffed animals. A couple of young, college-aged looking guys were staring at them, scratching their heads. Most likely they were trying to figure out how to spend the least amount of money without their girlfriends thinking they were cheap. Ah, to be young and concerned with only getting laid again.

Joe rolled his eyes and he and Annabelle turned towards the check out.

She tugged on his hand and he looked down.

"What, sweetie?"

"Aren't those flowers pretty, Uncle Joe?" Annabelle pointed towards the brightly-colored displays.

"They sure are."

She tugged him closer to the flowers and stopped in front of a stand filled with daisies and lilies in various vases and pots. She reached out and touched a vase that looked like it was made out of stone or concrete. "Isn't this soooooo cute?"

He looked at it closer. Actually, the vase was kind of neat. It looked more like a planter, and was a statue of a princess kissing a frog she held in her hands. Brightly colored daisies spilled out of it, the reds and pinks and yellows adding even more whimsy to the image.

It would be perfect for Molly.

"Yeah, it is cute." He picked up the planter. "Maybe we should get some flowers for Grandma, too. You think she would like that?"

Annabelle grinned up at him. "Grandma loves flowers."

Joe chose a pretty display of white lilies in a clear glass vase. "Think she'll like these?"

Annabelle nodded her agreement, her blue eyes sparkling up at him. He reached over and plucked a single pink rose from another display. "And this is for you."

Her eyes widened and her mouth formed into the shape of an "O." Moments like this, when Annabelle looked up at him like he was a super hero, made him realize how lucky he was. Sure, his situation wasn't ideal, but he wouldn't trade it in for anything.

"Thank you," she said softly.

He bent down and kissed her on the tip of her nose before ruffling her hair. "Every pretty girl deserves a pretty flower."

She giggled. "Who are the daisies for?"

He straightened and sighed. Sure enough, she hadn't missed a thing. "Those, sweetheart, are for another pretty girl."

"Oooh. Do you have a girlfriend, Uncle Joe?"

He rolled his eyes at her and they headed back towards the checkout line. "No, I don't have a girlfriend." *Yet, anyway.* That was a situation he planned on changing soon. Very soon.

♡

Ugh. Valentine's Day.

Molly rolled her eyes as she walked past a display of pink and white carnations perched on the receptionist's desk. She hated Valentine's Day. Hated it.

Of course, part of her hatred could probably be attributed to the fact that she rarely had a date—much less a boyfriend—on February fourteenth. Something about being told how much she sucked at life for being single just didn't seem to sit too well with her.

As she waited for the elevator to arrive, Molly's gaze kept being drawn back to the floral arrangement. Okay, so she was a sucker for flowers, even if they were cheap pink and white carnations in a hideous red plastic vase with lips all over it. Where did people find this stuff anyway?

The elevator dinged seconds before the doors opened, and Molly stepped inside.

Valentine's Day had always sucked for her. Even as a kid, when you had to get everyone in your class a card, Molly had known that the only reason she got cards was because the kids had to do it. She'd seen the pretty girls' construction paper envelopes, decorated with colorful hearts and butterflies with girly handwriting and glitter all over them. Those envelopes had been stuffed to the brim, always containing a little extra than everyone else's. And there hers had been, always meticulously made, her name neatly printed on it, hearts and flowers carefully drawn and holding the bare minimum.

Sure, there had been one year when Trevor McGlockson had given her a special Valentine, and Molly's lonely little heart had lit up with joy.

Until she'd found out Trevor McGlockson had also given a special Valentine to her best friend Suzanne, who had in turn given Trevor the friendship bracelet Molly had braided just for her.

The memory made Molly chuckle. Sure, being a kid had kind of sucked, what with being smart and chubby with coke bottle glasses and all, but she had to admit that the dating thing really had been much simpler in elementary school.

The elevator dinged and the doors opened up on her floor. Even though this was only her third day on the job, she'd already begun to relax in the newspaper's offices. Everyone was nice, if not busy, and the environment was simply so different from her previous job. Plus, she felt relaxed at the simple thought of no longer having to deal with Warren breathing down her neck every fifteen minutes.

She'd set her purse down on the desk and turned on the computer before catching sight of a bunch of bright colors sitting next to her phone. Molly turned and looked, surprise—and confusion—clouding her brain.

Where in the world had those come from?

She sat down—plopped, really—and stared at the flowers. Gerbera daisies. Her favorite. And they'd been planted in the most obnoxiously whimsical container she'd ever seen—a princess kissing a frog. She laughed, couldn't help it, really, as she reached for the small square card tucked in among the thick green stems.

Looking around, she noticed that no one was watching her. Curious, she knitted her brows together as she slid her finger under the flap and broke the seal of the envelope. She pulled the card out. It was simple, white with silver print that said, "Happy Valentine's Day" on the front. She opened it, read what had been written inside and promptly began laughing.

Still giggling, she picked up her phone and dialed Joe's extension.

"Yes?"

"So you won't turn into a frog, huh?"

"Nope. I came already evolved, no magic spells and fairy princesses necessary."

"So you're saying you're already a prince?"

"Well, I wouldn't go that far. I'm definitely not a frog, though."

She could hear the smile in his voice, and the sound was infectious. "The flowers are beautiful. I totally wasn't expecting them."

"I figured you weren't, but they looked like you and I couldn't resist."

"They looked like me? How, pray tell, do I look like a gerbera daisy? And if you dare say we're both round, I'll be doing more than turning you back into a frog."

He laughed. "They looked like you because they're bright, fun, not your typical hothouse rose or classic lily."

"So you're saying I'm neither sexy nor classic?" Her words didn't have much heat, though, considering she was barely restraining her laughter.

"Oh, you're both of those things. More so, though, you're the laid-back girl next door. The flowers caught my eye because they were different from the rest of the displays."

She swallowed. How was she supposed to respond to that?

Molly reached out and touched one dark pink petal with her fingertip. She'd always been amazed at how soft flower petals were, and yet how resilient they could be. Through rain and wind, soccer balls and kids' wayward feet, some flowers always managed to survive. They might look a little worse for the wear, but they were still standing, still alive.

She cleared her throat. "Okay, well, I should probably get to work now. Thanks again for the flowers; it was really sweet of you."

"No problem. You do realize you owe me a make out session now, though, right?"

A very unladylike snort escaped from Molly's nose. "I owe you a make out session now?"

"Yes, ma'am. I bought you flowers, now you owe me some hot and heavy lip and tongue action."

She wanted to sound offended, but knew that would be hard to do considering her stomach had turned into a carnival ride at the thought of making out with Joe. "So what, is this up-front payment for my services or something? If so, you must think I'm pretty cheap. I mean, I'm so worth an added balloon. And if you really want to get lucky, one of those obnoxious stuffed animals that makes kissing sounds. That's worth at least a good ten minutes of making out."

She could hear his laugh all the way from his cubicle. "Fair enough. I'll have you a balloon and an obnoxious stuffed animal after lunch. What do I get if I throw in some chocolate?"

"Well are we talking the good stuff or the cheap stuff?"

"Whatever I can find left on the shelves."

"In that case the cheap stuff."

"Unfortunately." His sigh was filled with an exaggerated heaviness.

"Well, for the cheap stuff I might let you kiss me a little longer than ten minutes."

"What if I managed to find the good stuff?"

"Definitely fifteen minutes. If it's dark chocolate,

though, I might think about letting you cop a feel."

I am so going to get fired for this.

"Only think about it?"

"Hey, that's better than nothing."

"Very true."

She heard his phone ring, indicating someone was trying to get through to him.

"Hey, I've got to go. Mr. Charles is calling me."

How was that for some timing?

"No problem. Thanks again for the flowers."

"You're welcome. I'll talk to you later. Bye."

"Later," Molly said before hanging up the phone. She sat back in her chair, a goofy grin playing over her face as she stared at Joe's Valentine's Day gift.

How wonderfully unexpected.

CHAPTER TWENTY

Molly was sitting on her couch, grinning wildly at the pair of kissing monkeys Joe had brought her after lunch, when a knock on her door jolted her from her reverie. She got up and looked through the peephole, and was surprised to see Benjamin standing there.

She opened the door. "What's wrong? You look like someone just ran over your dog."

Benjamin looked at Molly with blood shot eyes and shrugged as he entered her apartment. She took in the bags that were forming under his eyes, the disheveled hair and the generally unhappy expression on his face and said, "Seriously, hon, what's wrong?"

He sighed and flopped down onto her couch. Eyes closed, head thrown back, he said, "Emery and I just broke up."

On Valentine's Day? Now that was some crappy luck. "Why? What happened?"

He sighed. "She said she'd been thinking about this for a while, and thought breaking up was the right thing to do. Said that she doesn't think a long distance relationship will work any longer. She also has this crazy idea that I'm in love with you."

Molly felt as though she'd just been punched in the stomach. Luckily she was still standing behind him, so he couldn't see the expression on her face. "She what?"

"She thinks I'm in love with you."

"Why would she think that? You're not in love with me. Hell, you've been setting me up with men. You wouldn't do that if you were in love with me." *Besides, why would you want me when you've had Perfect Emery? Stop it, Molly!*

He opened his eyes. "I have no idea. I think you might have been right, though. Ever since that night we played I Never she's been acting weird. Even though she says she's fine with our past, I get the feeling she might not have been."

Molly sat down on the couch beside him. Somehow saying "I told you so" didn't seem like the right thing to do at the moment. She breathed deeply. "I was afraid that would happen. But still, just because you and I have that history doesn't mean there's anything more to it than that. There's a reason why it's history."

She didn't know how to handle this. A maelstrom of emotions swirled inside of her, the primary one being confusion.

She could see the kissing monkeys from the corner of her eye. Molly swallowed. She wondered if she should feel more excited, even though the thought of being happy over someone else's pain seemed slightly sadistic to her. But this was Benjamin. Her best friend. The guy she'd wanted to be with since her sophomore year of high school.

But you don't want that anymore, Molly. You're trying to get over him, remember?

She looked at the kissing monkeys again and felt more confused.

"I can't believe she broke up with me."

She patted his arm, not really knowing what else to do. "I know, hon. But look at it this way, at least the break up happened before you moved off to Oregon with her."

"Is that supposed to make me feel better?"

"Just trying to find a bright side."

"There is no bright side. Not right now."

They sat there in awkward silence for long moments. Molly figured he would talk when he needed to talk, and since she had no idea what to say she decided to keep her mouth shut. Figuring out what to say was pretty hard when you couldn't figure out how you felt.

"Who are those from?" he asked, breaking the silence.

"Who are what from?"

He nodded. "The monkeys."

She cleared her throat. "A guy I work with."

Why was she being so secretive about this? *Probably because he told you Joe wasn't your type.*

"You've been on the job three days and you already have a guy giving you kissing monkeys? Seriously?"

Was that jealousy or disbelief in his voice? Probably the former.

"Well, to be honest, we've known each other a little longer than three days."

"Oh really?"

She nodded.

"Is this one of the guys I set you up with? Because I'd thought you didn't really like any of them, except for Larry."

"Actually, no. He's a guy I met one night at the bookstore."

He looked at her and narrowed his eyes. "Okay, something's going on here. You would usually be bursting at the seams to tell me something like this."

"Is now really a good time for me to talk about this? All things considered?"

"All things considered, I think I need to get my mind off of what just happened. So spill."

She sighed, felt conflicted. "Well, like I said, we met at the bookstore one night. He was buying books for his mom and asked me for my opinion since we were in the same section. We got to talking and he asked me if I wanted to grab something to drink with him in the café. So we had some hot chocolate and talked for a while and that was that. Then we ran into each other at the gym a few days later, he got my phone number. He seemed like a nice guy, but totally out of my league. But then I bumped into him after my interview at the paper—ends up he works there as a copy editor. We went to lunch together, he asked me out on a date, I said yes, and today he brought me flowers and the monkeys." She didn't mention the Mylar balloon or dark chocolate truffles he'd brought after lunch along with the monkeys.

"He was buying romance novels for his mom?"

It figured Benjamin would latch on to that particular detail. "How do you know he was buying romance novels?"

"Because that's all you read."

"I could've been in the art section or something."

He laughed. "You're a horrible liar. So you actually believed him when he said he was buying romance novels? For his mom?"

"He had a list, in very feminine handwriting I might add."

"Maybe he writes like a girl."

She punched him in the arm. "I've seen his handwriting since, and no, he doesn't write like a girl. His is closer to chicken scratch."

"But you didn't know that at the time."

She crossed her arms over her chest. "No, I didn't. But I still talked to him and had hot chocolate with him, because doing so seemed pretty harmless considering we were in a public place. If he'd asked me to go get a drink with him at a bar I would have said no and that would have been that."

"So what's this guy like?"

Now this was the tricky part. Did she just tell Benjamin who Joe was or keep him in the dark? "Actually, you already know him."

"How?"

"From Clicks. Remember about a month ago when that guy came up to the table and greeted you? I said something later about him being cute and you told me he probably wasn't my type and to look elsewhere?"

Benjamin looked as though he were trying to remember. "Was I drunk?"

She punched him in the arm again. "You know I hate it when you say that."

"Which is why I say it." He thought again for a few moments before snapping his fingers. "Joe? Is that who you're talking about?"

Molly nodded her head.

"Well I'll be damned."

"In a good way or a bad way?"

He chuckled. "Is there a good way to be damned?"

"This is true."

"Joe. Wow. I never would have seen that coming."

"Why? Is he too far out of my league?"

"Not at all. He just seems to have some secrets is all."

She'd sensed the same thing, but wasn't about to tell Benjamin that. "Maybe I like secrets."

The secrets were driving her crazy.

"That's because you're nosy."

"Again, very true."

"So he brought you kissing monkeys for Valentine's Day. Why aren't you out with him right now?"

She shrugged. "We're going out again tomorrow, and both of us agreed that trying to do anything tonight would probably be pretty difficult."

"Smart man. So do you want me to keep setting you up

with other guys?"

She swallowed. That was what she wasn't too sure about. "Well, I don't know. I mean, as far as I know of Joe and I are just dating, we're not actually exclusively seeing each other. But on the other hand, the thought of going out with someone else just seems, weird, considering how much I like Joe."

"Don't put all your eggs into one basket, Molly."

"But what if I want to put all of my eggs into one basket?"

"Well, it's too late because I've already set you up with someone for Saturday night."

She groaned. "Seriously?"

"Yup. His name's Tony. I gave him your number and he should be calling you tomorrow."

She sighed. "Okay, I'll go out with this one guy. But no more after this unless I tell you to. I don't want to screw things up with Joe."

"Fair enough. Just give Tony a chance. He's a good guy. I think you'll like him."

Probably not as much as I like Joe.

"Okay. So, enough about me. Do you need to talk or anything about the Emery thing or are you okay?"

"I'm not okay, but I don't know what to say, either."

Come to think of it, Benjamin didn't seem to be very heartbroken over any of this. Distressed, sure, but not like he'd just had his heart crushed and trampled on. What was that about? "Well, if you need to talk I'm here."

"I know. Can we just watch *The Voice for a while?"*

"Sure, hon."

She turned up the volume on the TV as Blake and Christina fought over a blonde chick with a Stevie Nicks vibe.

She glanced at Benjamin from the corner of her eye. Could he really be in love with her? And if he was, what was she going to do about it?

After Benjamin left, Molly got on her laptop and pulled up her blog editor. Restlessly, she set her fingers on home row and began to type. At first, the words came slowly. But the more she thought, the more she felt, the faster the words came.

There's something weird going on in the universe because my life just got what looks a little like crazy.

I guess I should probably start at the beginning. Well, the beginning of today at least, because today's when things got strange.

First, I got to work, in a really bad mood. It's Valentine's Day. I hate Valentine's Day. It's a stupid holiday. But then I got to my desk and Joe had brought me flowers. Daisies, even, which are my favorite. They were in this adorable stone planter of a princess kissing a frog, and the note he'd left with them said he promised he wouldn't turn back into a frog. After lunch he brought me a pair of kissing monkeys and some dark chocolate.

The skeptic in me is thinking, "Oh, he just wants to get in my pants, and once he's done that he'll forget all about me." The hopeless romantic, though, thinks all of this is really sweet. I've never had a guy bring me stuff on Valentine's Day before, and I've never had a guy bring me flowers period. So he gets at least a few points.

This evening was when things got strange, though. Benjamin came over. He and Emery broke up.

The reason?

She thinks he's in love with me.

Yes, you read that right. Emery thinks Benjamin—Benjamin!—is in love with me.

Is she out of her freaking mind?

Benjamin isn't in love with me. Benjamin loves the idea of having me around and having me as his fall back crutch. It's been that way for years. I knew, though, that her finding out about us and the truth about what happened would freak her out. That's why I'd told him from the beginning to tell her everything, to explain our past to her so that she didn't worry and so that she understood the entire picture.

Even then, though, it's not like what happened between us meant anything to him. He says it did, that it still does, but I find it hard to believe him most of the time. If it had meant anything to him, he would have dated me. He would have been more careful with my feelings.

He's not in love with me. He loves me as a friend and that's it.

In all honesty, I don't know that I've ever been completely in love with him. I think that what I've felt all these years has been my warped idea of love. Let's face it, growing up I didn't exactly have the best example of love to go by. I didn't know what a healthy relationship looked like until I was in my twenties, and that was from the outside looking in. To me, love was about hurting, about being in misery and emotional hell. And when you feel like you're worthless and like you don't deserve to be loved—I have my ex-stepfather to thank for that—you don't exactly expect much from the people you do care for.

I've been stupid. Stupid and blind. Why have I put myself through this?

Tonight was so like Benjamin, though. Here I was, sitting on top of the world, happy and thinking that maybe this time I've found something good. And then he came over and burst my bubble. Why is it that whenever he's around all I feel is confused and unhappy? That can't be healthy. That can't be normal or right.

But he's my friend. My best friend. We've known each other since high school. I can't just throw over a dozen

*years of friendship away. We have some good times. We've
had some good times. We laugh together. He knows me
and I know him. The problem is that I sometimes wonder if
he understands me. He seems completely oblivious sometimes—okay, most of the time—to my thoughts and feelings.
I've brushed that off as him just "being a guy." Now I'm
starting to wonder if maybe that isn't the case, if maybe it's
just him.*

*Joe understands me. We haven't known each other
long at all, but he understands me. He seems to instinc-
tively know what to say and when to say it. He's giving me
time, taking this slow, letting things go where they will. But
he's made it clear he's attracted to me. I appreciate that.
Knowing what he wants actually makes this so much easier,
because I'm not sitting here over-thinking this and trying
to figure out what he wants from me. Okay, in all fairness I
am over-thinking this because that's what I do. And a part
of me does still have a hard time believing someone like Joe
would ever want someone like me, but I'm working on that.
I'm trying to allow myself to believe that maybe this time
could be different.*

*I've never had that before. I've never had honesty and
understanding and ease and laughter and a really strong
attraction.*

*He's kissed me a couple of times. Nothing really major,
but enough to make my knees weak and to let me know that
I want to kiss him again. Often. More. I want to do more
with him.*

*And, really, when was the last time I felt that way
about Benjamin? When was the last time I looked at him
and thought, "God, he's so hot. I wish he would kiss me."
or looked at him and got all tingly and mushy inside? When
was the last time Benjamin made me feel butterflies? Actually, I'm not sure Benjamin ever made me feel butterflies,
much less mushy and tingly and weak-kneed.*

God, I've been stupid. Even knowing that, it's still hard to completely let go of the safety net. I'm getting closer. I only have a couple fingers left hanging on, and those are starting to slip. But dammit, why'd he have to come over here and tell me that? Why'd he have to ruin the first good Valentine's Day I've ever had?

Why?

CHAPTER TWENTY-ONE

"What am I going to wear?" Molly asked herself—this was really becoming far too common of a question—as she pulled yet another shirt over her head and tossed it onto the bed.

It was Friday night, and Joe had once again told her to dress warm yet casual, and of course nothing fit or looked right on her.

She blew a strand of hair out of her eyes and glared at the clothes hanging in her closet. Part of the problem was that she desperately needed to do laundry. The other part was that she felt fat and bloated thanks to what the calendar—and her body—told her was PMS.

Note to self: never go out on a date again two days before you're due to start your period.

Deciding her closet had nothing to offer, Molly walked over to her dresser and rifled through drawers. T-shirt. Cami. T-shirt. T-shirt. T-shirt. Man, she could use a wardrobe readjustment.

She was going through the last drawer when she finally found something that could possibly be suitable. Molly pulled out the lightweight v-neck sweater, opened the drawer above it and pulled out a white cotton cami, and set both items down on her bed. She pulled the cami on over her head, and then followed that with the sweater, which was a pale green and thin enough so as to almost be sheer.

She turned this way and that in front of her floor length mirror, sighed, and decided it was the best she could do.

Fifteen minutes later she heard Joe's knock on her door, and she quickly walked into the living room to answer it.

"Hey."

"Hey."

"Come on in. I just need to put on some shoes."

He glanced down at her feet and then back up her face. "You have cute toes."

Those cute toes curled. "Um, thanks." She was suddenly glad she'd taken the time earlier to paint them.

A brief, somewhat awkward silence fell over them. "I'll be right back. Got to grab some socks."

She turned and hurried back into her bedroom, all the while feeling like the world's biggest idiot. *Come on, Molly. Just because a guy says you have cute toes it doesn't mean he wants to suck on those toes or anything.* Where had that thought come from? She glanced at the bedside drawer where she kept her vibrators. Maybe she should have spent some time with one of them rather than putting on and taking off twenty-six different shirts.

Socks in hand, she re-entered the living room to find Joe once again perusing her bookshelves. She sat down on the couch, feeling slightly unnerved at the sight of this very attractive man standing in her living room looking at her collection of romance novels and erotica.

"See anything interesting?" she asked. The question came out in a much more even tone than she'd expected.

He turned his head and glanced over his shoulder at her before turning his attention back to the brightly colored spines. "A few things. I recognize some of the titles and authors."

She raised an eyebrow as she pulled on her left boot. "Really? How is that?"

He shrugged. "My mom reads a lot of them, Nora Roberts especially."

"Yeah, she's kind of a big deal in the romance world."

"I gathered that." He turned around, his green eyes twinkling with humor.

Molly stood up. "Ready to go?"

They once again took his car, and headed south on Highway 84, away from town.

"Where are we going?"

"I told you, it's a surprise. But I think you'll like it."

"As long as there are no golf balls involved, I'm good."

"Aw, come on. You know you enjoyed Putt-Putt."

"Oh, I did. But I still feel bad for almost knocking that little boy upside the head with my golf ball."

"You shouldn't have been looking at my ass."

"Back to that, are we?"

He laughed as he turned onto Hewitt Drive. "Almost there."

What in the world were they doing out in Hewitt?

A few minutes later they pulled into Hewitt Park, and Molly saw that there were several other vehicles there, too. Odd.

They got out of the car and Joe popped the trunk before extracting two folding captain's chairs and a blanket.

"Do you need some help with that?"

"Want to carry the blanket?"

"Sure." She took the blanket from his hands and followed him into the park.

Apparently the city of Hewitt had decided to put up a giant movie screen in the park, and dozens of people lounged in lawn chairs, laughing and talking, eating popcorn and drinking various beverages.

"I had no idea they did this out here."

Joe grinned at her as he opened up the second captain's

chair. "This is the first time they've done it this year. One of the writers at the paper told me about it."

"How did I not hear about it?"

"Apparently you haven't been reading the paper like a good copy editor," he teased. "At any rate, the writer and I are friends and she thought this might be something I would be interested in doing."

Molly sat down in one of the chairs. "Does she know about us?" Furthermore, who the hell was she?

"No, she doesn't. I haven't said anything to anyone at work because frankly our personal life is no one's business but ours."

"You do have a point."

He jiggled his keys in his hand. "Do you want anything to drink?"

"Sure."

"Bottled water?"

She smiled. "You're figuring me out too quickly."

"I don't think I've got you anywhere near figured out yet." He winked at her and headed towards a snack stand that had bet set up off to the side.

Molly watched him as he walked away, and once again she caught herself staring at his ass. What was wrong with her? She'd never been an ass girl, in fact was usually more prone to looking at a guy's hands than anything else. But something about Joe's butt just grabbed her attention.

He yawned and stretched as he stood in line, causing the edge of his polo shirt to inch up and expose the waistband of his underwear riding just above the edge of his jeans. Her mouth got dry as she watched him stretch, the smooth line of tanned skin playing with her head and making her wonder what his happy trail looked like. God, she was a sucker for a man's happy trail.

She was jolted from her reverie by the feeling of her cell phone vibrating in her pocket. Who could that be? She looked at the screen and saw a text from Benjamin.

> Benjamin: You busy tonight?
> Molly: Date with Joe, remember?

She hit the home button on her phone. Seconds later, it vibrated again.

> Benjamin: Oh, yeah. I was just wondering
> if you wanted to catch a movie or some-
> thing.

Oh, the irony.

> Molly: Maybe Sunday.

She hit SEND, and a few seconds later he responded.

> Benjamin: Okay. Sounds like a plan. I'll
> talk to you later.
> Molly: Later.

She turned off the phone's screen and shoved it back in her pocket as Joe returned with drinks and popcorn.

"Everything okay?" he asked as he handed her a bottle of water.

"Yeah, everything's fine. Benjamin was just wondering if I wanted to catch a movie with him tonight."

Joe sat down and placed his drink in the cup holder in the arm of his chair. "He doesn't know you're out on a date?"

Molly shook her head. "He said he forgot. Although I didn't tell him about us until a few days ago anyway."

"Why is that?"

She shrugged, hoping the gesture came across as casual. "I was afraid I'd jinx it if I talked about it."

He leaned over and caressed her cheek with the smooth pad of his thumb before pecking her on the lips. "There's not a chance of that happening."

♡

"So how long have you been a closet Audrey Hepburn fan?" Molly teased as they left the park. She'd been pleasantly surprised to see that the movie was *Breakfast at Tiffany's,* one of her all time favorite films.

Apparently it was also one of Joe's since he'd mouthed lines along with the actors here and there.

"For a while now. She was a great actress. Classy yet fun, girl next door yet sexy as hell."

"So basically every guy's fantasy?"

"Not quite. To be that, you'd have to add a dash of Marilyn Monroe, and I'm not just talking about the sex and nudity, either."

"What are you talking about, then?"

"The body. The curves. Put Audrey Hepburn's face and personality on Marilyn's body and then you might have every guy's fantasy."

"But Marilyn had a gorgeous face, too."

"Yeah, but I like brunettes." His voice was low and sexy and Molly suddenly felt way too warm.

"Brunettes, huh?"

He grabbed her hand and brought it to his lips, kissed her palm before curling her hand up into a fist and wrapping his own hand around it.

"And curves."

"Hmmm?" Her brain was feeling a little fuzzy.

"I like brunettes with curves, women who are smart and sexy yet very much the girl next door."

"Good luck finding that."

They came to a stop light and he looked over at her. "So now I'm starting to get a peek under the surface."

She drew her eyebrows together. "What are you talking about?"

"You."

"Which part?"

"All of it."

"What did you mean by you're starting to get a peek

under the surface?"

The light turned green. "Just that you seem so confident and calm on the outside, but I know there's more going on inside than you let on. I already know that your brain goes a mile a minute and that you over think things. And I had a feeling you weren't as confident as you like to let people believe."

The warmth she'd been feeling was starting to feel more like discomfort. She wasn't sure she was ready to let Joe in. In fact, she wasn't sure she wanted to let anyone in. What if once he saw the real her, the insecure person inside, he wouldn't want her anymore? What if he suddenly decided he wasn't attracted to her anymore and that her self esteem issues were too much to deal with?

They pulled into her parking lot. Joe cut the engine, got out, and opened her door for her. Silently, they walked up to her apartment. Molly pulled her keys out of her purse, unlocked the door and stepped over the threshold, not entirely sure what to say.

Joe reached for her hand and pulled her back towards him. "Let me in, Molly. I promise you I'm not going to change my mind once you do."

She closed her eyes and breathed deep, whispered. "Get out of my head."

"But I like being there."

She opened her eyes. "Why? My head is a scary, scary place."

"No scarier than anyone else's."

"Somehow I find that hard to believe."

He chuckled and rested his forehead against hers. "If you knew half the things going through my head right now you'd probably run away screaming."

"Oh really? Like what?" Maybe if she got him talking about his own head it would get him out of hers.

"Like I can't stop thinking about you. And when I'm at

home at night I want to pick up the phone and talk to you or come see you. Like I want to kiss you so badly right now but I'm trying my damnedest to take things slow because I respect you and want far more from you than just sex."

He wanted to have sex with her? Good to know.

"And honestly, Molly?"

She swallowed the nervous lump in her throat. "Yeah?"

He inched away from her slightly and gazed at her, his green eyes intense. She felt him tighten his grip on her hands. "It's taking every bit of self restraint I have right now to not touch you."

There were those damned butterflies again.

Along with the butterflies, though, there was another feeling she hadn't felt in a very long time. Hope. Hope that maybe this one was for real and that he did want more from her than a football watching buddy or a blow job.

"Joe?"

"Yeah?"

"Feel free to touch me."

It took a few seconds for Molly's whispered words to sink into his brain. Slowly, he released her hands and rested his own on her hips. He knew she probably wouldn't believe him, but he really did love her body. He'd never been fond of overly skinny women who looked as though they spent all of their time figuring out the newest way to starve themselves.

Molly, however, was curvy and soft and looked like women should look, in his not so humble opinion. It was a shame, really, that women felt so much pressure to be thin when most of them were made to be soft and curvy and look like, well, women rather than twelve-year-old boys.

Molly was definitely all woman, he thought as he

flexed his hands on her hips. He brushed the tip of his nose against hers and she leaned into him. Joe vaguely felt her hands wrap around his waist as he brushed his lips over hers. Soft at first, because he'd also figured out that Molly was a little skittish when it came to men, and then increased the pressure when she didn't pull away.

Really kissing her was even better than he'd imagined, and he could feel himself falling head first into something he wasn't entirely sure he wanted or was ready for.

He flexed his hands on her hips again before slowly pulling away. If he didn't stop now he wasn't sure he would be able to any time soon, and he really was trying to take things slow.

"You're pretty good at that," he said, trying to lighten the mood.

She grinned back up at him, her eyelids still half shut and her cheeks pink. "You're not so bad yourself."

Unable to resist, he nibbled on her full lower lip.

"We really need to stop."

She brushed her mouth over his, and open invitation to continue what they'd been doing.

"Why do we need to stop?"

His lips brushed over hers, seemingly of their own volition. "Because if we don't this night might end in a way neither of us had expected."

He could feel her hands grip the bottom edge of his shirt. Did she know what she did to him? He didn't want to stop but he also knew that now was not the right time.

"I have amazing self restraint, Joe." She kissed him again.

She called this self restraint? He thought as Molly kissed him.

Wait a second, Molly had kissed him. And he didn't think she was even remotely aware of that fact, or that she'd made this particular move.

Deciding not to look a gift horse in the mouth, he kissed her back, felt her fingers tickle over the bare skin of his back under his shirt, and tightened his hold on her hips. A breathy sigh escaped from her lips and he wanted to do a happy dance and strip her naked all at once. He could slowly feel her body relaxing against his, but there was still enough tension in her limbs for him to know that they had a long ways to go before Molly would feel comfortable enough——and trust him enough—to let this go further. And that was fine with him, because earning Molly's trust was infinitely more important than sex.

Unfortunately, his body didn't seem to agree with his head.

Molly pulled away from Joe slowly, not wanting to break the kiss but knowing that if she didn't there was no way she was going to be able to stop.

"Jesus," she whispered, her thoughts still scattered.

She gulped in air and slowly became more aware of her surroundings. Huh. That hadn't happened before. She'd actually forgotten where she was.

Holy crap.

As her world slowly came back into focus, she became aware of two things. The first was the, ah, physical proof that Joe was indeed attracted to her. The second that his, ah, physical proof seemed to be vibrating.

"I think you're vibrating."

"Hmm?"

She pulled away from him a little bit more, knowing she needed to put some distance between them but feeling completely unwilling to do so. "You're vibrating."

"Oh!" He suddenly seemed to come out of his own fog, and Molly felt a certain sense of power that she'd never experienced before. Wow. She'd put that look on his face, made him dazed and confused and, well, that had felt like a sizeable amount of physical proof.

Joe reached into his jeans pocket and answered his cell phone.

"This is Joe."

Molly hung back in her doorway, trying not to make it obvious that she was listening to his conversation.

"Is she okay?"

He paused.

"That's not good. Okay, I'll be there in ten. Bye."

He ended the call and looked back at Molly.

"Sorry. That was Mrs. DeSoto. Annabelle's staying the night at a slumber party at their place, but she's apparently sick and throwing up, so I've got to go pick her up."

Molly briefly wondered why he would be the one having to pick up his niece, but the sexual haze still fogging her brain caused her to decide that the fact that he was even doing so was a completely good guy thing to do. Besides, she could always ask him about it later, since he seemed pretty worried.

"It's okay. Go pick her up. I'll talk to you later."

He leaned in and lightly kissed her one more time. "I'll call you tomorrow."

"Okay."

Molly watched as he made his way down the stairs before closing and locking her door. Her legs suddenly rubbery, she slid down to the floor and rested her head against the hard wooden surface.

Crap. She was officially deep into like.

CHAPTER TWENTY-TWO

"So what do you do, Molly?" Her latest date—Tony—asked her over his plate of shrimp scampi.

She swallowed a bite of stuffed flounder and took a sip of water before answering. "I actually just started working at a local paper as a copy editor."

"How do you like it so far?"

"I like it a lot, actually." She cut off a small piece of fish.

An awkward silence fell over the table. Tony turned his attention to his meal and Molly contemplated having another cheddar biscuit.

She thought it was a bit telling that Tony had chosen Red Lobster over some of the more local seafood restaurants, namely that he lacked a sense of adventure. Okay, in all fairness maybe he wasn't from the Waco area and thus didn't know that Waco had some really great local places.

You're supposed to be giving these guys a chance, remember, Molly? So stop judging.

Their waitress, Candace, stopped by their table to check on them and to make sure everything was good. Molly and Tony both murmured their approval and the bubbly teen walked away.

"So how long have you lived in Waco?" Molly asked, finally breaking the silence.

"My entire life. You?"

So he just wasn't adventurous. *Stop it, Molly! Maybe he just thought Red Lobster was a safe choice.* "Same here. Born and raised. Well, I moved away for college, lived out of state for a couple of months after I graduated, and lived down in Houston for a while after that. But other than those brief periods of time I've lived in Waco."

Tony speared a piece of shrimp with his fork and went back to eating his scampi.

Wow, this guy wasn't very talkative.

Molly polished off her flounder and smiled up at Candace when she stopped by to refill Molly's water glass. "Thank you."

"You're welcome. You all done here?"

"Yes. It was excellent."

Candace smiled and scooped up the nearly empty plate. "I'll be right back with y'all's ticket."

Tony's head snapped up. "Could you split it?"

"No problem. I'll be right back."

Molly took a sip of her water.

"You don't mind going Dutch, do you?"

She might still be pretty new at this whole dating thing, but shouldn't he have asked her that up front rather than waiting until the end of the date? "I don't mind, but shouldn't you have asked me that up front?"

"Yeah, I should have." At least he had the decency to look apologetic. "Listen, Molly, you're a nice girl and all. You're just not big enough."

Confusion filled her. "Excuse me?"

"You're not big enough. Sure, you have some meat on your bones, but I like my women bigger."

Was he seriously telling her she wasn't fat enough for him? Hell had officially frozen over. "You're a chubby chaser?"

"I don't call myself that. But yes, I like big women."

Of all the things she could have ever been rejected for, this had never even popped onto her radar screen. Morbid curiosity caused her to ask, "How big?"

"Big. You're just thick. I like my women with lots of meat and a side of rolls, if you get what I'm saying."

She wasn't sure if she should be offended or laugh at the absurdity of it all. "I've...I don't know what to say."

"I'm sorry if I hurt your feelings, Molly. You really are a pretty girl. I'm sure you're just the right size for some-one."

She almost laughed. Was tempted to laugh, really, because the situation was so absurd. Who would have ever thought she—a size twenty—would be accused of not be-ing big enough? It boggled the mind.

Candace's return broke through Molly's reverie. Molly pulled a twenty out of her wallet and handed it to the waitress. Tony handed Candace a VISA card. Molly wasn't sure what to say to Tony as they waited for the waitress to return.

"Here's your card and here's your change."

Molly looked at her receipt and counted out her tip, which she placed on the table. Tony signed his receipt and stuck his card back in his wallet.

They stood at the same time and walked to the exit. Once outside, Molly removed her keys from her purse and said, "Well, it was nice meeting you."

Tony nodded his head. "Nice meeting you, too." He turned to his right and walked off without so much as a backwards glance.

Molly headed towards her car and muttered to herself, "Well, how about that?"

CHAPTER TWENTY-THREE

Molly had just pulled into a space in the paper's parking lot Monday morning when Joe arrived and parked right beside her. They got out of their cars, and Molly saw that Joe was carrying two steaming cups from Starbucks, one of which he held out to her.

"Tall white mocha, right?" He grinned.

She wrapped her hand around the cup and its protective sleeve, their fingers touching as she did so. "How'd you remember?"

He removed his hand from her cup and tapped the side of his head with an index finger. "Good memory."

They'd covered coffee last week at lunch. He preferred a large Americano with an extra shot of espresso. Molly was a Frappuccino fan, but in the cooler months preferred a white chocolate mocha.

"Nice to know. Remind me not to tell you anything embarrassing." She grinned up at him.

He chuckled. "Come on. We better get inside. Can't be late to work."

Joe held the door open for her as they walked into the old brick building, his fingertips resting on the small of her back as she passed through the entryway. Molly readjusted the purse strap on her shoulder as they walked across the lobby towards the elevator, wondering if she should mention her date Saturday night to Joe. Especially since the kiss they'd shared Friday evening was still burning a hole in her brain.

A *ding* announced the elevator's arrival, and Molly stepped into the elevator first. The doors closed and Joe pressed the button for their floor. Molly leaned against the back wall and took a drink of her coffee.

"You're awfully quiet." He took a surreptitious sip of his coffee.

She glanced over at him and smiled. "I just have some stuff on my mind, that's all."

"Anything you care to talk about?"

Should she tell him? "I don't know yet."

He raised an eyebrow. "You don't know yet?"

"Are you a parrot now?"

As soon as the words left her mouth, Molly wanted to take them back. Instead of coming out sounding like she was teasing him, the tone was full of sarcasm.

"Sorry. I'll leave you alone."

The doors opened and Joe stepped off the elevator and walked briskly towards his cubicle.

"Joe, wait."

He continued walking.

Well, hell, Molly, way to screw that one up.

Molly waited until a few minutes before their lunch break to say anything to Joe.

"We still on for lunch?" She asked as she poked her head into his cubicle.

He turned his head and looked at her. "Sure. Schmaltz's sound okay to you?"

"Sounds fine. Let me go grab my purse." She headed back towards her cubicle so she could collect her bag.

When she turned around, Joe stood behind her, his

hands stuffed into the pockets of his khakis. "You ready?"

The lack of a smile on his face or in his voice threw Molly off a little bit. The only time she'd ever seen Joe without a smile was when she'd asked him about the photo on his cubicle wall. The thought that she'd somehow caused him to be in a bad mood left her with an unpleasant feeling in her stomach.

As they walked towards the elevator, the unpleasant sensation began to develop into full-blown nausea. Joe pressed the down arrow, and Molly reminded herself to breathe deeply.

They didn't speak as they waited for the elevator, and Molly's thoughts started running wild. She'd really managed to screw this one up. Although, honestly, she wasn't entirely sure just what she had screwed up. But Joe was mad at her and not talking to her and for some reason it was making her feel bad and nauseous and—crap—cold.

The elevator doors finally opened up and Joe motioned for Molly to step into the elevator first. The doors closed and he pressed the button for the first floor.

"Are you okay?"

His sudden question made her jump. He wrapped his hands around her upper arms to steady her. "Sorry. Didn't mean to startle you."

She looked up at him. "It's okay. I was just thinking too much."

"About what?"

Trying to stop this anxiety attack before it starts. "Just...stuff."

They stepped out of the elevator and crossed the lobby. Joe held the door open for her and she stepped out in the February sunshine. It was a pleasant day with temperatures in the lower 60s, so they decided to walk the few blocks to the locally-owned sandwich shop.

They'd just crossed over to the other side of Franklin

Avenue when Molly decided to address the proverbial elephant. "Listen, Joe, I'm sorry about this morning."

"Don't worry about it."

She sighed, but at least she wasn't feeling cold anymore. "But I am worried about it."

"Why?"

"Because I hurt your feelings and I didn't mean to. It just came out all wrong."

They came to a stop at the corner of Franklin and 7th and waited for the light to change. "Seriously, don't worry about it."

She sighed, trying to figure out if he was really okay or just trying to act like he was. She hated men sometimes. "But I'm going to."

"Why?"

"Because that's what I do. I worry incessantly about everything until I feel like I'm going crazy. I worry until I start having anxiety attacks and convince myself that I'm irrevocably screwed up. I worry that I've said the wrong thing or done the wrong thing, smiled the wrong way, laughed too loud, rambled too much, made a complete idiot out of myself and—"

He grabbed Molly's shoulders and lowered himself until they were eye level. "Molly."

She swallowed. "Yeah?"

"Just slow down for a second, okay? I know that brain of yours can go about a million miles a minute, but I promise you the world won't end if you let it slow down every now and then."

She looked at him and shook her head. "What?"

"I'm not mad, okay. Everyone has bad days, and you were obviously having an off morning. I know you didn't mean to sound snippy because that's just not your style." His eyes searched hers. "And if you want to tell me what's wrong, that's fine. If you don't, that's fine, too."

She closed her eyes and breathed deeply. "I had another blind date Saturday night." There. She'd said it. Her eyes popped open.

"Why'd you go out on a date Saturday night?"

The WALK signal started to flash, so they made their way across the street. "Because Benjamin had already set me up with the guy before I'd had a chance to tell him about us."

"Couldn't you have called it off?"

"I thought about it, but we haven't exactly discussed the parameters of whatever's going on between us, either."

Joe stopped walking.

Molly turned to look at him.

He started walking again. "You want us to discuss the parameters of our relationship?"

"I'm not used to this, Joe. This is completely new territory for me."

"I haven't exactly been here in a while myself. But I figured we both wanted something exclusive."

"You couldn't have said that sooner? I can't read minds."

They crossed over 6th street. "Don't try to blame this on me. You could've asked."

"Asked how, Joe? I didn't want to come across as some psycho, pushy chick who moves in for the kill too quickly."

"What are you now, a black widow?"

"Very funny. I'm just saying I don't know what the rules are."

"Fair enough."

"Besides, the guy told me I wasn't fat enough for him and we paid for our own meals. It was more like an awkward conversation with food than an actual date."

He stopped walking again. "He told you that?"

She waited for him to catch up with her. "Yes, he told me that. I couldn't believe it. I'm used to hearing I'm too fat, not skinny enough. But never not fat enough. Talk about strange."

They turned left onto 5th Street and headed towards Austin Avenue.

"I think you're perfect just the way you are."

This time Molly stopped walking. At this rate they would never get to Schmaltz's.

♡

Joe watched the expressions play over Molly's face. They ran the gamut from confused to thoughtful to down-right funny at one point. In the short time they'd known each other, he'd come to really enjoy the fact that Molly didn't have much of a filtering system. Every little thought and feeling tended to flit across her face, and while it would probably irritate her to know that, he found her face fascinating.

"I—" she paused and chewed on her bottom lip. "Do you really mean that?"

"Yes, I mean it." A car passed, the driver looking at them curiously. Joe took Molly's hand in his own and tugged gently. "Come on, we should get to Schmaltz's before our lunch break is over."

They walked the rest of the way to the sandwich shop, which thankfully wasn't very crowded. Molly ordered a turkey and Swiss and he ordered a club. Joe unwrapped his sandwich, took a bite and chewed before saying, "So what else is bothering you?"

"What makes you think something else is bothering me?"

"You seem keyed up, tense. Plus, you keep biting your lip and getting this confused look on your face."

"Confused?"

"Yes."

"I—"

"Molly, trust me, I'm not out to hurt you."

She took a drink of her water before answering. "Emery broke up with Benjamin last week."

"Oh?" Now that was interesting. He wondered why Molly hadn't said anything sooner.

"Yeah. She apparently thinks he's in love with me."

He tried to appear calm, even though the idea of Benjamin being in love with Molly made him nervous as hell. "What do you think?"

"I think she's crazy, quite honestly."

"What if he really is in love with you?"

She put her sandwich down and looked at him, sincerity written across her face. "Joe, I started off this year with a plan to get over Benjamin. At first it wasn't working, none of the guys were catching my attention and I honestly wasn't giving any of them a snowball's chance in hell. But then I met you and I had a good date and some fun and finally realized that I needed to let go of Benjamin once and for all, because holding on hasn't been healthy for me. Even if he were to come in here right now and profess his undying love for me, I'm pretty sure it would be too little too late."

He hated the note of uncertainty he thought he detected in her voice. He chose to ignore it, though, and address her words instead. "So what are you going to do if he really is in love with you and decides he wants to be with you?"

"Let him down gently?"

"And what if that doesn't work?"

"Why are we even talking about this? Benjamin isn't in love with me nor will he ever decide that he is much less attempt to do something about it."

"Why do you say that?" He took another bite of his sandwich. Man, their bacon was good.

"Because it's Benjamin and if he hasn't been willing

to commit to me at any point over the past four years, why would he be willing to now?"

"You have a good point. But what if all of a sudden he was willing to commit to you?"

Molly rolled her eyes. "It's not going to happen, Joe. I know Benjamin better than anyone and I know that he will never be willing to be with me and I don't think he'll ever be what I would need him to be anyway."

He polished off the rest of his sandwich before responding to her statement. "What do you need?"

She chewed and swallowed, took a thoughtful sip of water. "Someone who's emotionally available and who doesn't take me for granted." Her brows knit together. "Someone who has goals and who isn't content just standing still and never growing up. He's like Peter Pan, just blithely going through life, never wanting to grow up. I mean, sure, he got engaged but he had his doubts and he knew there was a good chance it wouldn't work, what with her leaving for Oregon and grad school soon. And I guarantee you that had Emery not broken up with him he would have found some way to screw it up because that's what he does. Any time something starts getting too serious or too adult he finds a way to back away from it.

"And y'know, I love Benjamin to death. He's my best friend and he has some great qualities and so much potential to do some really good things with his life, but he's just always too scared to try. Like, a few months ago he was at this little comedy club up in Dallas. It was open mic night, he'd had a few beers and he decided to go up and give it a shot. He had the audience laughing so hard they were in tears, and afterward the manager asked him if he would come back and be a regular performer. Big old scaredy cat that he is he said no. Stand up is something he's wanted to do for years and he finally gets a chance to follow his dream and the dumbass walks away from it because he's too damned scared to take a chance. It's infuriating."

"You've been letting that one build up for a while, haven't you?"

She stared at him for a few seconds before bursting into laughter. "I guess I have. I didn't realize all of that was bothering me so much."

"The fact that it does says a lot about you as a person, though."

She tilted her head to the side. "How so?"

"It says you care. You wouldn't be so upset about Benjamin's wasted opportunity if you didn't care about him. And even though he seems to be completely unwilling to pursue anything remotely resembling a goal, you see the potential in him and still manage to see the good."

The pink in her cheeks darkened, which caused her freckles to fade and blend in just slightly. It was damned cute.

"Thanks. I guess."

He winked at her. "It's just one of the many things I like about you."

The pink in her cheeks began to turn a nice shade of red. "Uh. Okay then."

He decided to back off the flirting for a few minutes, let her stop blushing long enough for her cheeks to return to their normal light pink.

"You ready to go?"

"Yeah."

They left the sandwich shop in companionable silence. Joe saw Molly readjust her purse strap on her shoulder before tucking her hair behind her ear. A sure sign she was nervous about something. "Spit it out."

She stumbled slightly. "What?"

"You have something to say. Spit it out."

They crossed Austin Avenue and headed back towards Franklin.

"Just, I'm glad I met you."

"I'm glad I met you, too."

They reached the corner of 5th and Franklin and turned right. He saw her tuck her hair behind her ear again from the corner of his eye. "So I have a question for you."

"What's that?"

"Why did you have to go pick up your niece the other night?"

He almost stumbled. He knew he needed to tell Molly the truth, but how in the world was he supposed to bring it up? When he'd said earlier this was new territory for him, he hadn't been lying. "Because she was sick. Ends up she had a stomach bug that kept her in bed the entire weekend."

They stopped at the corner of 6th.

"Yeah, but why were *you* the one who picked her up? Why didn't her parents pick her up?"

Crap. "I think we need to talk."

Molly could feel her body going cold, and knew it would only be seconds before the nausea kicked in. *Deep breaths, Molly, deep breaths.*

"She isn't really your niece, is she?"

"Why do you say that?"

"Too many secret baby romances as a teenager?" she asked in an attempt at levity.

"Annabelle's my niece. But it's complicated."

"Apparently so."

"Listen, Molly, it's a long story. How about you come over tonight? I'll cook dinner and explain the entire thing to you."

Should she trust him? Her gut was telling her yes, even though alarm bells were ringing in her head. She went with her gut. "What time?"

"Seven good for you?"

"Works for me."

They walked the rest of the way to the paper's office in awkward silence. Molly wasn't sure what was going on, or if she really wanted to find out. Something, though, told her things were about to get complicated.

CHAPTER TWENTY-FOUR

Molly arrived at Joe's at ten till seven. For some reason she wasn't surprised that he lived in Woodway.

She parked in the street in front of his house, cut the ignition and took a deep breath. For what had to be the nine-hundredth time that day Molly wondered just what it was that Joe needed to tell her about Annabelle.

Well, hiding out in her car wasn't going to garner any answers, so she got out and headed up the walkway to Joe's front door. Those damned butterflies were dancing in her belly again. She pressed the doorbell with a shaky index finger. Was this the beginning of the end? All the possible "what ifs" paraded through Molly's brain.

I really like this guy. Please, please let this work out.

Seconds later the door swung open. Molly swallowed hard, her mouth as dry as west Texas.

"Glad you found it okay."

She tried to smile and failed. "Yeah."

He stepped to the side and gestured for her to come in.

"Dinner's just about ready." His smile both calmed and unnerved her, mainly because he looked as nervous as she felt. "Want a tour while it finishes up in the oven?"

"Sure." She readjusted the strap of the purse that was slung over her shoulder.

"Here, let me take that for you." He set the large pink and tan bag on a small table in the house's entry way before reaching out his hand and saying, "Here, follow me."

Molly took his hand in hers and walked with him through the house. He showed her the living room first, which was nice and spacious with a well-worn but still in good shape living room set, a large entertainment center and a good-sized bookshelf crammed with what had to be at least two hundred brightly-colored paperbacks. Curious, she let go of Joe's hand and walked over to the shelves. If anything, books would surely calm her down.

"You weren't lying when you said you recognized some of the titles on my shelf."

She could have sworn Joe's cheeks turned a little pink. "They're my mom's."

"If you say so."

"They really are, I swear."

She walked back over to him. "I love the room, by the way. It looks comfortable."

"Thanks."

"So is this your place or do you still live at home?"

She could tell the question caught him a little off guard. "I'll get to that, too, I promise."

Butterflies danced in her stomach again.

He led her through the rest of the house, showing her the guest room, bathroom, Annabelle's bedroom and finally—

"Wait. Annabelle's bedroom?"

They stood in the doorway of a purple and cream room. Disney princesses lined the walls, dragonflies danced on the bedspread and Barbies popped their heads out of a wooden toy box.

Joe's grip on Molly's hand tightened. She looked up at him and saw uncertainty etched across his face. His hesitation, the discomfort all but radiating from him, had her gut churning and her heart racing. Oh, God, this really couldn't be good.

He sighed and tugged her further down the hall, towards the back of the house. Molly dug her heels into the carpet.

"Joe, answer me."

He sighed again. "I will, Molly. I promise you. Just… later. I'll explain everything later."

He tugged her hand again and she allowed him to pull her over the threshold of the very last room. His bedroom.

And here you only thought you were nervous before, Moll.

"Are you okay?"

She started at the sound of his voice and blurted out the first thing that came to mind. "I'm not going to sleep with you."

"That's not why I was bringing you in here, but thanks for letting me know up front."

He sounded kind of snippy. "I don't know where that came from. I'm sorry."

He pulled her closer so that she was almost flush with his body. "Molly, don't ever apologize for being honest with me. I know you're not ready to take that step, and I'm not going to coerce you into something you don't want."

She touched his face with shaky fingertips. "Are you really real? Because I swear you know just what to say."

"And that's a bad thing?"

"It's a suspicious thing. There has to be a reason why a guy like you is single. Women want guys like you. We dream about guys like you. So what's the deal, Joe? What's a guy like you doing single, living in your mom's house and picking up an eight-year-old when she gets a stomach bug?" *What's a guy like you doing with his arms wrapped around a girl like me?*

Hesitation clouded his face. "Just…just trust me, okay? Just, let's get through dinner and then I'll explain everything. I promise."

A beeping penetrated the confusion floating through her head. "What's that noise?"

Joe pulled away from her. "It's the timer. Dinner's ready."

Joe led Molly back towards the kitchen, thinking that it was probably a good thing the timer had gone off and essentially gotten him out of the bedroom and away from the wariness in Molly's eyes.

The smell of lemon pepper greeted his nostrils, the tang causing his mouth to water. He'd made his mom's lemon pepper chicken, remembering that she'd told him a few years prior that a man could never go wrong cooking lemon pepper chicken for a woman. Unless she was a vegetarian. And then he probably wouldn't want to be with her anyway because what kind of red-blooded Texas woman didn't eat meat?

The memory made him smile. He turned to Molly, covered his nerves as best he could, and said, "And this is the kitchen."

She searched the room, giving it the same thorough once over she'd given every other room in the house, but her eyes lit up when her gaze landed on the large kitchen island. "I love it, the island especially."

Relief flooded him with the subject change. "The island, huh?" He let go of her hand and walked over to the stove, where he picked up the two potholders he'd placed on the counter top next to it.

"Yes, the island. I've had a fascination with them ever since I was a kid, but I've never lived anywhere that had a kitchen big enough to hold one."

He pulled the casserole dish from the oven and set it on top of the stove. "I love having the island. It's a great workspace."

He pulled two plates from the cabinet to his right and set them down on the counter before placing a piece of chicken on each one. He then scooped a spoonful of buttery angel hair pasta onto each of their plates, followed by steamed broccoli.

"You didn't have to do that."

He looked over his shoulder at Molly, who was still standing next to the island and apparently watching his every move. He shrugged. "It's what a good host does, or at least that's what my mom always told me."

He picked up their plates and walked over to the round dining room table where he set them down next to the silverware he'd already laid out. "Dinner is served."

She smiled back at him and walked over to the table. "Why thank you. Have you ever thought about moonlighting as a waiter?"

He laughed as he took his seat and then waited for Molly to take hers next to him. "Well, I waited tables for a while in college, but got tired of that real quick."

She sat down. "Luckily that was one thing I somehow never managed to have to do in college. Granted, I'm not sure if working retail was that much better, though."

They chatted throughout dinner, sharing anecdotes about college, their childhoods and life as an adult. He found out Molly had grown up a bit poor, whereas he had grown up firmly middle class. Her biological parents had divorced when she was six, whereas his dad had passed away when he was four. Her mom had remarried a few times, mostly to some unsavory men who were best described as "abusive jerks," but the man her mom was married to now was wonderful and had become "Dad" to Molly. His mom had never remarried, said she could never find anyone good enough to replace his father.

"Sounds like you had a rough childhood," he said as

they moved into the living room.

She shrugged and sat down on the couch. "It could have been worse."

He sat down beside her and rested his arm on the back of the sofa. "Yeah, but it sounds like it could have been better, too." She'd skimmed over the details so matter of factly that he had to wonder what else there was to her story.

"Definitely. But it made me who I am today, and if it hadn't been for that crappy childhood I'm not sure I would have been so determined to go to college and make something of myself."

"I think you would've done those things even if you'd had an idyllic childhood."

"Yeah, probably. I was an overachiever long before things got bad."

"For some reason that doesn't surprise me." And it didn't. He'd pegged her as the driven type from the get-go.

She smiled back at him. "Dinner was fantastic, by the way."

"Thanks. It was my mom's recipe."

Molly turned so that her body was angled a little more towards his. "You know, you haven't said too much about your mom, just a few things here and there."

Joe twirled a piece of Molly's hair around his index finger, playing with it as he tried to figure out how to dive into this particular story. After all, it was the reason he'd invited her over in the first place.

"This is actually her house. You were right about that earlier. About a year ago she had a stroke due to a brain aneurysm, which left her paralyzed on the right side of her body. For months she could barely speak, and she still has trouble moving her leg. She's regained the ability to use her hand a little bit, or at least enough to function, but the doctors don't see her ever getting out of the wheelchair. It was unexpected, especially to someone in their early fifties.

Mom had always been in great health. The doctors said that probably was what saved her life in the end."

Molly placed her hand on his thigh in what he assumed was a comforting gesture. "I am so sorry."

"There's more." He grabbed her hand on his thigh with his left hand and lightly squeezed. He wasn't entirely sure how to lead into what he really needed to tell Molly, and he swallowed as he searched his brain for the proper words. "I had a sister. She was a couple of years younger than me. Jessica had just turned 18, was a senior in high school and started dating this guy Brad. He was a good guy. Ran track, played baseball, honor student, had been offered a full ride to Texas Christian. Jessica herself had been offered a pretty substantial scholarship herself to TCU, and they were planning on going to college together, dating for a while and getting married after they were both done with school.

"They were head over heels in love, and Mom wasn't stupid so she took Jessica to the doctor and got her on the Pill. Me being the overprotective big brother I had a talk with Jessica when I came home for Thanksgiving break, told her to be careful and that if Brad hurt her I would break his legs.

"A couple of weeks later Jessica found out she was pregnant. Since Mom made sure she took her pill every morning before she left for school, they were pretty sure it was just one of those weird flukes where the birth control failed. The doctor set her due date at the end of August, and Jessica had every intention of still going to college even after the baby was born. Brad stuck around, which honestly surprised me because even though he was mature for his age most guys that young wouldn't want to be saddled with that sort of responsibility.

"That July, on the Fourth, actually, they were headed back to his place after going to watch the fireworks down at the river when a drunk driver hit them. They said Brad was

killed on impact, but Jessica was still alive and barely con-
scious. They took her to Hillcrest, found she was bleeding
internally and did an emergency C-section to save the baby
and to try to save Jessica."

Joe stopped and grabbed a glass of water off the coffee
table, took a sip to soothe his parched throat and continued.
"Unfortunately too much damage had been done. They
did all they could, but they couldn't save her. Mom and I
were here, had actually just gotten home when we got the
call from the hospital telling us we needed to get there as
quickly as possible. When we got there Brad's parents were
just walking into the ER. The doctor found us, took us into
one of those family counseling rooms and explained the
situation. Mom started crying. Brad's mom started crying.
His dad started crying. I just stood there in shock. Jessica
and I had been close, more like best friends than brother
and sister, and I remember thinking that the doctors were
wrong, that she was still alive and was just playing dead
like we used to do as kids.

"She wasn't playing, though. She really was gone.
And here was this baby, who'd been forced into the world
almost two months early, tiny and helpless and without
her parents. Mom talked to Brad's family, asked if she
could have custody of Annabelle. His parents didn't put up
a fight, I guess because they were still so distraught over
losing their only child. So once Annabelle got out of NICU,
Mom brought her home and raised her.

"Brad's parents moved away a few years later. They fly
in a few times a year to see Annabelle, and call once a week
to see how she's doing. When Mom had the stroke I was
granted custody of Annabelle. Since Mom's in a rehabili-
tation home—which was her decision, not mine—and has
limited mobility we all thought me being her legal guardian
would be the best thing for Annabelle. That's why I had to
go pick her up the other night from the slumber party."

He inhaled deeply and watched Molly as several expressions flitted across her face. Joe was relieved to see that none of them looked quite like panic, because he'd honestly been scared to death that Molly would freak out.

"Why didn't you tell me this before?"

"Because I honestly haven't been in a situation where I've needed to explain it, therefore I wasn't sure how to go about doing it. You're the first woman I've dated since Mom's stroke, the first one I've explained any of this to, and trying to explain to people that you're the guardian of a kid who isn't yours isn't exactly the easiest thing to do."

"So weird question. It's eight o'clock on a Monday night. Where's Annabelle now?"

He smiled, feeling slightly relieved. "Mrs. Jasper, the next door neighbor, is watching her for me. Her daughter is Annabelle's age and they've pretty much grown up together, so she knows the situation. When I told her I'd invited a date over she jumped at the chance to babysit."

"Do I need to keep this quiet at work?"

"See, one of the things I like about you is that you pick up on things. And yes, you're correct. Mr. Charles knows but that's it. This hasn't exactly been a situation I've wanted to discuss with anyone and everyone, and I'm not really close enough to any of the other copy editors to divulge details of my life to them."

"That's understandable." She tilted her head to the side. "None of this can be easy for you."

"It isn't. I've gotten a crash course in parenting, and raising a girl is just weird. She wants to play with Barbie dolls and makeup and likes to play dress up. I finally mastered the art of the ponytail a month ago, but I'm completely lost if she asks for a braid or anything else."

Molly smiled. "I have a seven-year-old niece who's the same way. I was a total tomboy, so there are times when I just don't know what to do with her."

"Sometimes I just want to give her a bunch of G.I. Joes and say, 'Here, go have an imaginary war' or something."

"I totally did that with my G.I. Joes."

He raised an eyebrow. "You really were a tomboy."

"Oh yeah. Except I loved Scarlet—you know, the girl G.I. Joe with the red hair. They would go off to battle, defeat the evil Barbie army, go back to camp and then Joe and Scarlet would declare their love for each other and make out."

"How old were you when this happened?"

"About five." She shrugged. "What can I say? Even as a kid I was a sucker for a good romance."

They sat in companionable silence for a few moments before he asked, "So are we okay?"

Her thoughtful expression played across her face. "I think so. It might take a few days for all of this to digest, but I think we're okay."

She sounded slightly hesitant, but at least she wasn't telling him they weren't okay at all. Hell, he couldn't blame her, either. If their situations had been reversed he'd probably be just as hesitant to tell her everything was hunky dory. He sensed that she needed some time to process everything he'd told her, so he did the smart thing and changed the subject.

"Do you want some dessert?"

Later that night, Molly found herself sitting on her couch staring blankly at the television as one of the guys on *SportsCenter* went over the day's basketball scores. She was trying to process everything Joe had told her earlier in the evening, and was having a harder time with it than she'd thought she would.

On one hand, she felt Joe deserved to be commended

for taking on the responsibility of raising an eight-year-old girl. Most men their age would have run away screaming if they'd been thrust into his situation, but instead of freaking out he'd stepped up to the plate and taken on the role of caretaker. He didn't complain about his situation, either, just accepted it as one of life's curveballs and was doing what he could to ensure his niece had as stable a childhood as possible.

If anything, that alone almost pushed Molly over the edge of like into something far more intense.

She had to admit that even though she really admired him for doing what he was doing, the thought of dating a guy who for all intents and purposes had a kid kind of freaked her out.

Part of that was because she didn't want to be any-one's surrogate mom or step mama, but a bigger part of it was that she'd seen firsthand what introducing people into a child's life could do. Her younger sister was the world's worst about it, and just as Molly's niece would warm up to the latest boyfriend they would break up and another would take his place. Obviously Joe wasn't like that, and the fact that he'd had the next door neighbor babysit Annabelle while Molly had been there spoke volumes, but if they con-tinued to date Molly would eventually meet Annabelle and she didn't want to confuse the girl or make her afraid that Joe would pay less attention to her as a result.

To be honest, Molly was also afraid she would like Annabelle. Sure, that would be a good thing for most peo-ple, but not for Molly. She tended to get attached to kids, and she was having a hard enough time already keeping her heart intact. If he threw a puppy into the mix, she was totally screwed.

Joe had a kid, was essentially a single dad. No wonder Benjamin had warned her against him.

CHAPTER TWENTY-FIVE

I *should have known this was too good to be true.*

I should have known that Joe seemed a little too perfect, a little too much like every woman's fantasy brought to life (okay, my fantasy brought to life).

He has a kid.

In all fairness she isn't technically his. She's his niece, he's her legal guardian.

But still, for all intents and purposes, he has a kid.

Can I bang my head against the wall now?

I'm not sure how I feel about this. I don't know that I want to get too involved with someone who's essentially a single parent. At the same time, I like him, I really like him. And what he's doing is amazing. His story is sadder than mine in a way, and I was wrong about him, he isn't perfect and he's possibly just as damaged as I am.

His father died when he was four and his mom never re-married. So first there's the no father figure thing (I just never had a positive father figure—I'm not sure which one is worse, really). Then his younger sister and her boyfriend died when she was eighteen in a car accident. She was eight months pregnant, and they were able to save the baby. His mom got custody of the baby, but then about a year ago she had a stroke that left her paralyzed on one side of her body. That's how Joe got custody of Annabelle.

Here he is, twenty-eight years old and raising an eight-

year-old girl who isn't even his. I can't imagine doing that. As much as I love my "babies," I can't imagine having to step in and be their sole parent and guardian. How many men our age would take on that responsibility? Not many, that's for sure.

Still, though, I don't know that I want to get involved with someone who has a kid. Semantics aside, he's a single parent. That's a lot of responsibility. So far things have gone smoothly for us, aside from him getting a phone call the other night because Annabelle was at a friend's house and was sick. But how often is that going to happen? How many other kisses will be interrupted by his cell phone? If things start to get serious between us, if we start sleeping together, how are we going to handle that? I don't want to sneak in and out of his house. I'm not going to stay over if Annabelle's there. Actually, I doubt I would even go over if she was there, simply because I don't think it's right.

I know this isn't easy for him. I'm apparently the first woman he's dated since he got custody, and I'm flattered that he's that interested in me. I like him, he likes me. And knowing his story only makes me like him more. It makes me admire and respect him even more than I did before.

Despite that, though, is this really something I want to tackle? Is this something I'm ready to tackle? Am I emotionally stable enough to handle the fact that Annabelle comes first in his life? I know that when it comes down to it, I'll be the runner up. In a way, I think that's how it should be. But am I stable enough to share? To know that he might not always be available when I want to see him or need to see him?

Am I thinking too far ahead about things that may never come to pass?

Molly clicked on "save" and closed her blog editing program after she heard a knock on her door.

Must be Benjamin.

She glanced at the DVR unit and was shocked to see it was time for *The Voice* already.

She hadn't realized she'd been so deep into what she was writing.

She got up and opened the door. "Hey."

"Hey." He stepped inside. "Are you okay? You look a little confused."

She closed the door behind him and threw the locks. "Just thinking about stuff, that's all."

He plopped down onto the couch and turned on the TV. "Anything you care to talk about?"

"Not really. At least not right now."

She padded into the kitchen.

"Do you mind if I check my email?"

"Go ahead."

She pulled a jug of water from the fridge, and almost dropped it when she heard Benjamin ask, "Joe has a kid?"

She set the bottle down on the counter. "What are you doing opening my files?"

"I didn't open anything. It was just here, and I happened to see it as I was minimizing the window."

"No, I closed that file. I'm sure I closed that file."

"Are you calling me a liar?"

"Not exactly. But I know I closed that file."

"Maybe you thought you did but didn't."

She breathed deeply. He could be right. "Maybe. But still, you shouldn't be reading that."

"So you'll write a blog that everyone else can see, but you won't tell your best friend that the guy you're dating has a kid?"

He sounded offended.

"It's a private blog, Benjamin, no one can read it but me."

"Oh."

She picked the water back up and poured herself a

glass before returning it to the fridge. She took a sip, desperately trying to calm her nerves.

"I thought you didn't want to date a single parent." His statement sounded more like an accusation than a question.

"I didn't. Don't. The situation is complicated."

"Are you sure you can handle this sort of 'complicated'?"

She didn't know. "That's what I've been trying to figure out."

"When did you find out about the kid?"

"She has a name."

He rolled his eyes. "That isn't the point."

Molly shredded a paper towel, dropping the pieces onto the kitchen counter one by one. "Monday."

"You've been dating this guy for what, two weeks now and he just now told you he has a kid?"

"It isn't that simple, Benjamin."

"Well then explain it to me."

She ripped another paper towel off the roll. "She's not actually his. She's his niece, but he's her legal guardian."

"How did that come about?"

"Long story. To keep it short, his sister died after an emergency C-section, their mom got custody. Then she had a stroke and is paralyzed on one side of her body and now Joe is Annabelle's legal guardian."

"That's a lot of baggage, Molly."

"What are you trying to say, Benjamin?"

"That that's a lot of baggage. Are you sure you want to be involved with that?"

A choked laugh escaped from her lips. "Because, y'know, I don't have baggage of my own."

"That's my point. That's a lot of baggage for one couple."

"Like anyone else I could date wouldn't have baggage? Come on, Benjamin, so far I've gone out on a date with a guy who doesn't know what shampoo is, a guy who's a wannabe pimp slash dealer, a guy who requires that any girl he dates be as obsessed with World of Warcraft as he is and another who told me I wasn't fat enough for him. Call me crazy, but it sounds like every guy you've set me up with so far also has some baggage. I mean what kind of guy only dates fat chicks?"

"The same kind of woman who only dates big guys."

"What's that supposed to mean?"

"Just that everyone has their preferences is all."

"Whatever. My point is the men you've set me up with haven't exactly been perfect. They've all had their issues."

"You sure do seem like you're working overtime trying to convince yourself to keep dating Joe."

She ripped another paper towel off the roll. "I like him, Benjamin. He's a great guy. He's smart, funny, and hot, and he understands me. And how many men our age would take custody of an eight-year-old girl who isn't even their child? Not many. So what if he has baggage. What he's doing is admirable, and my respect level for him only went up when he finally told me all this."

"But you've said repeatedly you don't want to get involved with someone who has a kid."

"Don't you think I know that? I'm not taking this lightly. I'm thinking about this hard, really hard. But I like Joe. I think this could go somewhere. Maybe. If I could ever manage to get past all my insecurities."

"How are you going to get past your insecurities when you'll never come first with him? He has a kid, Molly, whether or not she's his niece or his actual daughter. For all intents and purposes he's a single parent. How are you going to be able to handle coming in second?"

"That's a really shitty way to put it."

"It's an honest way to put it."

She swallowed past the lump in her throat. "I wouldn't

expect him to put me first, not in this situation."

"But what about when your plans get canceled because he can't find a sitter? Or what if you stay the night at his place and she walks into the room in the middle of the night?"

"If our plans get canceled because he can't find a sitter, I'll be fine with that. Things happen. And I don't know when we'll even get to the point of staying the night with each other, but if we do I won't stay at his place if she's at home."

He turned his attention back to the computer screen. "I just don't think this is a good situation for you to be in."

"That's my decision to make, Benjamin, not yours. But at least Joe's honest with me. At least he makes me feel special and wanted and doesn't take me for granted like some people I know."

"What the hell are you saying?"

She could feel anger slowly beginning to simmer inside of her. The feeling was unexpected, yet somehow inevitable. "Something I should have said a long time ago, something I should have realized a long time ago but only recently has become clear to me."

"We're not back on this again, are we?"

She picked up her glass and sipped her water before speaking. "Back on what, Benjamin? The fact that you can be the most self-centered person I know? The fact that you took my virginity and acted like it was nothing? The fact that you conveniently leave out pieces of the story when it suits you to do so?"

Molly slammed the glass down on the counter top. Water sloshed over the rim and onto her arm. She didn't care. This had been building up for far too long, and now that she'd started letting it out she didn't want to stop.

"I'm so sick of this Benjamin. I've been in love with you since high school, and yet all you've ever given me are crumbs. I'm the person you come running to when you have no one else. I'm your backup plan, and frankly I'm sick and tired of never coming first with you. You want to talk about not coming first with Joe? That's understandable. If I came first with him over Annabelle I wouldn't like him as much. But you never even attempt to let anyone else come first where you're concerned. You're so narcissistic. It's all about Benjamin all the freaking time!

"If you cared about me as much as you say you do, you wouldn't just toss aside what happened between us all those years ago. You wouldn't be sitting here trying to convince me to throw away the best thing that's ever happened to me on a personal level just because the road might get a little bumpy from time to time. That's what *you* do, Benjamin. You run at the first sign of a pothole or a road block.

"Why do you think you never have a relationship that lasts? Emery was great. She was smart, pretty and fun to be around. And she loved you. But because you weren't honest with her from the beginning, because you chose to ignore the truth and the past you sabotaged the best relationship you've ever had. And this isn't the first time this has happened. Every other relationship you've ever had you've sabotaged in some way or another, usually by not being completely honest. So you want to talk about honesty? You want to try to accuse Joe of being dishonest? No, honey, you're the one who's dishonest, with yourself and with everyone else."

Suddenly feeling drained, Molly scooped up the shredded bits of paper towels and threw them in the trashcan. As thick silence permeated the apartment, she wiped up the water that had puddled on the counter top.

After what seemed like days rather than minutes, Benjamin spoke. "Are you PMSing or something?"

That's all he had to say? After everything she'd just said to him, all he could do was ask her if she had PMS?

Her voice quiet and much more calm sounding than she'd expected, she said, "Just go, Benjamin."

"What do you mean 'just go'?"

"Exactly what I said. If all you can do is make PMS jokes, I don't want to talk to you right now. So just leave."

"Molly, I—"

"Leave, Benjamin. Don't pass Go, don't collect two hundred dollars. Just leave."

He stood and dug his keys out of his jeans pocket. "Why do I have the feeling I need to apologize for something?"

She sighed. "Benjamin, go."

She didn't watch him as he walked out the door.

Thirty minutes later Molly was still standing at the kitchen counter. She hadn't moved, had just stared into her glass of water as though it held all the answers.

It didn't.

Not even so much as a *Jurassic Park*-like tremor.

She finally snapped out of her reverie and reached for her cell, which she'd stuck in her back pocket earlier. Without really thinking about what she was doing, she dialed Joe's phone number.

He picked up after two rings. "Hey gorgeous."

"Do you have my name programmed in or do you always answer the phone that way?"

"It's programmed in. Caller ID's a lifesaver."

"What did we do before it?"

"Get stuck in conversations we didn't want to be in."

"This is true." She fell silent.

"Everything okay?"

Where did she begin? "Not really. I think I might have just burnt a bridge I didn't know needed to be burned in the first place."

"Okay, back up, what happened?"

She sighed and leaned against the counter top. "Benjamin was over here."

"And?"

How did she explain this to him without making herself seem like some crazy teenage girl writing diary entries about her crush?

"Well, I'd written a journal entry about us, just thinking things through and trying to clear my head a little bit. I thought I'd closed out the window. In fact, I swear I closed out the window. But Benjamin got on the laptop to check his email and saw the journal entry. He asked me about Annabelle, and basically tried to persuade me to stop seeing you because of her."

"Are you serious?"

"Yes, I'm serious. It was so totally unexpected, especially considering how flimsy his argument was. He said it was a lot of baggage, but come on now, every guy he's set me up with so far has had enough baggage to fill at least the back of a Volkswagen."

"Why do you think he tried so hard to convince you to stop seeing me?"

She sighed. "Because he's selfish and narcissistic and can't stand the thought of me actually being happy and not catering to his every freaking whim."

"Whoa. You are not okay. Do you need me to come over?"

She felt something deep inside of her start to melt. "I don't want you to drop whatever you're doing to come over here and listen to me bitch and moan about Benjamin."

"Molly, you just had a pretty big fight with your best friend, and you sound upset and angry. I've never seen or heard you angry. If you need me to come over I'll get the next door neighbor to watch Annabelle for a while."

"Joe, you really don't have to do that."

"No arguing. I'll be over there in twenty minutes."

"Yes, sir."

"Smart ass. I'll see you in a few."

"Later."

She ended the call and stared at the blank screen for a few minutes before finally leaving her place in the kitchen. She hastily straightened up here and there, threw away an empty water bottle she'd had sitting on the coffee table, lit a candle. She told herself she did so because the scent relaxed her.

Twenty minutes later Joe was knocking on her door, and the next thing she knew he'd wrapped her in his arms and was holding her tight.

She allowed her cheek to rest against his chest. She could hear the steady *thump thump* of his heart, and the scent of fabric softener and Joe tickled her nose. His body was warm, strong, solid. For the first time in a long time she realized she felt safe.

What was that all about?

She pulled away from him and looked up at his face. "Thanks for coming over."

He tucked a strand of hair behind her ear and kissed the tip of her nose. "I got the feeling you didn't need to be alone right now."

Is he really real? Is this all some fantastic dream I'm going to wake up from? Men like Joe didn't exist in her world.

"Tell me what happened. How did you burn a bridge?"

They walked over to the couch and sat down. She told him everything, about Benjamin's behavior that night and about how fed up she was and how she'd realized that Benjamin didn't really know what friendship or love were.

He held her through it all, and when she started crying he wrapped his arms around her tighter and let her get it all out.

The tears at first were slow and lazy, but as she talked about what had happened, how she'd felt, they began to flow faster and faster.

"I don't think he knows what friendship is. I don't think he knows how to care about anyone but himself, and I'm not sure he even really does that. I feel like I've wasted so much time on him, and all for nothing."

She felt his lips brush across the top of her head. "I don't think you've wasted your time. Right now you're hurt and angry, and you have every reason to feel that way."

She twisted so that she was facing him. "The problem, though, is that I've waited around on him for so long. I held on to this idea that never came to exist. As long as I was waiting, as long as I was willing to pick up his crumbs, everything was fine between us. I deserve more than some-one's crumbs, Joe. I need more than that."

"I completely agree. You're amazing, and you deserve someone who sees just how wonderful you are."

She toyed with a loose thread on the collar of his t-shirt. "I have my own baggage, you know."

"I know."

"Why haven't you ever asked me what it is?"

He nudged her chin up with an index finger until she was looking at him straight in the eye. "I figured you would tell me when you were ready, when you trusted me enough."

She swallowed. Looked away and then looked back at him. "I was emotionally and mentally abused as a child. Actually, as a child and a teenager."

He smoothed a thumb over her freckles. "Who did it? So I can go beat the crap out of them."

A smile teased her lips before she turned serious again. "My ex-stepfather. He would tell me how fat I was, call me lazy and worthless and make up nicknames for me like

Triple Sow Cow. He would moo at me, berate me while I was doing the dishes or laundry. If we were eating dinner he would make oinking noises. He would tell me he was amazed I hadn't fallen through the floor because I was so fat."

"Why didn't your mom say anything?"

"She was just as abused as I was. The thing that people don't understand who have never been in a situation like that is that getting out is hard. It's not as simple as saying, 'No more,' packing your bags and leaving. People like him, they make you feel worthless, like no one would ever want you, that without them you're nothing."

"God, Molly." He pulled her tightly to him, kissed her cheek and massaged the back of her neck where tension had gathered. "You know you're not any of those things, right?"

She spoke into shoulder. "Logically, yes. On an intellectual level I know that I have a lot to offer, that I'm smart and funny and at least moderately attractive. Deep down inside, though, I still sometimes feel like the little girl gorging herself on Doritos because it made her feel better."

"Doritos, huh? What flavor?"

"Nacho cheese. I'm a classic sort of girl."

His hand slowed its ministrations. "Don't ever doubt for a second that I think you're amazing. You're smart and funny and gorgeous. I don't care how many times I have to tell you that until you believe it, either."

She pulled away so that she could look at him. "I might take a while to get there."

"That's okay. I have all the time in the world. You're worth it."

She leaned forward and kissed him, needing to show him how she felt since she couldn't quite find the words. His mouth responded to hers, their tongues danced and tangled. Butterflies once again danced in her stomach, and his hands drifted down to her waist, massaged her lower back right above her butt.

She slowly drew away and whispered, "I want you, Joe, but I want to take this slow."

"I don't see any need to rush this. Like I said, I have all the time in the world."

He kissed her again, and for the first time ever Molly felt like maybe some of the broken pieces inside of her were beginning to glue themselves back together.

CHAPTER TWENTY-SIX

The evening was not going as planned.

Joe closed his eyes and rested his head against the freezer door, his cell phone still clutched tightly in his hand.

He heard footsteps on the tile floor behind him and turned around, making sure to plaster a smile on his face.

"Uncle Joe? When's Kristy going to be here?"

"Kristy's sick, sweetie, so it looks like it's just you and me tonight."

Annabelle clapped her hands. Her smile spread across her entire face. "Yay! Can we order pizza and watch *Beauty and the Beast?*"

At least she hadn't asked for *Cinderella*. He'd seen that movie so many times over the past year he had entire pieces of dialogue memorized. "Sure. Just let me make a phone call real quick."

"To your girlfriend?" She said the word "girlfriend" in the way only eight-year-old females could say it.

"What makes you think I have a girlfriend?"

"You bought a girl flowers for Valentine's Day. Remember?"

He definitely remembered. How could he forget the happiness he'd heard in Molly's voice that morning when she thanked him for the flowers? Or the flirtatious way she'd told him chocolate would get him a make-out session.

"And you were on the phone with a girl the other night,

before you took me next door."

He sighed. How in the world did single parents handle dating? How did they explain dating to their children?

"Well, I have a friend who's a girl. I really like her. She really likes me. But she isn't my girlfriend."

"Why not?"

"It's complicated."

Annabelle placed her hands on her hips and looked up at him. "Why do grownups say stuff like that?"

"Stuff like what?"

"'It's complicated'," she mimicked.

"Because we're grownups and we can."

"I wish I were a grownup."

He sighed and rubbed a hand over his face. "Why don't you go find the movie and I'll be in the living room in just a minute?"

She stuck her bottom lip out and he was afraid she was going to pout. Annabelle was generally a good kid, but even she had her moments.

He snagged the phone off the kitchen island, pulled up Molly's contact info and hit the phone icon before stepping into the backyard. He didn't want to have to cancel their date tonight. He'd had a good one planned, too—a play at the Hippodrome followed by a walk across the Suspension Bridge. Plus, Molly had already had a tough week, and canceling their date tonight probably wouldn't help to make things better.

She picked up after a few rings. "Hello?"

"Hey, it's me."

Her voice warmed. "Hey you. So when are you planning on telling me what you have planned for tonight?"

He winced, and was glad she couldn't see his facial expression. "Well, I did have a good one planned. Annabelle's sitter has strep throat, though, and I couldn't find anyone else to cover for me for a few hours."

"I hope her sitter gets to feeling better. Strep throat sucks, for lack of a better word."

"That it does. I feel bad, though. You've had a rough week already, and I was really looking forward to tonight."

"Don't worry about it, Joe. I understand. Annabelle comes first and that's the way it should be. We can always do something another night."

"Thank you for understanding. If I don't get back inside Annabelle will probably try to start the movie without me."

"Aww. What are you watching?"

"*Beauty and the Beast.*"

"I love *Beauty and the Beast!*"

"Seriously?"

"Oh, yeah. It's my favorite Disney movie of all time, followed closely by *Pirates of the Caribbean.*"

"That's quite a combination."

"Yeah, well, I love Johnny Depp."

He chuckled. "Good to know. Are you sure you're okay with this?"

"I'm fine. I'll just watch *Say Yes to the Dress* and catch up on my reading."

"Alright. I might call you after I've put Annabelle to bed. Is that okay?"

"That's more than okay."

They said their goodbyes and Joe ended the call. He closed his eyes and inhaled the dry late February air, wishing he were with Molly rather than standing in his backyard, avoiding the questions of an eight-year-old.

Molly set her phone back down on the coffee table and sank into the couch cushions.

Okay, so that had sucked just a little bit.

She took a deep breath and turned on the television. In all fairness, she'd known this could eventually happen. The timing could have been better, considering the things Benjamin had said to her Wednesday night.

They hadn't talked since he'd left her apartment. On one hand that bothered her. On the other, she felt like she could breathe for the first time in years.

She picked up her tattered copy of Christie Ridgway's *Must Love Mistletoe* and opened it up to the page she'd bookmarked. If she had to take a break from her own romance tonight, she could at least submerse herself in someone else's.

Later that night, as the Beast was redeemed and turned back into a prince by Belle's love, Joe's thoughts turned to Molly.

After finding out the Disney classic was one of her favorite movies, he'd watched it in a new light. Her adoration of the film made sense, considering it was about loving the inside rather than the outside of a person. Knowing now what he did about her childhood, it made sense that this would be her favorite.

Annabelle stirred beside him, sat up and rubbed her eyes open with fisted hands. She yawned and Joe stood.

"Time for bed, sweetie."

She blinked up at him. "Did they live happily ever after?"

"Yes, they did."

She slid off the couch before heading to her bedroom. Joe followed her and made sure she brushed her teeth before putting on her nightgown and crawling into bed. When nothing but her face was peeking out from under the covers he bent down and kissed her on the forehead, tucked in the sides tight like she always asked him to and turned off the light.

"'Night Uncle Joe." Her speech was slurred, and Joe could tell she was already drifting back into sleep.

"Night, sweetie."

He pulled the door closed behind him with a soft *click* before heading back into the living room. He turned off the DVD player and picked up the empty pizza box on the coffee table. On his way to the garage and the trash bin he grabbed the phone and tapped on his most recent call.

"Hey there."

Just her voice made his mouth dry. "Hey there yourself."

"So how was movie night?"

"Well, I have a nice drool spot on my sleeve from where Annabelle fell asleep."

"Mmm. Sexy."

Her tone was teasing, but he could still feel his lower body coming to life. "You think so?"

"Oh, definitely. Nothing turns me on more than drooly sleeves."

"You wouldn't be able to keep your hands off me right now, then."

"Hot."

He laughed. "So how was your evening?"

"It was good. Read a little bit. Watched some TV."

"So what are you doing now?"

She was quiet for a few moments before responding. "Lying in bed thinking about you."

Yup, his lower body was definitely wide awake now. "Oh really? What are you thinking about?"

"Well, I was thinking about you wearing nothing but boxers and that polka-dotted tie you like so much, but now that you've mentioned a drool-covered sleeve I might have to readjust my fantasy a little bit."

"A tie and boxers, huh?" He chose to ignore the drool comment.

"I like a man in a tie."

"What were you wearing in this little fantasy of yours?"

"I hadn't really thought about that. What would you like me to be wearing?"

He closed his eyes and inhaled, immediately picturing Molly lying in his bed, her hair in disarray and a satisfied smile on her face. "Nothing at all."

"That's easy enough."

He walked back into the kitchen and shut the garage door behind him. His voice low, he asked, "So in this fantasy of yours, what am I doing?"

She cleared her throat, and considering how long it took her to answer he could tell she was nervous. Now more than ever, though, he wanted Molly to trust him. Needed her to trust him. "Don't be shy, Molly, not with me. You can tell me."

"Well, I—" he could hear her deep inhalation, "—I was thinking that first you would kiss me."

"I could do that."

"Then, well, you would play with my nipples."

"What would I do to them?"

"Uh, well, um, suck on them?"

Her nervousness was oddly endearing. "Are they sensitive?"

"Very."

Good to know. "And then?"

"Then you would, um, touch me."

"Where?" He was officially hard as a rock.

"You know where."

"Tell me."

"Down there."

"Australia?"

Her laugh was filled with nerves. "No. My clitoris."

Leave it to Molly to make phone sex sound clinical. The thought made him grin.

"How would I touch you down there?"

He could hear her swallow across the phone lines. "You would do it lightly at first, and then a little harder maybe."

"Would I be doing anything else?"

"You would—"

Just then he heard steps in the hallway. "Dammit. Could you hold on a second?"

Sure enough, Annabelle walked into the kitchen, her pink Hello Kitty nightgown askew and her hair sticking up in tufts here and there. He was glad he was standing behind the kitchen island rather than in front of it.

"Can I have some water?"

He sighed. "Sure, sweetie."

He poured her a quick glass of water, watched her drink it down and then ushered her back to bed. He waited until he'd heard the door click shut before putting the phone back up to his ear. "Sorry about that."

"It's okay. Annabelle, I take it?"

He sighed. "Yeah. Glass of water."

"This must be hard on you."

He glanced towards the fly of his jeans. "You have no idea."

"Why do I have the feeling there's a double entendre in that statement?"

"Because there is."

She sighed. "If it makes you feel any better, I'm pretty sure I'm going to cuddle up with a vibrator after we get off the phone."

"Why not while we're on the phone?"

"Oh, no, I don't think so."

He almost laughed at her quick response. "You're

right. Hearing you getting off would only make me wish I was there with you even more."

"I wish you were here, too."

"Are you saying what I think you're saying?"

"What do you think I'm saying?"

He'd been out of the dating game far too long, and Molly had never really been in it. He wasn't shocked that either of them was having a hard time figuring out how to move things to the next level. "Well, you told me the other night you weren't ready for that yet."

"For sex?"

"Yes."

"I'm not. Is that what you thought I was talking about?"

"Well, all things considered."

"True. I think about it. Obviously I think about it. And like I said the other night, I do want you. I want you so bad it hurts sometimes. I want to do this right, though. We haven't been dating for very long, and we're still getting to know each other. I just want it to mean something when it does happen."

He exhaled a pent up breath he hadn't realized he'd been holding. "It'll mean something, Molly, no matter when it happens. I'm not pushing you, but I do want you to know that if it happened tomorrow or next month or next year it would mean something."

"I really do wish you were here right now."

He sighed and closed his eyes. "Me, too, gorgeous, me too."

CHAPTER TWENTY-SEVEN

Joe sighed as Annabelle's lower lip began to quiver.

"But I don't wanna, Uncle Joe."

"Annabelle, you promised Jodi you would be at her party. This morning you couldn't wait for this sleepover. What happened?"

She crossed her arms over her chest and adopted the same petulant expression her mother used to have. He swallowed past the memory as he waited for Annabelle to answer.

"I just don't want to."

He raked his hands through his hair and looked at the clock. He was supposed to pick up Molly in thirty minutes and he still hadn't had a chance to shower or change out of his work clothes. "That isn't going to cut it."

"You're mean, Uncle Joe."

The first dozen or so times she'd told him that, the pain had been almost debilitating. He'd hated hearing her tell him he was mean. He'd picked up on her game, though, and had hardened himself as much as possible against the eight-year-old's tactics. "Fine, then. I guess if you don't want to go you can just go to your room."

She turned and began to stomp towards her bedroom.

"And no TV, no radio, no telephone, no Barbies."

She stopped and looked over her shoulder at him. "What am I going to do?"

"Your homework."

"But it's a Friday night!" she whined.

"And you could be going to a sleepover with all of your friends, where you could watch TV, listen to music and play with Barbies. But since you don't want to go, I figured you would rather do your homework."

She was quiet for a few moments before almost whispering, "Sarah laughed at me today because all the other girls had their hair braided and I didn't."

Why was this keeping her from going to Jodi's slumber party?

"And then she told me that I had to have my hair braided to go to Jodi's slumber party, or else they wouldn't let me stay."

So this entire thing was over braided hair? Man, he was glad to be a male.

Joe walked towards Annabelle and picked her up. "Sweetie, why didn't you just tell me that?"

"Because you don't know how to braid and I didn't want to hurt your feelings."

He closed his eyes and kissed her on the forehead. Love for his niece filled him, but so did sadness. An eight-year-old shouldn't be worried about hurting an adult's feelings. She should be playing and having fun and wearing as many braids in her hair as she liked. Instead, though, they'd been stuck together. A lonely little girl who'd never known her parents and a guy in his late twenties who hadn't planned on having kids until he was at least thirty-five and who couldn't braid hair if his life depended upon it. Not for the first time, he wished things would have turned out different, that life hadn't thrown his family the curve balls it had.

"Don't worry about hurting my feelings, okay? We'll just go next door and get Mrs. Jasper to braid it for you."

She picked at the top button on his shirt and worried

her lip. "Okay."

He kissed her on the nose before setting her back down on the ground. "Okay, let's go next door and get your hair braided, and then I'll take you over to Jodi's. Alright?"

She nodded her head. "You're not really mean, Uncle Joe."

"I know." His smile, though, felt strained.

♧

Joe picked Molly up an hour later. They'd agreed on Chuy's earlier that afternoon.

"You okay over there?" Molly smiled at him across the table.

"Sorry, I was just thinking."

"Those must have been some pretty deep thoughts."

"I was just thinking about how lucky I am that Anna-belle has so many friends who have sleepovers."

She laughed. "Kind of helps to free up your weekends, huh?"

"Definitely. Sometimes I think those sleepovers are the only thing that keeps me sane."

She took a sip of her margarita. "This has been hard on you, I would imagine."

"I'm not going to lie and say it's been easy. But she's a good kid, rarely gets into trouble. I'm more worried about when she's a teenager and boys want to start dating her."

"Uh oh. Is Uncle Joe going to get out his shot gun?"

"Probably. I know how teenage boys think."

"How do teenage boys think? Actually, do teenage boys think?"

He laughed, couldn't help it really. "They think about boobs and sex. That's about the extent of it."

"Funny, that's what a lot of teenage girls think about, too."

"Teenage girls think about boobs and sex?"

"Oh, yeah. They obsess over getting boobs and having sex. Or whether they should have sex."

"Huh. Who knew? All this time teenage boys and girls really haven't been all that different."

"I guess not. Knowing that probably would've made things a lot easier in high school."

"No kidding. And here I'd been thinking teenage girls obsessed over the cutest rock star and who was dating who."

"That's part of it."

"So did you obsess about getting boobs and having sex?"

She took another sip of her margarita. "Well, to be honest I was already an A cup in the fifth grade, so my obsession was more on how to make them look smaller by the time I was in high school. And as for sex, I was more curious about kissing. I mean, I thought about sex, but I really had no desire to do it. I just wanted someone to kiss me."

"Did you ever find someone to kiss you?"

A blush crept up her neck and cheeks. "Not until two days after I graduated."

"I can see you being a late bloomer. I don't think teenage boys could have appreciated you anyway."

Their waitress stopped and cleared their table. "Would y'all like dessert?"

Molly shook her head.

"No thanks," he responded.

The waitress returned a few moments later with the ticket. Joe handed over his credit card and the waitress disappeared once again.

He noticed Molly had started drinking water, leaving at least half of her margarita untouched. "Do you want the rest of that? We can stay if you would like."

She shook her head. "No. If I drink the rest of it I'll

wind up drunk."

He wiggled his eyebrows suggestively. "Maybe you should drink the rest of it then."

She laughed. "I think I'll stick with water for the remainder of the evening."

He glanced at his watch. "I'm sorry it took so long to get Annabelle to her friend's house. Now we can't catch that movie."

"That's okay. We can catch it some other time."

He shifted in his seat. "We could always rent a movie and go back to your place or my place." He tried to sound casual.

She gulped down some water before saying, "We can go back to my place."

Instead of renting a movie, they decided to watch her copy of *The Princess Bride.*

They'd cuddled up on her couch, Joe's arm wrapped around her and her head on his shoulder. When Princess Buttercup and the Dread Pirate Roberts kissed at the end, Joe kissed Molly. They'd been making out on the couch for a while, and all she really did know was that she felt good and didn't want this to stop.

"Do you have a condom?" Joe's breath tickled Molly's ear.

She backed away so that a few inches separated their faces. "I haven't had sex in two years. Why would I have a condom?"

"You haven't had sex in two years?"

She stared at a cobweb that was forming in the corner of her living room. "Um, no. Why don't you have a condom?"

His cheeks turned slightly pink. "Well, um, I wasn't

exactly planning on this happening tonight."

"Were you planning on it ever happening?"

"I hoped it would, but I figured it might take us a little while longer to get to this point."

She cocked her head to the side. "Why? Just out of curiosity."

"Because I respect you and I didn't want to push you into doing something you weren't ready for."

"Oh." Well then. How…how sweet.

He leaned in and kissed her, a light brushing of his lips over her own. Open mouth. No tongue. "If this is moving too fast let me know."

She swallowed and stared back at him. Crap. She could fall for him. Was scared she was falling for him. Hell, had already started to and was on the last leg of the trip and her parachute didn't want to open up.

She sighed, closed her eyes and felt his forehead bump against hers. Molly let it rest there, trying not to over think the fact that for the first time in, well, ever, she had an attractive, intelligent man in her apartment who apparently wanted her and yet respected her enough to wait if she wasn't ready to take the next step in their relationship.

Joe's lips lightly brushed over hers again and Molly couldn't help but to respond. For the first time in a long time she actually wanted someone other than Benjamin, wanted someone on a level she hadn't wanted anyone in a very, very long time if not ever. And he wanted her back.

"I don't know that I'm ready for sex yet," she whispered against his mouth, "but I am up for fooling around."

"Are you sure?"

She nodded, kissed him lightly. "I'm sure."

His grin briefly registered in her mind before he got up from the couch and pulled her with him. His mouth claimed hers and he backed her towards the bedroom. She vaguely felt the mattress bump against the backs of her thighs before she was lowered to the bed. Joe's weight followed, settled beside her.

His hands were all over her body, skimming over the curves, touching and sneaking under her clothes where they could. God, it felt good to be touched. To feel wanted.

Her hands followed suit, finding their way under his shirt, following the planes of his back and around to his chest where her fingertips were met with a light dusting of hair. He felt good. Solid. Strong. Warm. Male. Most importantly male.

She tugged at the hem of his shirt, pushed it up his torso and pulled it over his head. God, she wanted him naked.

He made quick work of her shirt and tossed it over his shoulder. Cool air hit her chest, and even though her nipples were fully covered by her bra she could still feel them pebble inside the cups. He traced the edge of her bra with a fingertip before dipping it inside to brush over a nipple.

Molly sighed and closed her eyes. God, it felt really, really good to be touched.

Her bra came off next thanks to Joe's very deft fingers—Molly wondered what else he was good at with his fingers—and her breasts were left bared, nipples hard and aching. He kissed her again and cupped a hand over one breast.

"Mmmmm." Oh, that felt good.

His other hand worked the snap of her jeans, got it loose and slid the zipper down. The man was definitely showing promise with his hands.

Molly lifted her hips and helped him to push the pants down and off her body.

"You're wearing too many clothes." She reached for his belt.

"Yes ma'am."

She loosened the buckle and unbuttoned his khakis before unzipping them and pushing them down his legs. He pushed them off the rest of the way, removed his socks and laid back down beside her, wearing nothing but a pair of boxers with Christmas trees on them.

"Nice underwear." She grinned at him.

"I need to do laundry." He nibbled on her neck, causing goose bumps to skitter across her body. "You, however, have very nice underwear. Sexy."

She laughed nervously. "Thanks."

His tongue toyed with her earlobe. "I mean it. They're sexy. You're sexy."

Oh, God, how was she supposed to respond when his tongue was doing such wonderful things to her ear? "Hmmm. Thanks."

His hands roamed over her nearly naked body, lingering over the curve of her tummy before skimming over a hip and moving towards her thigh. His mouth continued its slow path of torture, moving from her ear lobe to her throat to her collar bone and down to her breasts. Wet heat covered one nipple and Molly's hips shifted restlessly. Jesus, the man knew how to use his mouth, too.

She felt his hand casually resting on the inside of her thigh as his mouth turned its attention to her other breast, and she shifted her hips, silently begging him to touch her where she most needed to be touched.

His hand stayed where it was. His tongue traced the underside of one breast and then the other. Molly sighed and her eyelids slowly closed. Oh, this was nice.

She could feel his mouth leaving a moist trail down her stomach, pressing kisses here and there as it moved further down until he was kissing her through the material of her panties, applying light pressure and making her wish she was completely naked.

Her stomach and thigh muscles clenched, nerves and need causing her body to tighten. He seemed to have read her mind and he pulled her panties down and off. He shifted so that he was on his knees on the floor, grabbed her hips and pulled her forward so that her ass was almost hanging off the edge of the bed. Nerves and excitement mingled together as his head dipped down between her thighs and she felt him open her up to his gaze seconds before she felt his tongue lick over her.

Oh, Jesus, he really knew how to use his mouth.

Oh, God, did she taste okay?

She wasn't sure if it was seconds, minutes or days later, but his mouth felt so good and her hands were gripping the sheets underneath her and holy shit the man was a sex God. So close. She was so freaking close.

Knowing her body wasn't going to do what she wanted it to, she tugged on his hair and pulled him up towards her. He worked his way back up her torso, kissing her stomach, lightly nipping at her breasts, nibbling on the side of her neck, toying with her earlobe. He settled his weight onto her and she could feel his erection pressing up against her through the cotton of his underwear.

She turned her head so that their mouths met, tasted herself on his tongue and pushed his boxers down his legs and off his body. She wrapped a hand around him, lightly stroking. Mmm. She'd forgotten how good it felt to hold a penis in her hands, feel the length and girth and the contrast of silky smooth skin wrapped around the hard, hot shaft.

"Oh, God, Molly." Joe drew in a shaky breath.

She kissed him again before pushing him so that he was on his back. He'd tortured her with his mouth, now it was time to return the favor.

Molly kissed a path down his stomach, followed his happy trail all the way down, reminded herself that blow jobs were like riding a bicycle and touched the head of his penis with the tip of her tongue. Swirled her tongue around the head a few times, ran it along the underside, applying pressure to that fun little vein, and then wrapped her lips around the head.

Joe closed his eyes and sighed, and Molly barely kept from smiling. Oh, yeah, definitely like riding a bicycle.

Minutes went by as she bobbed her head up and down, swirled her tongue along the underside and reveled in the feeling of his hands tangled in her hair, gently tugging his approval. He moaned. She applied a little more pressure with her lips and tongue, sucked a little bit harder on the head on the upstroke, tightened her grip on the base just a little bit before moving her mouth back down.

"Oh, God, Molly. I'm going to come."

She felt him spill into her mouth, against the back of her throat and swallowed, moving her mouth back up, sucking on the head one last time. His hips jerked and he tightened his hands in her hair just a little bit before easing the pressure. She removed her mouth, looked up at him and smiled.

He was staring at her, watching her every movement.

"What?" She raised an eyebrow.

"Wow."

She laughed and reached for the bottle of water on the nightstand, took a drink and offered it to Joe. He sat up and took a drink, still watching her.

"What?" She asked again.

He shook his head. "Just…wow."

She smiled again. "One syllable. That must've been good." The thought warmed her. Well, more than she already was to begin with.

"Oh yeah." He lay back down on the bed and reached for her.

She placed the water back on the nightstand and lay down beside him, her head on his chest and her arm draped across his stomach.

They lay there in comfortable silence for long moments, and for once Molly's mind was quiet, even if her body wasn't.

$\heartsuit$

"You didn't come." He turned his head and kissed her lightly on the cheek.

She sighed from beside him. "I rarely do."

Now that was interesting. "Is that just with a partner or all the time?" Maybe they should have talked about this beforehand.

"Uh, well, just with a partner."

He propped himself up on an elbow and trailed the tip of his index finger over the slope of her breast. "Show me."

"What?" Her tone was sharp with nerves. And he guessed probably sexual frustration, considering her nipples were still hard and he could feel her heart racing underneath his wandering hand.

He nibbled on her bottom lip. "Show me."

She swallowed as he kissed her neck. "I, uh, have carpal tunnel."

"Then how do you help yourself out? Because I know you do, you're far too sexual not to."

"You think I'm sexual?"

"Sexual," he kissed the edge of her jaw. "Sensual." He kissed the side of her neck right below her ear. "Sexy as hell." He nipped at her earlobe and felt goose bumps raise on Molly's skin underneath his hand. She shifted her hips. Interesting. Earlobe nibbling turned her on.

He nipped again and she sighed.

"Definitely sexy as hell."

"Hmmm."

"Show me, Molly," he whispered into her ear, teasing the shell with his tongue. He felt her shiver. "Don't be embarrassed. You have no idea how much of a turn-on it is to think of you touching yourself."

"I usually use a vibrator." Her voice sounded strangled, and knew this couldn't be easy for her.

He looked up at her face, saw the closed eyes and the flushed cheeks and grinned. Couldn't help it, really. Oh, yeah, getting Molly to come out of her shell was definitely the most fun he'd had in a very, very long time.

I can't believe I just told him that.

Molly cracked her eyelids open and looked at Joe. He was propped up on an elbow, grinning. His dimple winked at her, and she felt a burning need to lick it. She refrained, but barely.

"Show me," he said again in that seductive voice that had her bones—and other places—melting.

Show him? She wasn't sure she could. That was just too…too…private.

But at the same time, God she was about ready to blow.

Embarrassment or orgasm, Molly, embarrassment or orgasm.

He nipped at her earlobe again before moving down her jaw and over to her mouth. She kissed him back, felt his hand on her breast. Her gaze wandered over to the drawer that held her vibrators. Oh, it was so tempting to reach in and pull one out.

"Show me," he whispered again.

She swallowed. "Okay."

He looked up at her, his expression hopeful and, okay, Molly had to admit he did look pretty turned on. And then he smiled, boyishly confident. She rolled her eyes. "This has nothing to do with you."

He pinched her nipple and she arched her hips. He looked far too all-knowing. "Sure it doesn't."

She rolled away from him and got off the bed, pulled open the drawer and looked at her choices. She had a feeling the rabbit might scare him, so she grabbed a small pink mini vibrator that packed a lot of punch before closing the drawer.

When she turned she saw that he'd been looking over her shoulder. "Interesting collection."

Her face flamed. "I, ah, they have different purposes."

"Oh really?"

"Yeah." She swallowed. "A couple are waterproof. Different speeds, different functions."

He nodded towards the one in her hand. "And that one?"

"It packs a lot of punch." *Was she really about to do this?*

He laughed and pulled her back onto the bed, wrapped his hand around the back of her neck and drew her down for a long, lingering kiss. When he finally broke it he looked up at her and said, "Don't be shy, Molly, not around me."

Don't be shy? He's crazy. How can I not be shy?

He rolled her over onto her back and resumed his propped up position, kissed her again and this time didn't stop for a while.

Oh, man, he could kiss.

Her entire body was tense and she could feel the tightness in her lower body and desperately craved release.

She turned on the vibrator and placed it against herself. Oh, God, that felt good, especially with Joe kissing her and his fingers tweaking her nipple.

Her eyes were closed and all she could do was feel. Feel his tongue in her mouth and his lips pressing against hers. His fingers on her nipples, the pleasure/pain that shot a straight trail to her core every time he pinched. The vibrations against her clit.

His mouth moved down to her left breast and her breathing grew thick and heavy. She cupped the back of his head with her free hand, grabbed his hair and held him close. She shifted her hips and the vibrator, needing more direct contact. Her hips jerked. There. There was the spot.

Her legs started shaking and Joe moved his attention to her right breast.

Too much it was too much.

She vaguely felt his hand brush over her stomach and across her hip, trail across the inside of her thigh. She shifted her hips and felt his finger slide into her. Oh, God. Too much.

Too much feeling. Too much heat. Too much intimacy. Too much vulnerability.

He slid a second finger inside her and she turned up the speed on the vibrator. He pried it out of her grasp with his free hand. Her hands floated down to the sheets.

Vaguely, she realized her control was slipping away. But Joe's fingers were inside of her and that little pink piece of silicon were all working together to create the most amazing sensations ever.

She moaned and Joe kissed her, long and deep, open-mouthed without finesse, stroking the inside of her mouth with his tongue. She kissed him back, completely lost in him, in the sensations, in actually feeling. One hand was on his back, the other tangled in the sheets. His fingers were rapidly, forcefully moving in and out of her and, "Holy fucking shit."

The tension gathered and released, her inner muscles pulsed around Joe's fingers, her hips lifted off the bed and she vaguely realized she'd curled her nails into Joe's back.

But she didn't care, because God it felt wonderful. So very, very wonderful, to let go and lose control.

She slowly came back to herself, felt like she was floating somewhere above the bed, above her body, above all of her worries and doubts and insecurities. Her heart was still racing, felt like it could jump out of her chest at any given moment, and her breathing was still ragged but she felt amazing. Absolutely amazing.

Molly realized Joe was no longer kissing her and opened up her eyes. How long had he been watching her?

He turned the vibrator off and tossed it onto the mattress beside them. He rubbed the tip of his nose against hers, lightly kissed her and smiled. "Feel better now?"

"You have no idea." She knew she probably looked like a wild-eyed crazy woman, but she didn't care.

He lay down next to her and gathered his arms around her, pulling her close against him. She felt his lips press against the back of her neck, his front pressed to her back and his hand resting on her tummy. Usually just the thought of a man's hand on her stomach would make her nervous, but considering what had just happened, she figured there was no place for nerves anymore where Joe was concerned.

Instead, she felt relaxed. She closed her eyes, felt his chest rising and falling and dozed off with a smile on her face.

CHAPTER TWENTY-EIGHT

Molly lightly knocked on Mr. Charles' door and plastered a smile on her face. When he'd called her a few minutes before he hadn't said anything other than, "Can I see you in my office real quick?"

She rubbed her palms on her thighs and walked into his office.

"You wanted to see me, sir?"

"Yes, yes. Close the door and sit down, would you?"

She did as he asked and tried to appear as calm as possible.

"Now, I know you've only been here a few weeks, but in those few weeks you've displayed some fantastic editorial instincts."

Molly blinked. "Well, thank you, sir."

He leaned forward in his chair and placed his folded hands on his desk blotter. "First, I wanted to tell you that your probationary period is officially over. Congratulations, you're now a full time staff writer."

"Thank you, Mr. Charles."

"Also, the senior editorial staff has been bandying about some ideas on how to gain readers and subscribers while continuing to engage the readers we already have. We've done a pretty good job of moving into the twenty-first century, so to speak, but we feel like our online content is lagging behind. Everyone's on Buzzfeed, Facebook or Twitter, and click-bait headlines are the norm. Content, however, is still king."

She agreed, but what did any of this have to do with her? "Yes, sir."

"All that's to say we've decided to have a contest among a few staff writers to see who can draw in the most blog readers, and we would like to give you first crack at it."

"Me? Really?"

Mr. Charles smiled. "Yes, you. Like I said, you've exhibited remarkable editorial skills. Plus, I dug up your columns from when you were a teenager and even then you were a succinct and engaging writer. I also performed a Google search and came across your own blog, and I have to say I love you're voice. You're young and hip and probably have much more of a social life than most of the old fuddy duddies around here and I think you'll do a great job at this."

"Well, thank you, sir. I appreciate it. And I'm very grateful for the opportunity." He'd checked out her private blog? Crap.

"I'm glad to hear that. The blog will start out as a once a week piece. Keep it fairly short and sweet, but fun. Like I said this is a competition, but you're free to talk about anything you like, whether it's a movie, a CD, pop culture or a local band. We're going to evaluate it after a month and see who's blog has received the most hits. Meanwhile, you'll still be copy editing, but this could be a stepping stone into reporting."

She had absolutely no idea what to say except, "Thank you."

He grinned at her and sat back in his chair. "You're welcome. Now get back to copy editing."

"I'll do that, sir. When's my first deadline?"

♡

"So why'd Mr. Charles pull you into his office earli-er?"

Molly sat down at the table across from Joe and un-wrapped her sandwich. "The senior editorial board appar-ently wants to compete with Buzzfeed, and he thought I would be a good blogger for the newspaper."

Joe raised his eyebrows. "Really? Nice to see they're finally trying to embrace pop culture."

"No kidding. It just struck me as odd since I've only been here a few weeks. I even said so."

"Mr. Charles is like that. Besides, I think you'd be great for the job."

"Yeah, but why not you? Or someone else who's been here longer than me?"

"I don't know. I'm sure the senior staff went with who they thought would be best for the job."

"I just think it should've gone to someone who's been here longer than me, is all."

He reached across the table and tucked a piece of hair behind her ear. "The fact that you're so damned nice is one of the things I like about you, but don't look a gift horse in the mouth. This could be a great opportunity for you."

"I know. I just feel guilty."

"Don't. And if you're worried I'm going to be jealous or something because you were offered the opportunity and I wasn't, don't. I'm not jealous at all."

There he was, getting inside her head again. "Stop doing that."

"What?"

"Reading my mind."

He took a bite of his sandwich. "So if I told you to take all the time you need to process everything that's happened over the past couple of weeks would I be reading your mind again?"

She hesitated, took a swallow of her water. It kind of freaked her out that Joe just seemed to "get" her after such a short period of time. "Yes, you would be reading my mind again. And thank you."

"Just don't take too much time, okay?"

She wasn't sure she could make any promises, so she said the next best thing she could think of. "I'll try."

Joe watched Molly as she entered the building the next morning, noticed the dark circles under her eyes and the way she moved slowly, as though walking through a thick sludgy fog.

"You okay?" He asked her as she joined him at the elevator.

She tucked a strand of hair behind her ear. "Yeah. Just didn't sleep well last night."

"Anything you need to talk about?"

The elevator dinged, signaling its arrival.

"Eventually. Maybe. I was just over-thinking stuff way too much."

Which meant she'd been up all night thinking about their relationship.

He didn't regret for a second following his mom's wishes and taking custody of Annabelle. His niece was the last link he had to his sister, but she was also more of a victim than any of them. Unlike most kids she'd never known her mom or dad, but she was surprisingly well-adjusted despite that fact.

He also understood Molly's hesitation, though. She was twenty-six and still trying to figure out herself and what she wanted. Things had happened a little quickly between the two of them, and then to suddenly find out there was a kid involved…yeah, Joe could understand why Molly would be up all night tossing and turning. Throw in what had happened last Friday night, and her hesitation was understandable.

The problem, though, was that he liked Molly and he couldn't let her walk away without giving their relationship a shot. The trick, though, was knowing when to push and when to back off.

Judging by the dark smudges under her eyes now was not the time to push.

"Got any plans this weekend?"

He hated how things had started to become awkward between the two of them.

"Not really. Benjamin and I are going to go see a movie tonight, and I still need to write this damned blog."

"Has he tried to talk you out of dating me anymore?"

Molly shrugged a shoulder. "No. This is actually going to be the first time we've seen each other since we got into that argument."

"You going to be okay tonight?"

"Yeah, I think so."

The elevator doors slid open and they stepped out onto their floor.

"Well, uh, I'll talk to you later." He walked towards his cubicle, wishing like hell he could just wave his hand and make everything okay again with Molly.

"Okay, was it just me or was that movie funny as hell?"

Molly and Benjamin were leaving the movie theater after watching the latest Judd Apatow flick, which had indeed been funny as hell.

"I've never laughed so hard in my life." Molly fished her keys out of her purse as they made their way to her car.

"Where to now?" Benjamin asked as they got in.

"Are you hungry?"

"I could eat."

She started the car. "You got any ideas?"

"How does Cotton Patch sound?"

"Good to me." She pulled out of the parking space and headed towards the restaurant he'd chosen.

"So how's work going?"

"It's going well. I have to write that blog over the weekend, but I think I might just do a movie review. Seems like a good way to go for an initial piece."

They chatted about their jobs and the movie the rest of the way to the restaurant, but once they'd settled into a booth Benjamin changed the subject on her.

"So how are things going with Joe?"

She glanced at him over the top of her menu. "Okay. He's giving me time to mull over the whole custody of a kid thing."

"So you still haven't slept with him?"

"Is that really any of your business?" She folded her menu and placed it on the table.

"So you have slept with him."

"Again, that's none of your business."

"I don't think he's right for you."

She tore apart a roll. "What would you know about that?"

"What does that mean?"

She slapped some butter onto the bread. "It means that you of all people have no clue who is and isn't 'right' for me, all things considered."

"If I don't know who's 'right' for you then why did you ask me to set you up on all those blind dates?"

She tossed the roll onto her plate. "Because I needed to

get over you once and for all and because you know every-one in this freaking town! That's why."

"You started dating to get over me?"

"Why do you sound so confused about that, Benja-min?"

"I didn't know you still had feelings for me."

She laughed harshly. "How could you not know that? I mean, come on, it's pretty hard to get over someone when they're always there, when they're always telling you that one day you'll get married to each other and live happily ever after, when he acts like he cares about you but really all he cares about is himself."

"First, I thought you knew I was joking about us get-ting married one day. Second, I don't care about no one but myself."

"You can't joke around with people about marriage, Benjamin. It isn't right, especially not to someone like me."

"Someone like you?"

"I shouldn't even have to explain that to you."

"Are you talking about your trust issues?"

"Yes, Benjamin my trust issues. My trust issues and my emotional intimacy issues and every other issue I have that has made me too neurotic for you to ever want to be with."

"I don't think you're neurotic."

"Oh, just own up to it already."

"Own up to what, Molly? I love you. You're my best friend and I love you. And there are times when I wonder about what could have been if I hadn't been such a chicken shit back when we were sleeping together, or any time be-fore or after that. And yes, I've wondered if maybe Emery was right when she said I have feelings for you."

Molly felt like she'd just been punched in the stomach. "You don't mean that."

"Yes, I do."

"No, you don't. You're grasping for straws. You had your chance and blew it. You weren't strong enough to admit your feelings, and I wasn't willing to fight for what I wanted. Love changes. People change. I'm not the same person I was just a few months ago, willing to beg for whatever scraps you would give me."

And suddenly she was angry. Angry for all the time she'd wasted waiting for him to love her. Angry for valuing herself so little that she'd made herself Benjamin's emotional plaything. Angry with her stepfather so scarring her for life. Angry with her ex for cheating on her and adding to the feeling of being unwanted, of being not good enough. She was angry with Benjamin for thinking she would drop Joe for his flimsy declaration.

Most of all, she was angry with herself for holding back and not allowing herself to trust.

Fed up, she tossed her napkin down onto the table, grabbed her purse and slid out of the booth.

"What are you doing?"

"Moving on with my life."

She left him with the tab for once and didn't look back.

CHAPTER TWENTY-NINE

"Molly, I have to say I loved your blog," Mr. Charles said Tuesday morning in his office.

"Thank you, sir. It was harder than I'd thought it would be to get back into a journalistic frame of mind writing-wise."

"Well, you did so beautifully. Your piece is smart and humorous and tells enough about the movie to let people know what it's about without giving away any spoilers."

"Considering that's what I was going for, it's a relief to hear that." Molly smiled and barely refrained from doing a happy dance in her chair.

"I think you're a natural at this, honestly, but it's still too early in the game to tell who's going to win. Just keep up the good work, young lady. I see great things in your future."

Molly stood up. "Thank you, sir."

Great things in her future, huh? Her gaze landed on Joe's cubicle. Maybe Mr. Charles wasn't too far off the mark with that statement.

♥

Later that night, Molly was just sitting down to eat dinner when her phone rang. She frowned at the unfamiliar number but answered anyway. What if it was work? Or Joe calling from his home phone or something?

"Hello?"

"Hi Molly, it's Larry."

Larry. Who the hell was Larry? She wracked her brain for a few seconds trying to remember…ohhh…Larry.

"Uh, hi, Larry."

"Hey there. Sorry it took so long to call you back. Work's been crazy and I've barely had any free time to myself."

"That's, um, okay." She smacked herself upside the head. For someone who was making her living using her words, she sure wasn't doing a very good job of it right now.

"So anyway. I was wondering if you were free Friday night?"

Oh. Well this was awkward. She took a deep breath before answering. "I actually have plans Friday night."

"Well what about Saturday?"

Molly swallowed the lump in her throat. How did other women let down nice, cute guys all the time without so much as batting an eyelash? "Well, I'm kind of, um, seeing someone now."

"Oh. Okay then." Was that disappointment in his voice? Holy crap, that was disappointment in his voice. "Well, if it doesn't work out, feel free to give me a call."

"Thanks, Larry. It was really nice meeting you."

"Nice meeting you, too. Take care."

The other end of the line went dead, and the call ended. Molly looked down at her phone and then stared at the bookshelf across from her. The rows of colorful spines shouted at her, beckoning her to hear their message. She set her phone down on the couch and walked over to the bookshelf. Without hesitation and feeling as if some unseen force were guiding her, she wrapped her fingers around her favorite book—Susan Elizabeth Phillips' *This Heart of*

Mine—and for the hundredth time dove into the story of the children's book author and the star quarterback who find someone to love them, faults, crappy childhood, hang-ups and all.

♡

The next morning Molly woke up a little earlier than usual and took a little more time getting ready for work, despite having a book hangover from staying up too late reading. During all of the thinking she'd been doing over the past couple of weeks, the one thing that kept circling around in her head was something Stacey and Clinton had been fond of saying on *What Not to Wear:* that wearing clothes that make you look good can also make you feel good.

She showered and used her favorite sugar scrub, which left her skin feeling extra soft and smelling good. She put on a pair of white lace boy shorts paired with a lacey white bra that made her feel both sexy and somehow innocent at the same time. Once she'd put in her contacts and brushed her teeth she stepped into black trousers and put on a white button down shirt with tiny black polka dots that she rarely wore but loved. She tied the matching black and white pol-ka dotted belt around her waist and looked at herself in the mirror. Oh, yeah. She was definitely feeling good. She then went into the bathroom and put on her makeup and blow dried her hair.

When she stood back up straight after being bent at the waist to dry her hair, she looked at herself in the mirror. Her cheeks were flushed, a smile curved her lips and her brown eyes were sparkling. Was that what she looked like when she felt happy and sure of herself? Go figure.

She walked into the living room and added the final pieces to her outfit—the piece de resistance, in a way—and slid her feet into her favorite pair of red high heels. Just putting them on made her feel good.

Molly grabbed her purse and headed out the door. Oh, yeah, great things were definitely in her future.

Joe just about swallowed his tongue when he saw Molly walk into the building thirty minutes later. He wasn't sure what it was, but something had changed.

He gave her a quick once over, and then a slower second over, before saying, "Good morning."

She smiled back at him, but not with one of her shy half smiles, but with one of her full smiles that indicated she was in a really good mood. "Morning."

"You seem to be in a good mood." Which was odd, considering Molly wasn't a morning person.

"I'm in a very good mood this morning."

"Mind if I ask why?"

"No reason. Just figured I might as well be in a good mood because it's certainly better than being in a bad one."

There was definitely something going on in that brain of hers, but he couldn't for the life of him figure out what. "You have a point."

He gave her a third over. "Nice shoes."

Her smile this time was slow and secretive and so sexy he felt like she'd touched him rather than simply looked at him. "Thanks."

The elevator arrived and the doors opened up. They stepped inside and Joe waited for the doors to close before speaking again. "They're kind of sexy."

She tossed him a sideways smile. "I know."

He raised an eyebrow but couldn't think of anything to say, primarily because he'd gotten a sudden image in his brain of Molly wearing nothing but those shoes.

The elevator slowly came to a stop. The doors opened and Molly walked out, her hips swaying and those red heels taunting him with every step she made. He took in the confident tilt of her head and set in her shoulders, remembered that knowing smile she'd had in the elevator and realized he maybe hadn't given Molly enough credit, because he had an inkling she'd done all of that on purpose, and she'd known exactly how he would react.

He ran his finger underneath the collar of his shirt as he stepped off the elevator.

Later that evening, Molly was at home, still wearing her clothes from work and trying to gather up the courage to do what she knew she needed to do.

Molly glanced at the clock on the DVR unit. Eight-oh-eight. Technically, the night was still young. Odds were he would still be awake.

But would he be home?

If he was home would Annabelle be with him?

She looked at the time again. Eight-ten.

Her right hand curled around the keys sitting on the couch beside her. Cool metal bit into her palms.

She took a deep breath and stood up, and before she could talk herself out of it grabbed her phone and purse.

She was doing this. She was really going to do this.

Fifteen minutes later she'd parked her car in front of Joe's house. She sat there for long moments, trying to drum up whatever vestiges of courage were still inside of her.

Stop being a chicken, Molly. Sometimes to get what you want you have to take a chance.

She opened her car door and quietly shut it, began walking up the long sidewalk leading to Joe's front door.

The feel of her phone vibrating in her hand startled her.

Breathing deeply to calm her racing heart, Molly tapped the answer icon.

"Hello?"

"Molly, this is Joe. Are you at home right now?"

"Well, I…"

"Just stay there. I'm coming over."

"But…"

"I'll see you in a few minutes."

"But Joe, I'm outsi…"

Just then his front door opened and he stepped out of the house.

"…side of your house."

He looked up, his expression one of surprise.

"Molly?" He still held the phone to his ear.

Molly ended the call and tossed her phone into her purse.

"What are you doing here?"

"I, ah," okay, this had been a much better idea when she'd been alone, "wanted to talk to you."

He finally ended the call, swallowed. "About what?"

"Can we talk about this inside?"

Joe pushed the door open. "Sorry. I'm just surprised is all."

Her smile felt shaky. "You and me both."

She closed the distance between the two of them and stepped inside. The quiet *snick* of the door closing reverberated like a shot gun blast inside of her brain. She tried to swallow past the sudden lump in her throat.

Joe was standing there, leaning with his back against the door like he didn't have a care in the world. This was so not going to be easy.

Might as well get it over with, Moll.

"There's something I need to tell you."

"I think you just stole my line," she thought she heard him say under his breath. Louder, though, he said, "Okay."

She took a deep breath and closed her eyes. "I'm screwed up, Joe."

"I wouldn't go that far."

Her eyelids popped open. "But I am. With the childhood I had, it's hard not to be screwed up. Having a stepfather like I had, it's hard not to be messed up. Even though now I know he was a cruel, sadistic bastard, it's hard to erase the damage he caused. When you add that to my ex cheating on me and Benjamin never really wanting me emotionally, well, my confidence in men—and myself—isn't very high.

"And then you come along, and you seem too good to be true and then I find out you essentially have a kid…I felt like you'd lied to me and betrayed my trust, and that hurt like hell.

"The thing is, though, I know you didn't purposely hurt me. You're just not that kind of guy. And honestly, I've been using Annabelle as an excuse, a shield of sorts because I've been so scared to let myself love you because I'm not sure you'll be there to catch me when I fall."

She took a hesitant step towards him. "I'm tired of being scared, Joe."

He stood there, simply stared at her for long moments before speaking. "I should have told you about Annabelle sooner, but the timing never seemed to be right."

Her smile was shaky. "Fair enough. So we both admit we messed up."

"Yes. And for the record, I'm just as scared as you are."

"Somehow I find that hard to believe."

He pushed away from the door. "Oh, I am. See, I think I started to fall for you that first night at Barnes & Noble, and here you were trying to get over your best friend by dating all these men. And there I was, wanting you so badly I felt like I was going crazy, but you kept holding me at a distance."

"It's a self-preservation thing."

He snorted. "No kidding."

She smiled as he closed the remaining distance between the two of them. Their gazes caught and held, and she felt her breath hitch in her throat. The smile slowly died.

Joe reached out and ran the pad of his thumb over the curve of her jaw line. "Your ex-stepfather was wrong, by the way. You're gorgeous, and I'll tell you that every single day if I have to, if that's what it takes to erase his words from your mind. And you're not lazy or worthless. You're one of the most hard-working, intelligent, worthwhile people I've ever known."

He cupped her face with both hands, gently, tenderly. "Furthermore, your ex and Benjamin are obviously idiots, but their loss is definitely my gain."

"Mine, too," she whispered, for the first time realizing that their stupidity had been her gain.

"I'm falling in love with you, Molly. That's what I was going to tell you. I'm falling head over heels for you. I'm falling for your brain and your smile and your curves. I'm falling for your sense of humor and your way with words and the way you kiss me. I'm even falling for your neuroses—they're what make you you. I love the fact that you wear sexy underwear just because they make you feel good, and I love how you look when you're wearing nothing but that. And I know this isn't going to be easy. I know this situation isn't ideal, or what you were looking for, but we can make it work. We owe it to ourselves to at least try to make it work, and I'm not willing to just let you walk away from this, from us, without giving it our best shot."

Molly's nose was burning and her eyes were stinging, a sure sign she was about to cry. But she didn't care. Instead, she let it out, because for once these were happy tears.

These were relief tears. Tears of joy and pain and fear and all the pent-up emotions she was sick and tired of burying inside.

"Oh, God. I've said the wrong thing. Don't cry, Molly." Joe's voice was panicked.

She shook her head and smiled. "They're happy tears."

She stood on tiptoe and kissed him gently. "For the record, I'm falling for you, too. That's what I was coming over here to tell you. Well, that and the whole me being screwed up thing and that I'm sorry I've ignored you the past week or so. But since that apparently doesn't bother you, I think this is a much better conversation."

He chuckled. "So you're willing to really give this a shot?"

She nodded. "We would be stupid not to."

"Thank God. Maybe now I can get all those PTA moms to stop pinching my ass during meetings."

She raised her eyebrows. "You're in the PTA?"

"Yeah. Sometimes I wish I wasn't, though. You have no idea how nasty those moms can get."

"Oh really?"

"Uh huh. I've been propositioned so many times I've lost count."

She wrapped her arms around his neck. "Well, I guess you're just going to have to set them straight now, since you're a taken man and all."

He rested his hands on her hips and pulled her closer. "One mom made the most outrageous suggestion last week."

"Hmmm?" She managed to get out, as Joe had started nuzzling the side of her neck.

He whispered in her ear.

"She really suggested that?"

"Mmmhmmm."

"Sounds interesting."

He laughed. "I figured you would say that."

"Unfortunately that isn't a toy I happen to own."

He ran his tongue along the outer shell of her ear. "Damn."

She shivered as goose bumps skittered across her body. "We can order one, though. I've always wondered that one would feel like."

He nipped gently at her earlobe. "Sounds like a plan to me."

Molly turned her head and fastened her mouth to his. Their kiss was slow and sweet at first, but quickly caught fire. Their tongues danced together and she pushed her body as close to his as possible.

After long moments, she pulled away just enough to whisper, "I'm guessing we have the house to ourselves right now?"

"All night. Annabelle's at another slumber party and won't be back until tomorrow afternoon."

He kissed her again, and Molly felt herself sinking under, into him, and for the first time in her life the sensation didn't scare her. This time it was just Molly and Joe. No thoughts. No worries. No inhibitions. No insecurities. It was freeing in a way she'd never imagined it would be.

They broke the kiss and Joe looked down at her, his eyes heavy-lidded and a darker green than usual, but filled with all the things she'd never known she'd wanted or needed. Silently, he started backing her out of the foyer. Her purse dropped to the floor with a heavy thud. Vaguely, she heard the clank of her keys as they hit the ground. The backs of her knees finally came into contact with something soft yet firm, unmovable.

She looked over her shoulder and saw it was the couch.

He grinned at her. "Later we'll christen the kitchen island, I promise."

She burst into laughter. Of course he'd remembered

that. "So is that your way of saying we're now going to christen every piece of furniture you own?"

"I love how you always manage to read my mind."

She kissed him again and they tumbled onto the couch, laughing and removing each other's clothing like they couldn't get naked fast enough. As his hands and then his mouth ran over her body, all thoughts fled her mind. Instead, there was just blissful quiet. Just her and Joe and the way they made each other feel.

He was working his magic with his fingers again, making her moan and writhe on the couch underneath him. God, she wanted him inside of her.

"Shit!"

He stopped what he was doing and looked up at her, an expression of worry spread across his face. "What? What happened? Did I hurt you?"

"No, no. Condoms."

He grinned. "I have some in my bedroom. I bought them after the other night, hoping I'd get you naked again soon."

"Thank God." She pulled him up and kissed him thoroughly. "Maybe we should make our way to your bedroom, then."

He nibbled on her bottom lip. "Only if you leave on those heels."

"You like the heels, huh?"

"You have no idea how sexy they are."

She raised her eyebrows.

"Okay, maybe you do."

He got up from the couch and she followed, their steps quick and hurried. Not quickly enough they were tumbling onto his bed, their mouths fused together and hands everywhere.

Joe leaned over and reached into his nightstand, took out a black foil packet and ripped it open.

"Here, let me." She took the condom from him and rolled it on, savoring the feel of him in her hand.

He gently pushed her back down onto the mattress and kissed her, soft and slow. Molly felt his weight settle between her thighs, could feel him rubbing against her. She moaned, and he moved so that he was poised to enter her.

"Are you sure about this?"

She wrapped her legs around his waist and nodded before pulling his body closer. He slid in slowly, and her eyes drifted shut. God, he felt good.

The air in the room grew thick and heavy, their breathing labored. Molly's hands were fisted on Joe's back, and she kept moving her legs further and further up his back.

"Oh, God, there."

He kissed her and slid into her again, the same way he had the last time. *Jesus.* And then she felt his finger on that magical bundle of nerves, rubbing in slow, circular motions.

She moaned into his mouth, arched her hips and let herself go completely.

Her orgasm ripped through her, curled her toes in her red high heels. She dug her nails into his back and gasped for air.

Vaguely, she heard Joe call out her name, felt his body stiffen above hers and realized, as though from far away, that he'd just come.

Slowly she floated back to herself. Her heart rate eventually slowed down and she finally got her breathing back under control. Molly kissed the side of Joe's neck, his jaw, his cheek, his ear before kissing him on the mouth.

They lay there for long moments before Joe finally pulled away, got up and went to the bathroom to clean up. Molly toed off her shoes and pulled the covers over her, suddenly chilly.

Joe returned to the bedroom and smiled at her, climbed

into bed with her and drew her flush against his body.

"Stay the night?"

She smiled. "I'll stay every night if you ask nicely enough."

"Stay every night?"

She nodded her head and closed her eyes, feeling content and peaceful. "I'll stay every night."

"Good. You have to promise to wear those heels every now and then, though."

She laughed. "You've got it."

EPILOGUE

Benjamin stood under a palm tree, a hat shading his face and his arms crossed over his chest as he watched the small group about two hundred yards away. The feeling of sand in between his feet and his flip flops grated, whereas usually it would have made him feel free.

In the past year and a half, everything had grated, though.

The words of the preacher floated towards him, muffled by the waves crashing into the shore and the sound of gulls crying out overhead. He barely managed to not close his eyes when the man said, "You may now kiss the bride."

As much as he didn't want to see this, he felt like he needed to. The dull ache in his chest and the throbbing in his head only helped to amplify the fact that this was a punishment he deserved.

His stomach churned as Molly and Joe consummated their vows with the traditional kiss. The small group of family and friends that was there to witness the nuptials applauded, and the newlyweds finally came up for air. Even from a distance, he could feel Molly's love for Joe, and Joe's love for Molly.

His former best friend beamed up at her new husband, the ocean breeze tossing her hair around her head. Something in his heart lurched, and he wondered if he was going to be sick.

Again, nothing less than he deserved.

Before anyone could spot him, he turned away from the wedding party and headed back down the beach towards his hotel. He hadn't seen or spoken to Molly since that day she'd left him at Cotton Patch, and he doubted she wanted to see him on what was the happiest day of her life.

He'd been an idiot, had treated her like crap and taken her for granted. He'd figured she would always be there. Waiting for him to be ready.

As he slid onto a stool at the hotel bar, the thought occurred to him that she was happier with Joe than she ever would have been with him.

He rubbed his chest, the thought hitting him where it counted.

He ordered a Bud Light, and took a drink once it was placed in front of him. The hell of it was, everything she'd said to him that day had been true. And furthermore, the things she hadn't said but that had been all over her face were also true.

No one deserved love more than Molly.

No one.

He lifted his beer in a silent toast. *Here's to you, Molly. The best damned woman I've ever known. Sorry I was such a dick.*

Wait. That didn't sound quite right.

Here's to you, Molly. I hope you've found everything you wanted and needed.

He finished his beer, set the empty bottle on the bar along with a handful of dollar bills and walked out of the hotel and into the sunshine.

Acknowledgments

This book would not have been possible without the tremendous support of the Seton Hill University Writing Popular Fiction program. The end product is SO much better than what I submitted for that very first workshop. Many, many thanks go out to my mentors: the wonderful Barbara Miller and amazing Victoria Thompson; and my critique partners: Stephanie, Jen, and Monica. You ladies rock! Also, a big thank you to Maria Snyder and Mary SanGiovanni for being so tough on me in that first critique session—and then approaching me afterwards and helping me talk through and process everything you'd said. I will never forget your advice or support.

Like I mentioned in the dedication, I never would have been a part of the SHUWPF program if it hadn't been for my brain twin—Shara Saunsaucie White—convincing me I had nothing to lose other than postage by applying. Going through grad school with you was beyond fun. Oh, and to Betsy Whitt and Sherry Peters, I can never thank y'all enough for your friendship, encouragement, brainstorming, and laughter-filled car rides while we got lost on the turnpike (rollin' with my homies forever, yo!). And Traci Castleberry, thank you for being kind enough to share your hotel room (and employee discount) with me. All of you have been amazing friends, and it really sucks that we all live so far apart and don't get to see each other more often.

Big Girls Need Love Too has had a long, winding path to publication. I've gone back and forth on whether or not I should publish this over the years, have submitted it to New York agents and publishers, and got close to publishing it at one point, but the timing was never quite right. For writers, all of our books are our babies. This book, however, is the closest to me and the hardest to let go of. I have my husband to thank (as always) for gently nudging me, loving me, and believing in me enough for me to finally feel like it's time to push this particular baby out of the nest, so to speak.

And to all the big girls and not so big girls out there—we all need and deserve love. Don't ever let yourself forget that.

Aubrey

P.S. Love what you read? Share the love and leave a review and/or rating so other readers can find books to read!

Want to Read more from Aubrey?
Check out her Devils Ranch Series, featuring
Between the Seams and
Baseball and Other Lessons. Also, be sure to keep
an eye out for the next two books in the series!

Keep reading for excerpts from the books readers
are calling "a homerun" and "a grand slam!"

Excerpt: Between the Seams

What happens when life throws you a curveball?

Chase Roberts is the quintessential Good Guy. Attractive, athletic, intelligent and successful, the former college baseball star and one-time major league prospect is the kind of guy any woman would love to take home to Mama. Except there's one small problem: Chase has never really gotten over his former best friend—and first love—Jolene "Jo" Westwood, who broke his heart as a teen. Now, all grown up with two thriving businesses, Chase has enough to worry about.

Jo Westwood just wants to come home to Del Rio, Texas, help nurse her grandmother back to health and go back to her calm--okay, boring and lonely--life in Austin once the summer's over. Unfortunately (fortunately?), her best-laid plans come to a screaming halt the moment she accidentally bumps into her former best friend--and first love--Chase Roberts in the feminine hygiene aisle. The cute boy she once knew has become a HOT man. A hot man who seemingly hates her. Great.

As the long, hot summer drags on, Chase and Jo find themselves spending more and more time together, resurrecting not-so dead feelings and putting the past behind them. Unfortunately, summer only lasts so long, and even love may not be able to survive long-held secrets that threaten to tear them apart.

Chapter One

"Yo, Chase, did you hear a word of what I just said?"

Chase Roberts snapped out of his reverie and glanced over at Owen Daniels, his best friend, business partner and occasional pain in the ass. "Sure."

Owen snorted. "No, you didn't."

A pretty blonde entered the building across the street, and Chase fought the overwhelming urge to follow her. "Did you see the blonde across the street just now?" He asked instead.

Owen opened the driver's side door of his car. "I thought you'd sworn off women? Called them all second-hand groupies or something like that."

Chase looked at the building—Mitchell's Drug Store—one more time before climbing into the passenger seat of the low-slung Mustang. "I didn't say they were all second-hand groupies. There just happen to be more than I would like."

"Must be tough, being chased by hot, scantily-clad women all the time."

Owen pulled away from the curb and Chase fought the urge to turn and watch to see if the blonde came out of the drug store.

"It is when the only reason they're chasing after me is because of my brother." Chase's brother, Matt, was Mr. Baseball. The long-time ace for the Texas Wranglers, Matt was well-loved in their hometown of Del Rio, Texas. So well-loved the high school baseball fields now bore his name. Without a sponsorship. So well-loved that he had his own menu item at Francine's Diner. So well-loved that there was a freaking Matt Roberts Day, complete with a downtown parade. In November. After the World Series and before Winter Ball started. Hell, his brother had been given keys to the damned city.

As much as Chase loved his brother, he got tired of the groupies who decided that if they couldn't have Matt they would just settle for Chase. After one too many stories posted about him on internet message boards and questionable websites, Chase had decided about a year ago that maybe a female hiatus was in order.

Besides, he had a business to run, and even with his last name he still wanted to project the image of responsible, trustworthy businessman—not wannabe playboy.

"Boo-freaking-hoo."

Chase ignored Owen's sarcasm. "Anyway. Did you happen to see her?"

"Who? The curvy blonde going into Mitchell's?"

"Yes. That one. Apparently you did."

Owen shrugged. "She looked like she had a nice ass."

"She looked familiar."

Owen turned into the parking lot of Roberts Ventures, LLC, and swung into the space next to Chase's pickup. "Previous one-night stand?"

Chase snorted. "No. Definitely not one of those." Hell, Chase could count on one hand the number of one-night stands he'd had over his entire lifetime. His brother's groupies just made it sound like he was, well, a player.

They got out of Owen's Mustang and entered the building. Chase's executive assistant and all-around office goddess looked up and smiled at Chase. As soon as Kimberly's gaze landed on Owen, her smile quickly turned to a frown.

Chase didn't know why Kim didn't like Owen, and no amount of gentle prying had managed to get the information out of her. "Good morning, Kim."

"Mornin', Chase. We got the Sutton contract in, and Frank Wimbly called earlier, said he found a spot out by the lake that he would like to take a look at."

Chase nodded. "Thanks. I'll take a look at the Sutton contract and give Frank a call back."

He made his way to his office, shaking his head as the sound of Kim scolding Owen could be heard from down the hall.

Never a dull moment he thought as he got back to work.

Jolene Westwood was usually pretty hard to embarrass. As a high school guidance counselor, she'd heard—and discussed—some of the most embarrassing things human beings experienced. From high school crushes to missed periods to kids grappling with their sexuality, she thought she'd heard—and seen—it all.

But embarrassment was much easier to deal with when it wasn't your own, and unfortunately she was currently knee-deep in it on this lovely evening.

She'd just been standing there, in front of the pads, tampons and Monistat cream that lined the back wall of the Del Rio Walmart, debating small pack versus value pack, when she accidentally backed up into someone.

A solid someone who radiated warmth and *man*.

Slowly, she turned around, her hands still paused mid-air, holding the bright yellow and blue boxes up like some sort of offering.

Or maybe as a big fat red light.

No pun intended.

Her gaze wandered up from the box of Crest toothpaste in one hand to the center of what was definitely a polo-clad male chest and up to a jaw shadowed with dark stubble. Firm lips. Slightly crooked nose. Brown eyes that made her think of warm, cinnamony Mexican chocolate. Dark eyebrows. Dark brown, almost black hair that curled out from under a blue YETI coolers ball cap.

Jo swallowed a gasp—or, more realistically, a longing-filled sigh—and took a quick step back.

Chase Roberts.

Childhood best friend.

Teenage crush.

The boy she'd long ago said goodbye to.

Her stomach flip-flopped as she slowly lowered her hands and her gaze. Mentally drank him in.

Six-one.

Two hundred pounds.

1.87 ERA.

At least, those had been his college stats. If anything, he looked like he might have gained a couple of inches, and whatever he weighed, it sure looked like it was pure muscle.

Realizing she was staring like an idiot, she mentally shook herself and somehow found her voice. "I am so sorry, Chase. I didn't see you behind me."

Stupid, Jolene. Of course you couldn't see him behind you, it isn't like you have eyes in the back of your head.

His melted chocolate gaze traveled up and down her body before settling on her face. "I'm sorry, you seem to have me at a disadvantage—you know my name, but I don't know yours."

Jo smiled, even though she was cringing on the inside, and she fought back the sense of disappointment his words evoked. They'd been friends for years and he didn't remember her? Hell, her mother had tried to end his parents' marriage, until the truth finally came out years later that Chandra Sommers had never slept with Bo Roberts. Ends up Sarah Roberts had known that for far longer than Jo had—Chandra was more than happy to let her daughter believe the worst. And he didn't remember her?

Serves you right, for ending things the way you did.

Her voice tinged with the disappointment she apparently couldn't hide, Jo responded. "Sorry. I've changed some since the last time we saw each other. Jolene Westwood."

Chase's brows drew together over those hot chocolate eyes. "I feel awful, but I don't remember a Jolene Westwo—wait a second. Jo? Jo Sommers?"

Jo could feel her cheeks warming and knew she was probably beet red by now. Could this be any more awkward? "Sorry. I changed my name a few years back, after my parents died."

"Westwood is your grandma's name, right?"

Jolene nodded and swallowed. "Yeah."

Lame, Jolene, lame.

Chase stood before her, a brown-eyed god with a 92 mile per hour fastball and a nasty curveball, looking for all the world like a pitcher who couldn't understand a single one of the signals the catcher was sending him.

Jo. Jo Sommers. His childhood friend and teenage crush. The captain of the cheerleading squad and smartest girl in the room (and hell, their class).

He'd known it was her as soon as she'd turned around and allowed that sea glass gaze to travel up his body oh so slowly. He'd never be able to forget those eyes——they'd haunted him for so long they were a permanent part of his psyche at this point.

She may have changed a little bit—her blonde hair was softer, longer and wavier than he remembered, and she'd gained some curves since he'd last seen her when they were in college, but he sure as hell would never be able to forget her.

So why was he playing stupid now?

She'd fueled more than one of his teenage fantasies, even after she'd suddenly stopped talking to him their freshman year of high school. As a teen he wondered if it had to do with the health issues—and eventual scarring—he'd had as a kid and young teen. Had she been embarrassed to be around him?

As an adult, he realized there could have been other reasons, but even a cocky teenage athlete can be felled by one simple brush off from the prettiest girl in school.

"So, uh, what brings you back to town?"

Smooth, Roberts, real smooth.

Worry briefly turned those sea glass eyes stormy, but the expression was gone so fast he wondered if he'd imagined it.

"Gran had a hip replaced. She refused to go to a rehab facility, and pretty much ordered me to come take care of her." A small grin played at the corners of Jo's generous mouth, and for a brief second Chase was reminded of the girl she used to be. The one who'd been his playmate and confidante.

"How's she doing?"

Jo waved her hand, and then blushed as she looked at the box she still held.

"I'm really not trying to accost you with tampons, I swear."

Chase barely managed to choke back the laughter that threatened to escape. "Well, at least they're not used."

Jesus, Roberts, that was awful.

Her blush deepened, and the chuckle that had been threatening to escape somehow managed to rumble out. Jo shook her head, smiled, and tossed the box into her cart.

"I'm glad to see you still have a sophomoric sense of humor, Chase."

"At times, yes." Unfortunately.

Their gazes met, held, and then a slow smile bloomed over Jo's face before she, too, was laughing. "How about we try this again?" She held out her hand. "Hey, Chase! Nice to see you again."

Chase wrapped his hand around hers, and he swore he felt tingles shoot up his arm. "Jo, it's good to see you, too."

Unsettled, he dropped her hand and stepped back. A look of confusion flitted across her pretty face before she once again replaced it with an odd, too-placid-to-be-real smile.

Had she felt it, too?

"Well, uh, I better get going." She gestured to her cart, which held a small amount of groceries and toiletries. "Gran's waiting for me to get back so I can cook supper. Can't let her starve."

Chase took another step back, feeling the need to put some amount of distance between them. He flexed his hand, still feeling slight tingles in his fingertips. "No, can't let her starve."

Jo began to push her cart away, and before he could take the words back he blurted out, "We should do lunch some time. Or supper. Catch up. For old time's sake."

God, he sounded like an effing idiot. Catch up for old time's sake? Yeah, because *that* sounded like a brilliant idea.

An expression Chase couldn't identify clouded Jo's eyes before it, too, was gone almost as quickly as it came. "Um, sure." She nodded her head once, her wavy blonde hair falling over one shoulder. "We'll have to do that."

Chase nodded in ascent and shoved his hands into his pockets. Jo shot him one last glance before turning from him. Chase allowed himself to enjoy the view as she walked away.

Couldn't not appreciate it, really, as it was a damned fine view. The same damned fine view he'd seen just this morning walking into Mitchell's Drug Store.

"Jolene, is that you?"

Jo set down her grocery bags and blew a strand of hair out of her eyes. "Yes, Gran, it's me."

"Good, that rehab woman just left and I'm starving."

Jo rolled her eyes. "I think that rehab woman has a name."

"Yes, the Devil's Harlot!" Gran shouted back from the living room.

Jo sighed and yelled back. "She's not a harlot, Gran." Who even used the word "harlot" anymore? "She works for Val Verde Regional Medical Center. Last I checked, Satan wasn't on their payroll."

Gran harrumphed from the living room. Jo finished putting up the groceries and walked into the living room. "Did she make you do something new today?"

Her grandmother sat in a big, somewhat comfortable chair. She waved a hand in the air dismissively. "Just a new exercise. Nothing too bad."

"Then why the name-calling, Gran?"

Gran gestured towards the flat screen TV mounted on the wall across from her. "She was lusting after that Roberts boy. Acting like a cat in heat."

"Roberts boy? Chase? Why was Chase on TV?" Jo's mind went back to the embarrassing scene in Walmart, and realized it was a good thing Gran couldn't read *her* thoughts. *Chase Roberts all grown up was definitely worth lusting after.*

Gran waved the remote. "No, not the sick one, bless his heart. The older one."

Sick? Was Gran referring to Chase's childhood illness, or did he only look like the picture of health? Hot, hot health.

"And we're back at the top of the eighth inning, and Wranglers ace Matt Roberts is back out on the mound."

Jo looked at the television and saw Chase's older brother, Matt, readying the mound for another inning. The camera zoomed in on his face, and Jo had to admit that he was definitely attractive. Always had been. Problem was, he'd always known it, too.

While Chase had been popular and well-liked in his own right, Matt had always had that "it" factor that just drew people to him. Throw in obnoxiously good looks and talent that had scouts looking at him as a freshman, and you had a combination that was hard for any girl to resist.

"The PT was openly lusting after Matt in front of you?"

Gran pursed her lips. "The shameless hussy wouldn't shut up about him. Went on and on about how 'hot' he is. Cat in heat, I tell you!"

Jo loved her Gran, she truly did, and while Jo was by no means remotely promiscuous, her grandmother's old-fashioned views sometimes came across as a little, well, old-fashioned.

"Well, Gran, in all fairness he's not an unattractive man."

"Don't you start acting like a hussy too, Jolene!"

Jo sighed. "Gran, just because a woman thinks a man is attractive, that doesn't make her a hussy. Come on, you thought Pawpaw was handsome before you married him, didn't you?"

Gran's eyes misted over and a small smile tugged at her lips. "Oh, your Pawpaw was so handsome in his dress blues. He had the most beautiful eyes—that's where you get yours, you know—and the sweetest smile. Curly black hair. Such a fine figure the first time I saw him. I knew right then I was going to marry him."

Jo smiled. "You just proved my point, Gran."

The older woman shrugged and absently massaged her hip. "Always been too smart for you own damned good."

Jo leaned over and kissed her grandmother's wrinkled cheek. "And you know you wouldn't have it any other way, young woman."

Gran couldn't hide her smile. "Don't go getting a big head, young lady. Now what's for supper?"

Later that night, feeling restless and crampy and borderline maudlin, Jo climbed out of the full size bed in the room that had been her's as a teen and pulled a box from the top shelf of the closet. She set it on the floor, brushed the dust off and opened it.

Inside were high school mementos.

Her Homecoming mum from her senior year, the bells still shiny but missing a glittery letter from her name. A set of royal blue and white pom poms. The corsage Billy Walther gave her for senior prom, the roses dried and in a protective plastic case, the lilac elastic band's color still as vivid as the day he'd slid it on to her wrist. There were other pieces of flotsam and jetsam, memories of years gone by.

A newspaper article talking about how she'd made valedictorian. The notecards from her graduation speech. An old report card. Her acceptance letter to Baylor. Notes she and her best friend Jenn McDonnel had passed during algebra.

At the bottom of the box lay her senior memory book and four yearbooks. She withdrew all of them and returned to the bed, leaving the other items on the floor where she'd left them.

She wasn't sure what had her feeling nostalgic. Maybe it was being back here in Del Rio, sleeping in the same room she'd slept in as a teen far too often when things went downhill at home. Maybe it was seeing Chase tonight. Or maybe Aunt Flo was just a mean bitch who made her do crazy things.

She opened the memory book, smiling at the memories and the thoughts of an eighteen-year-old girl hell-bent on changing the world. Or at least her little corner of it.

10 Years From Now I...
Will be Oprah's go-to psychologist on all of her shows
Will own my own practice
Will be married with two kids—boy and girl—to a gorgeous man who owns his own business, makes a lot of money and will never cheat on me
Will be a great mom who never cheats on her husband or abandons her kids
Will be living somewhere super cool, like New York City or Chicago or San Francisco
Will be making a six-figure salary with no debt, a nice house and driving a BMW
Will no longer feel the need to be perfect
Will know what love really is
Will be a member of the Junior League
Will be gearing up to run for office

Funny how the only one of those things that had happened was number seven.

Jo brushed away a lone tear that rolled down her cheek, hating herself for feeling maudlin but realizing that if she was there was probably a good reason for it.

She hadn't gone on to become Oprah's therapist, and instead of opening her own practice had decided to help out high school kids. God knew as a high school counselor she certainly wasn't making a six-figure salary, her student loan

debt was mind-boggling and her dreams of owning a shiny
new BMW had been replaced with the reality of driving
a Ford Fusion. Mr. Right still hadn't come along, and at
thirty-two she was beginning to wonder if he ever would.
The only guy she'd loved as an adult had been shipped off
to Afghanistan, and he'd ended things before leaving the
States. And she certainly wasn't a member of the Junior
League or planning on running for office any time soon.
As for her current town......well, she sure hadn't pictured
herself back in Del Rio taking care of her grandmother, but
she supposed her adopted town of Austin was pretty cool.
At least that's what people and dozens of weekly Top Ten
lists always told her.

Jo continued to flip through the memory book, smiling
at the photos and random pieces of high school life she'd
glued to the pages. Towards the back, folded up and tucked
underneath a photo of her, Jenn and Chase, was a lined
piece of notebook paper, which she unfolded.

Dear Chase,
I'm sorry.
I'm sorry I haven't been talking to you much. I think
I've hurt your feelings. I never meant to do that.
But I can't. I can't talk to you knowing that my mom
has a thing for your dad. It's weird and gross and makes me
embarrassed and ashamed.
My dad doesn't care who she sleeps with. I think the
whole town knows that by now. He probably doesn't care if
I sleep with someone, either.
But I'm not my mom. And I can't be around you be-
cause I'm too embarrassed and hurt and afraid you'll hate
me.
You're my best friend. You, Jenn and me. We're the
Three Amigos. I don't want to hurt you.
I'm so sorry.

Love,
Jo

She folded the paper back up and placed it in the book again, tucked neatly under the photo of her, Jenn and Chase. They'd been going into the ninth grade, the best of friends since elementary school. Until that awful day when Jo had overheard her mom on the phone with Chase's dad. The things her mom had said had made her hot with embarrassment and shame, and even though she didn't think Chase's dad would ever cheat on his wife, Jo still felt awful and as if it was somehow her fault. If she and Chase hadn't been such good friends, her mom might not have ever met his dad. So she'd done what seemed best to a fourteen-year-old girl—she'd distanced herself from her best friend even though it had killed her.

She'd written the note to him to try to explain, but in the end had chickened out. She couldn't. She was too embarrassed and ashamed and didn't want Chase to think she was like her mom.

Instead, she'd folded the note and tucked it into her diary. That night, after eating supper with her parents and being told not to eat so much—that "thinness is perfection!"—by the woman everyone thought of as The Easy Mom, was the first time Jo made herself throw up.

Want to keep reading? Purchase *Between the Seams* now, available at the following retailers:

Amazon
Barnes & Noble
Kobo
iBooks

Excerpt: Baseball and Other Lessons

The hardest lessons are a lot like a line drive to the heart.

Texas Wranglers' ace Matt Roberts had it all: fame, fortune, his dream job. Until one line drive to the head ended it. Well, at least that was the case according to Twitter. Needing time to let his fractured skull heal—along with his psyche—Matt heads home to Del Rio, Texas, with one goal in mind—getting back to baseball. Unfortunately a certain redhead keeps driving him to distraction.

Seventh grade English teacher Jenn McDonnell is not happy that Matt's come home and is staying with his brother—aka her best friend—while his thick skull heals. And she certainly could do without all the questions their group of friends suddenly has, like, "Why do you hate Matt so much?" Yeah, she totally has no desire to answer that one.

Unfortunately for Jenn the questions aren't letting up, and unfortunately for Matt he can't get Jenn off of his mind. Can Jenn put past hurt aside and teach Matt that there's more to life than baseball? Furthermore, can Matt convince Jenn that this relationship isn't doomed to strike out?

Chapter One

MATT ROBERTS' CAREER ENDED with a tweet.

@ESPN: Sources confirm @MattRobertsTX career likely over. 35yo pitcher suffered cracked skull, brain bleed. Surgery successful.

Next came the *Deadspin* article.

ESPN Reporting Matt Roberts, Texas' Ace, Out Forever

Followed by the piece from Bleacher Report.

Texas' Matt Roberts' Career Over, Next Steps for Texas to Fill Gap

Sports Illustrated jumped on it next, followed by the *Sporting News*, *Yahoo! Sports*, *The Dallas Morning News* and *SB Nation*. From there, the barrage was endless as social media took one stupid—and highly inaccurate to his knowledge—tweet as gospel.

Matt's head pounded. He wasn't sure if it was because of his stitched up head or if his blood pressure was getting too high. When he noticed his hands were shaking, he figured it was probably his blood pressure.

He sat back on his brother, Chase's couch, closed his eyes and took a few deep breaths, trying to find some internal peace. Instead, all he could find was that damned tweet. Sighing, he opened his eyes and looked back at his open laptop, giving the offending tweet the evil eye, before picking up his cell phone and dialing his agent.

Darrin answered on the first ring. "Hey, Matt. Don't

worry, man, we're on it. I don't know who ESPN's sources are, but they're wrong. We haven't heard anything from the front office other than they want you to have a full recovery and that your health comes first."

Matt sighed and pinched the bridge of his nose. "Dammit, Darrin, where the fuck did this shit come from? I've barely been out of the hospital for a week. Nobody knows the future of my career right now, especially not some low-life who'll give crap information to ESPN."

"I know. Like I said, we're trying to track down the source. I also have a call in to Reed. Hopefully I'll hear something soon and can get this mess cleared up."

Reed Thornhill was the team's president and general manager, and the person who would ultimately decide Matt's professional fate. He and Reed had a pretty good relationship, and Matt couldn't see him making such a definite statement without having all the facts. And the facts were, Matt couldn't even begin rehab until the stitches were out, and after that he had to be cleared by his neurologist. It could take weeks, if not months.

"Thanks, Darrin."

"No problem, man. So how are you doing?"

Matt blew out a breath. How was he doing? He was going fucking stir crazy. That's how he was doing. "Fucking crazy, D. I'm bored out of my mind."

"You know you could have stayed in Dallas, in the comfort of your own condo and all the take out you desire at your fingertips."

Matt snorted. "I know. Mom was worried sick, and I knew she'd be calling me multiple times a day. I also didn't feel like having the media breathing down my neck."

Darrin changed the subject. "How's the ranch doing?"

Matt, along with Chase, Chase's friend Owen, and Darrin were all owners of a managed game ranch just north of Del Rio, on the Devils River. "You know about as much as I do. Chase and Owen do a great job keeping up with it, and Daniel runs the place flawlessly. I'm hoping to get up there some time soon, just have to have clearance to drive."

"Any word on when that'll be?"

"I have an appointment in San Antonio next Monday. Hopefully he'll give me the go-ahead then."

"Keep me up to date. In the meantime, I've gotta go— lunch with Mercer to discuss the contract extension the Cowboys offered him."

Clint Mercer was the Dallas Cowboys' all-pro tight end, Darrin's client, Matt's friend, and all-around good guy. "Getting ready to milk them dry?"

"As dry as I can." Darrin chuckled. "Anyway. Stay off of Twitter and message boards for a while, and I'll call you as soon as I know something."

"Thanks, D." Matt ended the call and tossed the phone back onto the couch beside him. He rested his head against the plush back and stared up at the ceiling. God, he was bored.

Needing to do something—anything—he texted Chase.

> Matt: I've gotta get out and do some-
> thing. I'm losing my mind.
> Chase: Dude, you're supposed to take it
> easy.
> Matt: I know, but if I take it too easy I'm
> going to jump off a bridge. I just need to
> get out.
> Chase: Whatever. We were planning on
> going to April's tonight. I guess you can
> tag along.
> Matt: Great. And thanks.

Jenn McDonnell surreptitiously watched Matt as she and Owen played a game of pool in the corner of their usual group's favorite bar, silently cursing her best friend Chase for letting his older brother tag along.

The guy was a jerk, and she so did not want to be around him.

She hadn't always felt that way. Once upon a time they'd been friends. Well, kind of. They'd once gotten along okay, sort of like siblings but not quite. As kids he'd teased her and made her laugh, and she'd almost enjoyed hanging out with him.

Somewhere along the way, though, that had changed. Their family and friends sometimes pried a little too much, curious as to the sudden shift in emotions. She would just shrug her shoulders and say something flippant, or that maybe it was the fact that since he'd made it to the majors eleven years ago he'd rarely come back home to see his family (and Jenn had it on good authority that Sarah Roberts missed her "baby boy"). Sometimes she'd say it was because he came across as an arrogant dick, like being blessed with a ninety-eight mile per hour fastball and a nasty slider somehow made him better than the mere mortals who wore his jersey and cheered his name.

Somewhere along the way, she'd gotten pretty good at evading the truth.

So she would put up with him—when she had to—because Chase was his brother and one of her best friends. Like a brother, really. And tonight she was putting up with Matt more than she wanted to because she was trying to give Chase and Jo—her other best friend since childhood—some time alone together to try and figure out whatever was going on between the two of them (they were obviously meant for each other, but still hadn't come to terms with that fact).

Speaking of…

From the corner of her eye, she saw Chase lead Jo out onto the dance floor, took note of the way they looked at each other and smiled. It may have been the night before the Fourth of July, but Jenn was willing to bet money that there would be fireworks tonight.

She missed her shot, turning the table over to Owen Daniels. As her other best friend—she really was lucky, wasn't she, to have three best friends?—lined up to take his shot, Jenn sipped from her margarita and tried to watch Matt without anyone noticing.

Even with his current crazy haircut, the man was hot. Her gaze kept wanting to skitter up to the stitches on the shaved side of his head—stitches that had happened after he'd been hit by a line drive and suffered a cracked skull and brain bleeding just a few weeks ago.

Looking at the stitches, though, did funny things to her stomach. She'd never been good with blood or injuries; they always made her feel squeamish and jittery inside. Seeing Matt's head—and remembering the moment the injury had happened since she, Chase, Jo and Owen had been watching the game together—made her uncomfortable.

It made her want to care.

Jenn sipped her margarita and focused her gaze on the row of cue sticks on the opposite wall.

"You can look at them, y'know."

Matt's voice, deep and low, a whisper against her ear, startled her. She jolted. Slushy liquid sloshed in the glass in her hand.

She took a half step to the side, away from him. "Look at what?" she asked, not looking at him.

"The stitches. My head."

She shrugged.

"Unless you're one of those women who gets turned on by pain. That shit's too kinky, even for me."

Jenn closed her eyes. Gritted her teeth. "They make me feel squeamish."

She could feel him beside her, hot and big and the epitome of Alpha Male. If he'd been a character in the Regency romances she loved to read, he most definitely would have been a rake.

And she? She would have been a wallflower. Or a governess.

A woman who most definitely did not garner attention from outrageously attractive males with hazel eyes, a lean body sculpted with muscle and lips that would make most women think about hot kisses and raunchy sex.

Jenn, though? She really just wanted to wipe the smirk from those sinful lips and not be aware of that muscled body.

"Stitches make you squeamish?"

Matt's voice was deep and seductive, like the promise of silk sheets, dark chocolate and a bottle of wine. She steeled herself against it, knowing that he was all too aware of his…potency.

"Yes," she ground out.

He sighed. "You're a strange woman, Jenn McDonnell."

She snorted. Owen lined up to pocket the eight ball. "I'm strange? You're the one walking around with half of your head shaved."

"It's different. I like it."

"Or you just haven't gotten to a stylist yet." She somehow doubted he was a Super Cuts sort of guy.

Owen sank the eight ball and asked, "You up for another game?"

"Nah. I'm gonna go grab another drink and make sure Jo and Chase haven't been arrested for public indecency or anything yet."

Jenn made her way through the bar, set her empty glass on a table holding other discarded drinks, and headed for the ladies' room. She sang along as the DJ switched from Josh Abbott Band's "Oh, Tonight" to "Fuzzy" by The Randy Rogers Band. The song's tale of drunken escapades always made her think of *The Hangover*, which never failed to make her smile.

She finished up in the bathroom and walked out to the main bar area, didn't see Jo and Chase and figured they'd stepped out to the back patio to get some air. She stepped up to the bar, ordered another margarita and walked back to the pool tables.

There were three women surrounding Matt, the same three that had fluttered around him when Jenn and Jo had first arrived. They'd scattered for a while, but apparently had decided that Jenn and Jo weren't competition.

Jenn stayed back, sipped her margarita as the fake redhead with fake boobs leaned into Matt and trailed her fingers down his chest and towards the waistband of his jeans. Owen caught her eye and shook his head as he lined up a shot. Jenn stifled a giggle.

The redhead's fingers trailed lower, dipped inside Matt's jeans. He rolled his eyes before removing her hand. Jenn couldn't hear what he said, but apparently Ms. Wandering Fingers wasn't too happy about it, if the mulish expression on her face was any indication.

Jenn was stifling laughter when someone tapped on her shoulder. She turned around and saw Jo, her cheeks flushed, eyes bright and hair slightly mussed. Jenn raised her eyebrows.

"I, uh, feel a migraine coming on. Chase is going to take me home. I'll see you later."

"Migraine, huh?" Jenn teased.

Jo's blush deepened, but Jenn could tell she was trying not to smile. "Yeah. A migraine."

Jenn laughed and hugged her best friend. "Well, I hope you find a way to get rid of it."

Jo did laugh then, before turning and walking away. Jenn contemplated the sugar crystals on the rim of her glass as a smile tugged at her lips.

She'd so been right about those fireworks tonight.

Matt watched the exchange between Jo and Jenn, vaguely aware of the three women surrounding him. He'd never been a huge fan of jersey chasers to begin with, but having them surround him in his hometown while he was on the disabled list seemed like a little too much even for him to take right now. Jo shook her head at something Jenn said, and Matt noted the tousled hair, swollen lips and beard burn on her neck.

Looked like little brother was finally going to score.

At least someone was.

Disgusted with his self-pitying thoughts, because, really, he was one of the best pitchers in the league with a healthy bank account, wise investments and women at his beck and call if he wanted them, Matt breathed deeply and tuned back in to the jersey chasers currently trying to score with him.

Yeah, that wasn't happening.

Even if he'd been interested, the doctor had specifically told him no sex. Apparently repetitive motions and strenuous activities could still cause complications with the damned head wound.

Fan-fucking-tastic.

"So, Mattie, how 'bout we go back to my place?" The brunette—Kara or Katie or Karma—asked with a pout as she trailed an index finger over his left bicep. "We could play pitcher and catcher, if you know what I mean."

Jesus. Talk about a bad pickup line. "Thanks but, uh, no thanks."

"Oh, come on, Mattie. It'll be fun. Jeanine could join us if you like." The brunette batted her eyelashes at him. Matt couldn't remember which one Jeanine was, nor did he really care.

"Sorry. But I can't. Doctor's orders." He shrugged, adopted an innocent expression and hoped like hell it worked. Despite not liking jersey chasers, he only got tough on them when he had to.

Kara/Katie/Karma lifted up onto her toes and whispered in his ear, "I'll let you do me any way you want, Mattie. My pussy's dripping wet and aching for that cock of yours."

She nipped his ear lobe before lowering herself to her normal height, bit her lower lip and looked up at him with big blue eyes. Matt sighed. Time to play hardball, apparently.

Normally, he would have someone with him he could pawn the girls off on—whether it be Darrin, a teammate, or a friend who was more than willing to take one for the team. Tonight, though, he had Owen—a guy who would be more likely to crack a joke than show any interest in any of the three women—and Jenn, who he was pretty sure would outright refuse to help him, especially after what had happened the last time she'd assisted in a Jersey Chaser Extraction.

Feeling somewhat hopeful, despite the feeling in his gut, he caught Jenn's gaze, mouthed, "Help me" and hoped like hell she'd put that last Extraction behind her.

Want to keep reading? Purchase Baseball and Other Lessons now, available at the following retailers:

Amazon
Barnes & Noble
Kobo
iBooks

About the Author

Aubrey has been reading and writing since she was about two and a half and has been an avid romance reader since she read her first romance novel in the 6th grade. She wrote her first novel in high school. It was an ~~awful~~ imaginative historical romance that involved a cross-country trip via covered wagon, and maybe some Indians. She thinks it's still on a floppy disk somewhere (DOS computer, y'all), but can't be too sure. These days, she writes contemporary romance with a lot of humor and sass and characters that have issues.

She graduated from Seton Hill University's Writing Popular Fiction program with a Master of Arts in 2008. When she's not writing, she can be found with her husband and their two dogs at home in Austin, on their ranch in west Texas, watching a football or baseball game, or with her nose stuck in a (usually virtual) book.

Connect with Aubrey:

Website: http://aubreygross.com

You can also find me on Facebook, Twitter and Goodreads. And while you're at my website, be sure to join the readers' list for updates on new releases!